NOT JUST GAL PALS

A SAPPHIC, SMALL-TOWN, ROMANTIC COMEDY

ELIZABETH LULY

ISBN 978-0-6455808-3-9 (paperback)

ISBN 978-0-6455808-2-2 (ebook)

PROLOGUE

JENNY

"So you're telling me I've been canceled?" I blinked away tears, struggling to keep my voice steady.

"'Canceled' is too strong a word. More like, um, put on hold?" Serena, sitting behind her glass desk in her expansive office in West Hollywood, shot me an unconvincing smile, showcasing her gleaming white teeth. "Look, I'm sure this will all blow over soon. We've just got to sit tight and ride it out."

That was all very well for Serena to say. She had a whole raft of superstar clients providing a steady income stream that paid the mortgage on her gorgeous Beverly Hills home. Being a fashion-slash-dog-mom-influencer was my only source of funds. A source that was quickly drying up.

I swallowed. "How...how soon are we talking? Days? Weeks? Months?" The rent for my small studio apartment in Los Feliz had increased last month. And my dog Walter's little mishap with an Instagram-famous cat who, unprovoked, had bitten him at a photoshoot for a "Ten Pets

Taking Social Media by Storm" article two weeks ago had resulted in an expensive vet bill. I had some savings, but not enough to keep me going for more than a month or two.

"Maybe a few months?"

Oh god. I swallowed again, the lump in my throat bigger this time. "Didn't the thing with Tom Henson only last a few days, and then he was back on TikTok like nothing happened? And that was sexual harassment. This was...this was just a stupid mistake, which I've completely owned."

Serena pursed her lips. "That's true. But I hate to say this, Jenny... He's a man. And people forgive and forget men faster than women when it comes to social media scandals. So, I'm sorry, but I wouldn't count on things bouncing as quickly as they did for him." Either my tear blinking wasn't as surreptitious as I hoped, or there was an edge of panic to my voice, because Serena's face softened. "Look, Jenny. You're going home next week for that wedding, right?"

I nodded.

"Well, why don't you stay for the holidays and come back in January? You can sublet your apartment and post lots of wholesome content of you in the country." Serena's eyes lit up. "You know what? I actually think this is a great idea. You could get pics of you and Walter wearing lots of flannel and walking down cute little country lanes lined with gorgeous fall trees. I bet Bridgewater & Molten would snap you up as a brand ambassador in no time!" Serena stood up and started to pace up and down, clearly excited at the prospect of a new deal, no matter how improbable. Serena was a great agent, but sometimes she got a little carried away.

"Um, I'm not really sure I'm a good fit for their demographic. Don't they target well-off, middle-aged women who are into gardening and horse riding? I'm almost a decade off being middle-aged, even further away from being well-off, I kill all the potted plants I own, and I like to admire horses from a safe distance of at least ten feet. Anyway, weren't they just in the news for having terrible conditions in their factories? Given my current 'not quite canceled' status, I don't think that would be the best move. And, of course, I'm against bad labor practices as well," I added, wincing. I probably should have started with that, but Serena didn't seem to notice.

"Yeah, okay, maybe. But you know what I mean. It could be a chance to do something different, to show people the 'real you.' And rest and recharge." A dreamy look crossed Serena's eyes. She stopped walking and leaned against the glass wall. "You might even meet a hot lumber-jack and have a holiday fling. You know, make out on a bale of hay in a rustic barn, cozy up in front of a fire in a log cabin, and go on romantic hikes together." It was clear from the way Serena bit her lip that she was living out her own fantasy—and that she'd never tried to make out on a bale of hay before. Trust me, it was *not* comfortable. Despite how worried I was, I stifled a giggle. "And document it all for your followers, of course! Just don't get too serious. I want you back here early next year. We've still got the Whamz promotion booked for January. I called them today, and as long as your followers don't drop below 2.7 million, they're happy to go ahead. By that time, I'm sure all will be forgotten, and we'll be back to business as usual."

As unrealistic as Serena's fantasy was—hot lumberjacks were in short supply in Sapphire Springs, and I'd sworn off flings in any event—spending a couple of months back home wasn't a terrible idea. If I was being honest with myself, I was in a slump, tired of my life in LA, tired of thinking up new content, and tired of the unpredictability of my career.

Being almost canceled was a wake-up call. Something had to change. Perhaps time away from LA would help me work out what it was.

CHAPTER ONE

JENNY

Goddamnit.

I refreshed the page, chewing on my lip and glaring at my phone, willing the numbers to increase. Still only 1,234 views and twenty likes. *Urgh.*

Apparently, videos of me and Walter in matching flannel, standing in front of a rustic barn in the Hudson Valley with fall leaves floating down on us, didn't have the public appeal Serena had predicted. I thought we looked super cute, but it appeared my followers weren't into lumbersexual attire and wholesome fall scenes. I'd roped poor Dad into standing on a ladder and throwing leaves over us for nothing.

A message from Amanda popped onto the screen.

Where are you? We're starting in 5 mins!

I stood up from the toilet seat I'd been perching on and was reaching for the door when I heard footsteps. My heart sank. I was not in the mood for any awkward restroom encounters, especially not with my former teachers. And since I was in the teachers' restroom at Sapphire Springs High, that was a clear and present danger.

In fact, the first person I saw when I stepped foot in the high school twenty minutes ago was Mrs. Harding, the English teacher who'd been the bane of my existence in sophomore year. Memories of reading aloud in her class, my face hot with embarrassment as I stumbled over the pages of *To Kill a Mockingbird*, came flooding back. I had fought a strong urge to turn right around and run as fast as my jump-suit would allow in the other direction. While I'd enjoyed the social aspects of high school, the academic side of things had been a struggle. A dyslexia diagnosis in my early twenties had explained a lot. Unfortunately, I didn't get that diagnosis in time to make school a less painful experience.

I breathed out in relief as two women began to speak. They most definitely weren't Mrs. Harding. I would recognize her voice anywhere.

"Are you coming to the careers talk?"

The other woman sighed. "Yes. Did you see who the panelists are? One of them is a social media influencer." I winced at the derision in her voice, positive she'd paired her words with a dramatic eye roll. "That's not exactly a career."

Usually these types of comments rolled over me like water off a duck's back. A lot more hard work and creativity went into being an influencer than most people realized, and I was proud of what I'd achieved. But her words hit me harder than usual.

"Yeah. I don't know what Amanda was thinking. The kids are obsessed enough with their phones as it is. We shouldn't be promoting *influencing* as a career option."

I silently cursed Amanda for convincing me to do this.

My phone buzzed. Amanda had sent me another message.

> Meet me in the auditorium ASAP! We're about to start and Walter is getting antsy!

I suspected Amanda was projecting her own emotions onto Walter, who took pretty much everything in stride. When @charlietheinstagramcat had taken a chunk out of his leg a few weeks ago, Walter had only let out one plaintive yelp and then gracefully removed himself from the situation by leaping into my arms.

I checked the time. *Shit.* I needed to leave now, or I would be late. Unfortunately, that meant I couldn't hide in the stall until the women left. I took a deep breath, braced myself, and opened the door.

Two women in their forties were reapplying lipstick over the sinks. They glanced at my reflection in the mirror without recognition. Thank god. One awkward encounter avoided.

I washed my hands, checked I looked presentable in the mirror, and rushed out of the bathroom.

I knew this was a terrible idea when Amanda had FaceTimed me in a panic yesterday morning, only hours after I'd arrived in Sapphire Springs, exhausted after the red-eye flight. The journalist she'd lined up for the careers panel had dropped out at the last minute, and she was desperate.

"The journalist was the only person the kids were actually excited about. Without her, I'm worried they're going to totally zone out. Having a homegrown TikTok sensation who lives a glamorous Hollywood lifestyle would really zhuzh up the panel, and they'll love Walter too. I need you. *Please*," Amanda had begged. I'd always found it difficult to say no to Amanda, and yesterday was no exception.

I also found it hard to tell her bad news. Amanda didn't have TikTok or Instagram and hadn't visited me in LA recently, so she was oblivious to the fact that, lately, I'd been living anything but a glamorous Hollywood lifestyle.

I'd grudgingly agreed to be on the panel, hoping none of the kids asked about the scandal. My main demographic was twenty- to forty-year-old women interested in fashion and dogs, so there was a decent chance they didn't even follow me. And even if they did, they could have easily missed the whole thing—I'd just made an Instagram story refuting the allegations, which had only been up for twenty-four hours and otherwise hadn't addressed them.

I was almost at the auditorium when my phone started ringing. Amanda again.

"Where the hell are you?" she whispered, sounding stressed.

"Sorry, sorry. I'm almost there."

I entered the auditorium, which hadn't changed in a decade. The familiar blue and white painted walls, the scuffed wooden floors covered in markings for the basketball court, the stale smell of sweat, the rickety gray plastic folding chairs set up in rows to hold the senior students, and the raised wooden stage at one end. As I walked toward the stage, memories of boring school assemblies, stressful exams, awkward school dances, and embarrassing P.E. classes came rushing back.

I picked up pace when I realized the other two panelists were already seated onstage. Amanda, wearing her standard teacher uniform of black pants, floral blouse and cardigan, her shiny black hair in a tight ponytail she only ever wore at work—she claimed it helped her get into 'Ms. Lui' mode—

glared at me from her moderator's seat. In contrast, Walter, a caramel ball of fluff lying by her side, was the picture of canine calm. Amanda had definitely been projecting.

I took the stairs to the stage two at a time, heading toward the empty seat.

And then I saw her and nearly tripped.

What the...?!

My heart skipped a beat. The world suddenly veered off kilter. I'd been psyching myself up all morning for the panel, but I had not prepared myself for this.

For the second time today, I fought the urge to turn and run.

Why the hell didn't Amanda tell me *she'd* be here? On the panel with me. Sitting next to me. And looking just as good as I remembered. Actually, better. She'd cut her brown hair into a pixie cut—short on the sides with a wave of hair at the top—and it suited her. The navy jeans, gray oxford shoes, and a gray-and-blue plaid blazer also suited her. A lot. Damn it.

But I knew why Amanda hadn't warned me. Because I wouldn't have agreed to come if I'd known.

I'd been hoping to avoid Blake Mitchell for as long as possible.

Blake shot me a forced smile, and I managed something —which at best felt like a grimace—in return and then glanced away, avoiding direct eye contact. I sat down next to her, desperately wishing I could fast forward the next hour until my escape.

But before I had time to dwell on Blake's unwelcome presence, Amanda cleared her throat.

"Thanks, everyone, for coming. We've got an amazing panel of alumni with us today to talk about their very different careers. I'll ask them some questions, and then

we'll have time for Q&A afterward. But first, let me intro-
duce them. Next to me, we have Tom Harrison, who graduated in 2007 and owns his own car repair business in
Sapphire Springs. To his left, we have Blake Mitchell, who
graduated in 2010 and moved back two years ago to set up
Sapphire Springs' only medical clinic after completing her
medical degree at Columbia University and working in
New York. And finally, we have Jenny Lynton, who also
graduated in 2010, and her adorable toy poodle, Walter.
They live in LA and have over three million followers
combined on TikTok and Instagram." It had dropped to 2.8
million in the last month, but I wasn't about to correct her.

After the students finished half-hearted clapping,
Amanda launched into her questions. To my relief, she
turned to Blake first.

"Blake, thanks again for agreeing to be on our panel. So,
what made you decide to go into medicine?"

Blake flashed a genuine smile at Amanda, her whole
face lighting up. "Since I was a little kid, I've always
dreamed about being a nurse or a doctor. I wanted a job that
was rewarding, something that would allow me to help
other people and contribute to society. So, when I was lucky
enough to get into med school, it was a no-brainer for me."

Amanda turned to me. "And what about you, Jenny?
What drew you to working in the media and as a social
influencer?"

Heat crept up my face. How the hell could I answer
that question in a way that wouldn't make me sound like a
superficial fool after Blake's response? All my pride and
confidence in my work had disappeared. Whether it was
due to scandal, being back at high school, or Blake, I wasn't
sure.

I looked out at the crowd, hoping inspiration would hit

me, and immediately spotted Mrs. Harding seated in the front row, that familiar look of disapproval on her face. Farther along the row sat the two women from the bathroom, looking similarly unimpressed.

My eyes darted to the tired wooden floor of the stage in front of me, wishing it would open up and swallow me.

"I...um, I..." I took a deep breath. Fuck it. I wasn't academically brilliant or driven like Blake, but that was okay. "To be honest, I didn't set out with this career in mind. When I graduated from high school, I had no idea what I wanted to do. I didn't have the grades to get into a good college, and I didn't want to go to one either. All I knew was that I had to see the world." *Get the hell out of Sapphire Springs* more like it, but I didn't think Amanda would appreciate me saying that.

"My aunt, who lived in LA, offered to get me a job working at her friend's cafe, so I jumped at the chance. I stayed with her until I'd saved enough money to move out. At the cafe, I made friends with some struggling actors who worked there. One night, I went to a party where I met Vanessa Milan. We hit it off, and she offered me a job on the spot as Chris Trent's personal assistant." A murmur of excitement rippled among the students as I mentioned the celebrities' names, and I smiled, feeling more like my usual self.

"Initially, I didn't know what I was doing. But I learned on the job, and it turned out I was actually pretty good at it. It was while I was working for Chris that I started doing TikTok videos with his dog, Alfie, and then, when I got Walter, with this little guy." I looked down affectionately at Walter, who'd trundled over to me and was now curled at my feet. "And things kind of...blew up. Before I knew it, Walter and I were being offered advertising deals, invited to parties, and sent a *lot* of free dog food." The audience laughed. Seriously, the local dog shelter loved us. We were sent far more food than Walter could ever eat, and I was constantly lugging massive bags of the stuff to them. A wave of guilt washed over me, but I pushed it down. Now was not the time to think about the scandal.

I looked at the students, giving my best reassuring smile. "So, hopefully, that gives you some comfort that even if you're not sure what you want to do right now, things can just...work out, especially if you're open to new opportunities. You don't need to have your whole life planned out. And it's okay if you don't want to go to, or don't get into, college."

Regardless of recent events, I stood by my words. Society put so much emphasis on academic success, on college, on knowing what you wanted to do by senior year. In other words, on being a Blake. I wanted the kids to know it was fine if they weren't a Blake, either. I was lucky I had my Mom, who also hadn't gone to college, as a role model. She'd tried a few jobs, before apprenticing for a builder, a tough gig as a young woman. But she'd worked hard, and eventually gained the skills, experience and savings required to start her own, very successful, construction business. While her career was pretty much polar opposite to mine, she'd always been an inspiration to me.

"Thanks, Jenny. I'm sure our students will find that very reassuring." Amanda smiled and then turned to Tom, who spoke passionately for over five minutes about his love of cars. I had absolutely no interest in cars, but Tom's passion was genuine and contagious, so much so I began wondering if he needed any staff. Given my current situation, getting a job wouldn't be a terrible idea.

"Blake, what's the highlight of your career so far?"

Blake paused for a moment. "There've been so many highlights, but I'd say probably moving back to my hometown to set up its first medical practice."

"Jenny, what's your biggest highlight?" Amanda smiled at me.

"Um, maybe the time I met Beyonce at a Grammy's after-party?" I winced. *Way to go not sounding like a superficial fool, Jenny.* As soon as it was out of my mouth, I thought of so many better responses: running my own business before turning thirty, signing multi-year sponsorship deals, and using my platform to support animal-welfare charities, advocate for reproductive rights, and other worthy causes.

"And Tom?"

Tom grinned. "I'd say the time I got to work on a 1964 Aston Martin DB. An absolutely stunning car. They don't make 'em like they used to."

Amanda turned back to Blake. "What are the biggest challenges of your job?"

Blake furrowed her brow. "Giving people bad news is very difficult. And also knowing that you've got people's lives in your hands. If you make a mistake, it really could be life or death."

Goddamn. How did Blake manage to look so attractive even when she was frowning? There was an intensity to her eyes that was very distracting.

"Jenny?"

It took me a second to realize Amanda was asking for my response. *Focus, Jenny.*

"While my job is definitely *not* life or death, there are some challenges. The pressure to constantly think up new creative posts, the unpredictable income, and the trolls."

While they were genuine struggles I faced, they sounded trivial compared to Blake's challenges.

The rest of the talk continued in that vein. Blake was the poster child for a carefully planned career that she'd tirelessly worked toward achieving. I was the poster child for things just falling into place, for saying yes to opportunities without any higher purpose or grand plan. And Tom... well, Tom was the poster child for pursuing his passions.

Amanda opened it up for questions. The teens asked Blake about how many lives she'd saved (too many to count) and the goriest thing she'd ever seen (she declined to answer). I was grilled about the famous people I'd met (I blanked on most of the celebrities they'd actually care about, like Billie or Harry, and said Adele and Oprah) and if they could get a selfie with Walter (yes). And Tom was quizzed about particular car issues the students had faced (which he answered with enthusiasm). To my relief, I got through the session without any questions about the sponsorship fiasco.

Thirty-eight selfies later—Walter really was the most wonderful, patient dog on the planet—we were finally free of students. I looked around for Amanda and spotted her deep in conversation with Blake in the now almost empty auditorium. I sighed. I wanted to speak to Amanda, but I did *not* feel like interacting with Blake, especially not after hearing how wonderful she was for the last hour. Lying on my parents' couch, checking how my latest post had performed, and brainstorming content ideas seemed a much more appealing option. I turned toward the exit. I'd talk to Amanda later. I was two feet from the door when Amanda called my name.

"Jenny!" *Damn.* I eyed the door with longing before

turning around and walking back toward Amanda and Blake.

"You weren't leaving, were you?" Amanda narrowed her eyes.

"Me? No!" I responded unconvincingly. "Just taking Walter outside to pee."

"Uh-huh." Amanda raised her eyebrows, but then her face softened. "Thanks again for stepping in at the last minute. You were great."

"No problem." I was genuinely glad I'd been able to share my different career path with the students.

I avoided looking at Blake, but out of the corner of my eye, I could see her nod in agreement.

"Well, I'd better be off," Blake said abruptly, glancing at her watch. "I've got a patient in fifteen minutes."

"Good to see you again," I managed.

Blake gave a smile that didn't reach her eyes and walked to the door.

I waited until Blake left the building before I turned to Amanda. "I can't believe you didn't tell me she'd be here."

"Sorry, I was desperate. And if I had, you would have weaseled your way out of it. Anyway, you need to get used to being around her."

This was true. Amanda's bachelorette party was this weekend, and her wedding was in a week. Not only that, but we were both bridesmaids. When Amanda told me that Blake was also in the bridal party, I was taken aback. I didn't realize how close the two had become in the past few years. I mentally shook myself. For Amanda's sake, I needed to put my feelings for Blake aside—at least until her wedding was over.

Amanda inspected me closely. "I know she can be a

little gruff, but I still don't understand why you dislike her so much."

"You know she's more than a little gruff around me, and she's been like that for years." Since high school, to be precise. And it didn't help that not only was she rude and standoffish, but she was also annoyingly perfect. "I know it's not like all queer people have to be friends, but it would have been nice if we could have at least been friend-*ly*." We'd been the only two "out" girls in our class. I'd come out as bi as a sophomore, Blake as a lesbian a year later. But Blake had brushed off all my attempts at friendship.

"How's all the wedding prep going?" I asked, hoping to change the subject.

Amanda's eyes lit up. "Great! My wedding planner is a superstar, despite being run off her feet with weddings while pregnant. To be honest, I thought it would be a lot more stressful than it has been, but she's got everything under control. Which is just as well because I've got a whole lot of essays to grade this week." She grimaced.

"That's great! Well, let me know if there is anything I can do to help."

Amanda bit her lip. "Actually, on that note..." Her voice trailed off. "Could you give Blake a hand with the bachelorette party? I get the impression she's stressed about it. She's had a lot going on at work, and I don't think she's had as much time as she expected to plan it. She's terrible at asking for help, but I think she could really use some. And you're so good at that kind of thing."

My heart sank. I'd just survived one Blake interaction and wasn't keen for another one so soon. "If you'd agreed to let me plan it in the first place, you wouldn't be in this predicament," I said, sounding more petulant than I'd intended. But I had a point.

Instead of appointing a single maid of honor with all the usual responsibilities, Amanda had distributed tasks amongst her bridesmaids. She claimed it was to avoid over-burdening any one person, but I suspected it was really to avoid hurting anyone's feelings. While I'd put up my hand to plan the bachelorette party, Amanda had insisted it would be too difficult to do from LA. Instead, I'd been assigned to give a toast at the rehearsal dinner and provide emotional support.

"I know, I know, but it's done now. Can you just help her, Jen? Please?" I sighed. As much as I wanted to avoid Blake, I loved Amanda and wanted her wedding to be a success. And if that meant having to deal with Blake, then I'd have to suck it up. And at least, for once, Blake was the one struggling.

"Ok, fine," I said. "But have you spoken to her about this? I can't just show up at her clinic and announce I'm taking over the bachelorette night."

Amanda's face broke into a broad smile. "Just to clarify, you're not taking it over. Just helping her. And yes, I did mention that I'd see if you could help her. I'll text you her number."

Out of the corner of my eye, I saw the back door open, and Mrs. Harding appeared. She began walking toward us.

"Oh shit," I muttered. "Mrs. Harding is on her way over. I gotta go."

"She's really quite a sweetheart when you get to know her," Amanda said.

I raised an eyebrow, unconvinced. "Do I need to remind you of the *To Kill a Mockingbird* incident? Or the time she failed me because she didn't think I'd actually read *The Great Gatsby*? Or the time—"

"Okay, point taken," Amanda said hastily. "Just promise me you'll reach out to Blake."

"Yes, don't worry. I'll sort it out." And with that, I turned and walked quickly toward the other exit before Mrs. Harding reached us and I was forced to relive any more high school trauma.

CHAPTER TWO

BLAKE

I winced as Dad thumped the printer and swore loudly. Multiple times a day, I questioned whether employing Dad as my receptionist was a good idea. This was one of those times. At least there weren't any patients in the waiting room to witness his assault on my poor printer.

"Have you tried turning it off and on?" I yelled from my desk.

I turned back to the financial aid application I was completing for Mrs. Alvarez and sighed. She wasn't able to navigate the complex financial aid system herself, and she desperately needed treatment for her diabetes complications. It wasn't part of my job, but I couldn't just sit back and watch her suffer. Hopefully I could convince the hospital to give her the treatment she needed for free.

Once I finished, I'd head home to my little cottage, microwave a frozen meal, log back on from the couch to do some insurance paperwork and then sort out Amanda's bachelorette party, which had been hanging over my head for weeks. I'd been so busy at work I'd struggled to find the time and inspiration to focus on it. But with only a few days to go, I had to make it my top priority. I couldn't let Amanda down.

After a few moments of silence, Dad poked his head around the door, grinning. "Turns out I hadn't turned it on. Thanks, pumpkin. I'm going to head home now. Have a good night."

I shook my head, smiling. God, he was hopeless. But he was hopeless in a lovable, well-meaning way, which made it impossible to fire him. And of course, the fact he was my dad added an extra layer of difficulty. He'd retired from the bank a couple of years ago. But after about three months of retirement—during which he'd driven Mom, who'd retired five years earlier from teaching and gotten used to having the house to herself, up the wall—both Dad and Mom agreed it was best he returned to work. It just so happened that decision coincided with my homecoming. When I announced that I needed a receptionist, Mom immediately submitted his resumé for my consideration.

From Dad's perspective, it was the perfect job. He got to spend time with his eldest daughter, chit-chat with my patients, and during his lunch break, he'd wander down Main Street to meet his buddies at the pub for a steak or pop into my sister Olivia's flower shop to say hi. Mom was thrilled she had the house to herself again, to read in peace and potter around the garden without interruption. And the arrangement had its benefits for me as well. I hadn't liked the idea of relying on someone I didn't know or trust to help manage my practice. But I trusted Dad completely, despite his incompetence when it came to technology. I could also pay him minimum wage without feeling guilty, because I knew he didn't need the money. That was an enormous relief, given money was tight. And with that thought, the headache I'd been fending off all afternoon with a concoction of ibuprofen and acetaminophen picked up, throbbing behind my temples.

I refocused my attention on Mrs. Alvarez's application, but before I'd made much progress, my phone pinged. and a message lit up my screen.

> Hi, this is Jenny. Amanda mentioned you might need some help with the bachelorette party?

I sighed. Jenny Lynton was not who I needed right now. After a long day and the headache that showed no sign of subsiding, I wasn't in the mood for painful social encounters. And a painful social encounter was almost guaranteed when it came to Jenny.

I'd had a crush on Jenny since I was fourteen, when the zip on my backpack malfunctioned just before a math exam, trapping all my pens inside. She'd seen me struggling with the zip outside the exam room and offered to help. As she knelt beside me and made a valiant effort to dislodge the zip, I went from freaking out that I'd be late to being transfixed by Jenny's face, deep in concentration. The adorably furrowed brow and pursed lips. The intensity of her blue eyes focused on the zip. When that failed, she lent me two of her pens, handing them over with a radiant smile that made me weak at the knees. I couldn't believe my luck when she came out as bi a year later.

Unfortunately, ever since the zip incident, in Jenny's presence I transformed from normal, confident Blake to awkward, shy Blake who somehow always said the wrong thing or said nothing at all. My brain had a tendency to blank in her vicinity. I could tell Jenny wasn't my biggest fan, and I didn't blame her. I was a mess around her.

When Jenny had sauntered into the auditorium earlier, without a care in the world, all those familiar, disconcerting feelings came flooding back. My heart picked up pace, and I suddenly became very aware of how I was sitting and my facial expression. Was I all hunched over? What should I do with my hands? Was I looking at her funny? It was like we were back in high school again. Okay, yes, we *were* physically back in high school, but seeing Jenny transported me emotionally and mentally back there as well.

One benefit of your high school crush becoming a social media influencer was that it made it very easy to follow (I preferred that word over "stalk") her career from afar. So, while I'd hardly seen Jenny in person since graduation, I'd thought about her. A lot.

Checking Jenny's TikTok and Instagram accounts was one of my guilty pleasures, albeit one I tried not to do too frequently because it did feel slightly creepy. It turned out all the traits that had attracted me to her in high school—she was outgoing, funny, warm, genuine, and I had to admit, super hot—also attracted millions of fans on TikTok and Instagram. Of course, today on the panel, all the kids loved her.

I massaged my forehead. While I didn't need all the emotions Jenny Lynton stirred up right now, I did desperately need help with Amanda's bachelorette party, and as Amanda's closest friend and someone who—based on her Instagram feed, at least—was a skilled entertainer, Jenny was the perfect person to help me.

I stared at my phone, my thumb hovering over the keyboard.

As much as I hated asking anyone for help, especially Jenny Lynton, I really didn't want to screw this up for Amanda. Planning parties was not my strength.

I took a deep breath, swallowed my pride, and shot off a text.

> Thanks. Are you free tonight? Builders Arms at 7?

The bachelorette party was on Saturday, just three days from now. If I was going to accept Jenny's help, I needed to do it quickly. The insurance paperwork would just have to wait.

I PUSHED the door open and looked around the gorgeous old pub. Wooden beams crisscrossed the ceiling, matching the dark oak floors. Exposed red brick walls and two cozy log fires added warmth to the interior. Builders Arms was always busy, and tonight was no exception. Half the town seemed to be enjoying their craft beer and delicious food, which, in my opinion, rivaled New York City's finest gourmet pubs. Despite my nerves, my stomach rumbled at the thought.

I spotted Jenny sitting at a circular table near the back of the pub, staring at her phone, and the rumbling in my stomach was replaced with churning. I took a deep, fortifying breath and attempted a cool saunter over to her, immediately walking into the corner of a table. *Ouch.* Pain shot through my thigh. *Very cool, Blake.* My eyes darted over to Jenny, who thankfully still had her head down and hadn't witnessed my lack of coordination.

I collected myself and hobbled the remaining four feet to the table, my heart thumping. Jenny was so absorbed in her phone, frowning in either concentration or concern, she didn't notice I was standing awkwardly right in front of her.

Jenny looked as good in real life as she did on my phone, her long blond hair falling in waves down her back, wearing a colorful jumpsuit that flattered her curves, with a cozy, soft-looking cardigan over it. I had an alarming urge to reach out and stroke it. *Keep your arms by your sides, Blake.* It was a strange sensation to be this close to someone I'd primarily only seen on my phone screen for the last decade. She was so...three dimensional.

I cleared my throat. "Hi," I said, slightly strangled. I swallowed.

Jenny looked up from her phone. Her blue eyes connected with mine, instantly erasing all my social and language skills. *Shit.*

"Hi," she said, a wary smile on her face as she stood up.

How did Jenny always manage to look like she'd made absolutely no effort but still be fucking gorgeous? Meanwhile, I'd spent thirty minutes picking out my outfit for the panel because Amanda mentioned this morning that Jenny would be there.

She was still standing, and I realized I'd been staring at her for a beat too long. Multiple beats too long. *Oh god.* What was the social etiquette when meeting your unrequited high school crush for a bachelorette planning session? Should I hug her? Shake hands? Sit down? Mumble a pathetic excuse and sprint out of the pub? The last option held a strong appeal right now, although I wasn't sure my bruised thigh would allow for a speedy exit.

It was ridiculous that, in my early thirties, with an Ivy League medical degree under my belt, a pretty woman could reduce me to a blubbering mess. Well, not just any pretty woman. Jenny. Not even my ex, Grace, had this effect on me.

To my relief, Jenny sat down, and I followed suit. The

chair had a grounding effect, pressing into my back and legs and reminding me I was human and capable of basic human interactions. My brain started whirring, and some vocabulary returned.

"Have you ordered?" I picked up the menu and studied it intently—even though I knew exactly what I wanted to order—thankful it gave me something to do with my hands. And my eyes. While not a long-term strategy, avoiding eye contact with Jenny gave me an opportunity to finish pulling myself together.

"No, I was waiting for you. Are you hungry? If you are, I might grab a burger."

"Yeah, food sounds good," I replied, attempting casual but sounding more like my brother in his surly teenage years. I inwardly cringed but didn't have time to dwell on it because Dan, Builders Arms' owner, appeared in front of us.

"Doctor Mitchell. Jenny. What can I get you?" Dan smiled down at us. His daughter had been in our grade at school, so he knew us both well. Despite that, he insisted on addressing me as Doctor Mitchell even though I'd told him a million times to call me Blake.

"I'll get the burger and an IPA, thanks." Jenny smiled at him.

"And the steak with a glass of pinot noir for me. Thanks." I reluctantly handed the menu to Dan, not ready to relinquish my safety blanket.

Once he'd gone, Jenny got down to business. She leaned across the table, her hair falling forward over her shoulders, staring directly at me. An electric current shot down my back. "So, what's the plan for the bachelorette so far?"

"Well, um," I said and swallowed again, "so I hired out Old Cedar Tea Parlor, and I thought we could have afternoon tea there and then come here for dinner." I trailed off, but Jenny continued to stare at me, clearly expecting further detail. I cleared my throat. "So, yeah, that's about as far as I've got. I've been trying to think of activities to do. It's just...the whole thing doesn't feel very special, you know?"

"I see." Jenny bit her lip, a gesture that would have been absolutely adorable if she hadn't also been frowning and looking generally concerned. "How many people are coming? Amanda, me, you, Jacinta, Heather..."

"And Maya and Evie," I finished. Maya and Evie had both been in our grade at school, and Maya now worked with Amanda as the art and drama teacher at Sapphire Springs High.

"Hmmm." Jenny continued biting her lip, and I couldn't stop staring at it. Soft, full, pink...

Bang! I jumped in my seat as Jenny's hand smashed down on the table, crashing me out of my reverie.

"I've got it!" she exclaimed as a few older men at the table nearby turned to look at us. "Sorry!" Jenny smiled. "I can get a bit too excited when it comes to party planning. Okay, so as I'm sure you know, Amanda is a huge Jane Austen fan..." Unfortunately, I did know, having been subjected to at least three Jane Austen movie nights since returning and being dragged to the high school's production of *Emma* in May. "And didn't the school put on *Emma* a few months ago? I'm sure Amanda mentioned it."

"Yes..." I didn't see where this was going.

Jenny clapped her hands. "Great! Do you have Maya's number, by any chance?"

I did. I read it out to Jenny, who typed it into her phone and pressed the call button.

"Maya, hi, it's Jenny. Look, Blake and I are just putting the finishing touches on Amanda's bachelorette party. Do you still have the *Emma* outfits? Are they those flowy ones that aren't too fitted? Okay, great. That should work, then. Could we borrow them for Saturday? Seven, if you have them." Each time Jenny said "we," it lit a warm spark inside me, even though I knew Jenny was only doing this for Amanda, not me.

Dan carefully placed our drinks on the table while Jenny listened to Maya. I gave him an appreciative smile and reached for my wine. Maybe wine would help me relax.

"Uh-huh, six, okay. Well, I'm sure we can work out something. Let me talk to Blake, and we'll get back to you. Thanks. You're a lifesaver. See you Saturday!"

Jenny hung up the phone and took a sip of her beer. "So, what I'm thinking is a Jane Austen tea party. We can dress up, take photos, play some Jane Austen-related games. For dinner, we could see if Dan has the event room free and try to give it a little Regency style. Then, knowing Amanda, she'll want to head to Frankie's for a drink and dancing, then . . . done!" Jenny dusted her hands, smiling. "So, what do you think?"

A weight lifted off my chest. "That sounds great!" Powered by a surge of relief, I managed to string some more words together while maintaining eye contact with Jenny. "She'll love that. Party planning is not my strength. Thank you."

"Well, I might be good at party planning, but you save lives on a regular basis, so I think you win," Jenny responded. I looked at her closely. Despite her smile, there was an edge to her voice.

"This isn't a competition, you know." I bit down hard as soon as the words left my mouth, regretting them immediately. I'd intended my tone to be teasing, but it came out gruff and abrupt, verging on rude.

Jenny stared at me, her smile vanished, and her voice went flat. "Oh, there is one problem. There are seven of us, but Maya only has six Regency dresses available. So, we'll have to see if we can find another one somewhere."

"I can sort something out for me," I said. I was not a fan of dresses. I hadn't worn one since prom, so I was quite happy to have an excuse to avoid them.

"Ok, thanks, if you're sure." Jenny eyed me with trepidation, clearly not trusting me to get the dress code right.

"Don't worry. Amanda has forced me to watch enough period movies. I know what to wear." I cringed again. The words came out all wrong, sounding terse and offhand. *Goddamnit.* Why couldn't I just act normal when Jenny was around? It was like high school 2.0 all over again.

CHAPTER THREE

JENNY

Fall was, in my opinion, the best time to visit Sapphire Springs. Walking up Main Street, everywhere I looked the trees flamed red. Decorative gourds were on display in shop front windows, and enormous carving pumpkins were piled up on rustic carts outside the Sapphire Springs General Store. The ivy clinging to the two-story red brick buildings that lined the lower part of Main Street was a resplendent mix of red, yellow, orange, and green. American flags gently swayed in the breeze. The sky was blue, and the air was crisp. It was the perfect weather for pumpkin spice lattes, warm cinnamon donuts, s'mores, and hot toddies. I let out a happy sigh. I was surprised by how much I'd missed this.

Dan, out walking his dog before starting work at the pub, called out across the street and waved at me. I waved back. As a teenager, I'd found the lack of anonymity small-town living offered claustrophobic, but now it was kind of refreshing. So very different from LA.

I peered in the window of Blake's clinic as I passed, spotting her father behind the reception desk. I kept walking. Since Wednesday night, I'd texted Blake a few updates so she knew I had things under control—not because I kept thinking about her or anything like that. Definitely not. But I didn't want to be caught snooping in her window.

Dinner with Blake had gone better than expected. Yes, conversation had been stilted, and she'd been curt and dismissive a few times, but every so often, I'd get flash of the Blake everyone else knew and liked. Having said that, I was relieved when Blake excused herself shortly after finishing her steak, citing a headache. If our strained small talk had continued much longer, I probably would have been struck down with one as well.

Just before Blake arrived at the pub, I'd discovered another animal activist had tagged me in a TikTok video, sending my stomach and my follower count plummeting even further. Meanwhile, my fall flannel post was still not performing well. At least preparations for Amanda's bachelorette party were a welcome distraction from my algorithmic woes. Since Blake had a demanding day job and I did not, I'd offered to do all the grunt work.

I reached my destination, the florist, with no awkward Blake encounters and pushed open the shop door, a rush of sweet-scented warm air greeting me. Olivia Mitchell, the owner of the florist shop—and yes, Blake's younger sister—looked up from the flowers she was arranging, her eyes crinkling as her face broke into a big smile.

"Jenny! How lovely to see you. How's Walter? You should have brought him with you." Olivia and Blake shared the same dark hair and lashes, big brown eyes, strong jawline, and full lips, but that was where the resemblance ended. Olivia was warm and friendly, wore her wavy brown hair cut just above her shoulders, and had an impressive wardrobe of floral clothes. Today she was wearing a loose-fitting dress covered in red flowers and brown ankle boots. How the hell had they turned out so different?

"He's good. Great, actually. He loves Mom and Dad's yard. Much better than my tiny apartment in LA. I would have brought him, but I'm running a few errands this morning and thought he'd slow me down. I'm actually here to purchase some flowers."

"Oooh! How can I help?" Olivia's eyes lit up.

"So...and this is a surprise, so please don't tell Amanda..." I said, conscious of just how small Sapphire Springs was. "We're doing a Jane Austen-themed afternoon tea at Old Cedar and dinner at Builders Arms for her bachelorette. I was hoping to get some flowers to decorate the event room at Builders Arms to make it a bit more *Pride and Prejudice* and a bit less..."—I searched for the words—"pints and penises?" God, that was terrible, but Olivia giggled. So different from Blake, who I'm sure would have responded with an unimpressed stare. "I'm, um, on a budget. So, if you have any suggestions that aren't too pricey, that would be great."

"I'd love to help. If you only need them for tomorrow, I have some gorgeous flowers I haven't sold this week. They'd be perfect for this, and I could give them to you at cost since they're on their way out."

"Oh wow, that would be amazing, thank you." Given my financial situation, at-cost price was music to my ears. Blake and I hadn't discussed money last night, so I was proceeding on the basis that any money I spent would be coming out of my own depleted pockets.

"Since Amanda's buying all her wedding flowers from me, it's the least I can do."

Olivia bustled about, gathering flowers and animatedly talking me through her ideas for the flower arrangements.

While she was showing me some pink dahlias in the back corner of the store, I spotted a display of candles. I had a weakness for warm baths with lavender candles, but my parents' house was disappointingly candle free. After agreeing the dahlias would make a gorgeous centerpiece, I drifted over to the candle display and began inspecting them. While their packaging was plain—brown glass jars and simple white labels—their scents were not. Bourbon and wood smoke. Peach and cedarwood. Pear and bergamot. Coffee and leather.

I inhaled them deeply, closing my eyes and feeling slightly giddy from excess oxygen. They were divine. "These all smell incredible." I inspected the labels more closely, wondering if I'd be able to find a store that stocked them in LA when my financial situation improved, but they revealed nothing. "Do you know where they're made?" I looked up at Olivia, who was pink-cheeked and smiling.

"They're made here...by me. I started it as a hobby last year and then decided to make some to sell in the shop. I'm glad you like them."

"I love them! I consider myself quite the candle connoisseur, and these are really, really good." Now I knew Olivia had made the candles herself, I had to buy some. The peach-and-cedarwood candles would add ambience at dinner tomorrow night, and I could take what was left back to my parents' house to enjoy for the rest of my stay. And the bourbon-and-wood-smoke one would be perfect as the weather got colder. "I'll take three of the peach, and one bourbon."

Olivia carefully wrapped the candles in paper and then placed them in a cardboard box. "Here you go. Enjoy! And I'll have the flowers ready for you tomorrow morning."

I walked back down Main Street with a spring in my

step, pleased with my purchases. I couldn't wait to lower myself into a warm, relaxing bath with a good book and a candle lit.

As I reached Blake's clinic, I resisted the temptation to peer in. Instead, I stared across the road, pretending to admire the foliage on a particularly vibrant tree. Unfortunately, my pretense was too successful. I completely missed the door of the clinic opening and someone walking out until...wham! I walked, box of candles and all, right into them.

"Ouch!" yelped the person.

"Shit, I'm sorry," I said as the person staggered back.

My heart sank.

Blake.

Of course it was Blake.

I put the box on the ground, hoping the candles had survived the impact. "Are you okay?"

"You scared the shit out of me," Blake said abruptly, her voice gruff.

"I'm sorry." I tried to think of an explanation other than, *I was trying to avoid you, which ironically resulted in me running right into you*, but I came up blank.

"You could really injure someone storming down the street like that." Disapproval was clear in Blake's voice. My chest tightened. Seriously, what did Amanda see in this woman? And how the hell was she related to lovely Olivia?

"Just trying to help you drum up some business," I tried joking, hiding my annoyance that Blake didn't seem to accept it was an honest mistake.

Blake stared at me silently, unimpressed. Any warmth I'd harbored toward her after our dinner vanished. It was a genuine mistake and had only happened because I was doing *her* a favor.

"Okay, well, I'd better be off. I've got a lot of work to do for Amanda's bachelorette. I'll see you tomorrow," I said curtly, less than enthused at the prospect. I picked up the box and tried to walk around Blake just as she tried to walk around me the same way, and we bumped into each other again. "Shit, sorry."

We did the awkward side-to-side dance another couple of times before Blake took control.

"Okay, I'll stay still until you go around me."

With anyone else, this would have been funny, but Blake's mouth was pressed into a line. I sighed and walked past Blake, resisting the urge to look back to see where she went. Blake Mitchell really rubbed me the wrong way. At least it was just over a week until the wedding, and after that, I wouldn't have to interact with her again, barring any more awkward run-ins, of course.

CHAPTER FOUR

JENNY

Where the hell is Blake?

She'd said she'd be here early to help me set up. All the other guests would be arriving any minute to change into the dresses, so we'd be ready to surprise Amanda when she arrived.

I'd actually set everything up already, and to be honest, there hadn't been a lot to do. Old Cedar Tea Room was a gorgeous, "ye olde worlde" parlor, and the private event room Blake had rented was already decorated to perfection: white lace tablecloths; delicate floral china; three-tiered cake stands laden with miniature cakes, tarts, and savory treats; and vases of gorgeous flowers picked from their impressive garden.

But still, it was the principle of the thing. I was just meant to be helping Blake with the bachelorette party, not doing the entire thing myself. And after our run-in yesterday, I wasn't feeling particularly favorable toward her.

My phone pinged. It was Blake.

Sorry, running late. Caught at work.

I sighed and looked down at Walter who, after excitedly sniffing the room for the past hour, had finally calmed down and was sitting near my feet. "What do you think, Mister? Is she telling the truth or just trying to avoid helping?"

He looked up and cocked his head. Walter clearly didn't know either.

"Well, we'd better get that photo over and done with, little guy."

I really needed to do another post today. I popped Walter, wearing a little blue bowtie attached to his collar, on a chair so it looked like he was having an elegant high tea by himself. That would have to do. I added some music, wrote *While I have a repawtation as a pawty animal, sometimes I just wanna woof back some treats in style* over the image, and posted it. Walter posts usually performed well, so fingers crossed it would do better than my other recent posts.

I was giving Walter a treat for being such a champ when I saw Maya walking up the path, struggling under the weight of the dresses. I rushed to help her with the door. "Thank you so much for this!"

"No problem. I thought we could save this one for Amanda, since it's the nicest." Maya, already dressed in a pale-yellow gown that looked stunning against her brown skin and hair, handed me a gorgeous purple, Regency-style gown to put aside for Amanda.

As the other guests arrived, they picked out a dress and headed to the restroom to change. I was left with a light-blue dress with short, puffed sleeves. Looking at my reflection in the restroom mirror, I was surprised by how flattering and comfortable it was. The "waist" of the dress sat just under my boobs, leaving plenty of room for me to devour a few of the cakes I'd been eyeing, and the blue complemented my blond hair. The only problem was that it was way too long for my 5'4" frame. In order to walk properly, I had to hitch the dress up. Good thing I hadn't planned any physical activities for this phase of the bachelorette party, or I'd probably trip over it and humiliate myself in front of Blake. That is, if she actually showed. But Blake or no Blake, I'd definitely be changing before we went dancing at Frankie's.

Amanda was usually punctual, so after touching up my lipstick, I exited the restroom and joined the other women, who were chatting amongst themselves. A few minutes later, we heard a car pull up.

Maya peered through the window. "Yep, it's her!"

We stopped talking and assembled at the entrance, ready to greet Amanda. She stepped out of the car and almost lost balance when she saw us all standing there in our Regency dresses with enormous grins on our faces.

I cleared my throat, putting on my best posh British accent. "Welcome to Pemberley, my dear. Goodness, what are you wearing? Please, put this on." After eyeing Amanda's outfit—which consisted of a cute cocktail dress and matching heels—up and down in mock horror, I handed her the purple gown and ushered her into the room.

"Oh my god! This is amazing." Amanda gave me a big hug. "Thanks, Jenny and..." Amanda looked around, presumably for Blake.

As if on cue, the door opened, and Blake strode in, wearing long black boots over cream jodhpurs, a white shirt with a high collar, a white cravat, and a dark-blue waistcoat with a matching long tailcoat.

I froze.

And swallowed.

She looked absolutely incredible.

It was Mr. Darcy, crossed with...a very hot woman. And I was here for it. *Really* here for it.

"Jenny, are you okay?" Maya asked as I stared open-jawed at Blake.

No. No, I was not okay.

I knew I should be annoyed at Blake for running late, for being rude yesterday, and for ignoring me in high school, but all I felt was full-blown, all-consuming attraction.

Hormones flooded my body, sending my heart racing and my head giddy. I forced my mouth shut before I started drooling.

Damn. Who knew a woman in a fancy suit could have this effect on me? I certainly didn't until a minute ago. Come to think of it, I had seen plenty of women in tuxes and similar outfits before. But I'd never seen *Blake Mitchell* in one.

I cleared my throat. "Okay, everyone! First up, Jane Austen trivia. And yes, Amanda starts off at negative five points, so the rest of you have a chance."

CHAPTER FIVE

BLAKE

Thank god for Jenny.

Amanda, already on a high after trouncing us all at trivia, was almost peeing herself laughing. Blindfolded, she was trying to kiss a picture of Colin Firth stuck to the wall, her mouth caked with red lipstick. It was the adult version of Pin the Tail on the Donkey. While the doctor in me worried about the risk of communicable diseases being spread, the friend in me was thrilled Amanda was having such a great time. Without Jenny's help, I shuddered to think how the party would be going right now. We'd probably be sipping tea and making boring small talk.

Amanda finally kissed the wall, leaving a bright-red mark at least a foot away from Colin, and pulled off the blindfold dramatically.

"Damn!" She looked over at Colin's face. "I'm sorry, Colin. You know I love you, despite being betrothed to another. Actually, fuck it." She landed another passionate smooch directly on his lips—*Good lord, was she tonguing the paper?*—and we all cackled.

"Okay, that one doesn't count," Jenny said, still laughing. "Maya, since you kissed his eyeball *while still blindfolded...*" she said, shooting a stern look at Amanda, "you're officially Mrs. Darcy. Congratulations!" Jenny handed Maya a box of chocolates.

Jenny looked adorable in a baby-blue dress that was far too big for her. Her hair, which she'd curled into ringlets, perfectly framed her face. Her cheeks were flushed, possibly from the prosecco or from the exertion of running the party. A pang of guilt shot through me.

As we took a break to refill our glasses and help ourselves to more cake, I walked over to Jenny, who I could have sworn had been trying to avoid me. Each time I approached, she suddenly needed to tend to Walter or set up the next game. Every so often, I thought I sensed her eyes on me, but when I looked over to her, she was always intently focused on something else.

To be honest, I didn't blame her if she was pissed off at me. Not only had she had to step in to save the bachelorette party at the last minute, but I'd also arrived late for it and had been a dick to her yesterday. It was no excuse, but I'd just received Mr. Jeffries' scans, and it wasn't good news. Desperate to clear my head, I'd rushed outside to get some fresh air. To say I hadn't been in the best frame of mind for a literal collision with the woman whose presence sent me into a tailspin was an understatement. And to top that off, the corner of the box Jenny had been holding had made impact just below my rib cage, sending a shooting pain through my abdomen. As per usual, my words had come out wrong. I'd sounded curt, maybe even rude. I cringed just thinking about it.

I took a deep breath and strode over to Jenny, who was

giving Walter a treat. I was determined to catch her this time. I wouldn't be able to relax until I did.

"Hey, thanks very much for all of this. I'm sorry I was late. It's really great—much better than anything I could've done. Please let me know how much this all cost, and I'll pay you back. And can I do anything to help?" My words came out stilted, awkward.

"No thanks, I've got it all under control." Jenny's voice sounded polite, cordial, but not exactly warm.

Her eyes darted down my outfit, a strange expression on her face. Oh shit, maybe she was annoyed I hadn't worn a dress.

"I, uh, I hope my outfit is okay. I ended up borrowing the top half from Maya—it was Mr. Knightley's costume. I couldn't fit into any of the pants, though, but I thought the jodhpurs and boots would work." One benefit of being relatively flat chested was that I could fit into some men's clothing.

"It's...great." Jenny's strange expression lingered. Was it discomfort? Distaste? Uneasiness swelled in my belly.

Okay, Blake. Now is the time to apologize properly—for yesterday, for running late, for making Jenny do all the work.

I swallowed and opened my mouth, but nothing came out. I cleared my throat, preparing to try again, when Jenny shot me another indecipherable look and clapped her hands, her face breaking into a smile as she turned away from me. My heart sank.

"Okay, everyone! Pass the Parcel is next. Please form a circle. Yes, I know this sounds very elementary school, but I can guarantee you that the prizes are most definitely *not* elementary school—or Jane Austen themed, for that matter!" Jenny winked, and despite being frustrated at myself for my botched apology, I was intrigued. We hadn't discussed this game.

Jenny changed the background music to Lizzo, turned it up, and then handed a large parcel to Amanda, who was sitting next to me.

It quickly became clear that Jenny had done a run to one of the adult stores in Oldburgh, because each time the music stopped and another layer of wrapping paper was ripped off, an X-rated gift was revealed. A small black bullet vibrator, candy underwear, and a rose-scented, vulva-shaped candle. We all got a prize. I was the new owner of a pair of plastic handcuffs that looked like they would either not lock properly and ruin any S&M play, or they would lock too well and require a humiliating trip to the hardware store to buy a saw. Not that it mattered since I had no one to use them on anyway.

"Okay, everyone, we're down to the very last prize," Jenny announced, a cheeky grin on her face, turning "Juice" up to full blast. We passed the parcel around the circle a few times.

Amanda had just handed me the parcel when the music halted.

I looked over at Jenny, surprised. Given the game was obviously rigged, with Jenny stopping the music to make sure everyone got something, I'd assumed Amanda would get the final present. Jenny muttered something under her breath. I'm not a lip reader, but I was fairly confident it was, "Shit." I inwardly chuckled. She'd clearly intended for the music to stop while Amanda was holding the parcel.

"I think this was for you," I said to Amanda, holding up the parcel.

Amanda shook her head, grinning. "Nope, you won it fair and square. It's yours."

Jenny, pink-cheeked, chimed in. "Um, Blake's right. It was meant for you, Amanda."

Amanda stubbornly shook her head again. "No, I insist. Blake was holding it when the music stopped. I'm not going to steal a present from the true winner! What kind of bridezilla do you think I am? C'mon Blake, open it."

Everyone started chanting, "Open it! Open it! Open it!" Under peer pressure, I reluctantly peeled back the wrapping paper.

The present was more substantial than the others and also wrapped more tightly, with layers of pink wrapping paper to remove.

I clumsily ripped off pieces of paper, my eyes darting up to Jenny who sat frozen, watching me.

A pink, rounded end poked through the wrapping paper. I stared at it blankly for a moment before realizing what it was.

I scratched my neck and took a deep breath. Well, there was no turning back now. Better get this over and done with. I pulled off the last piece of wrapping paper.

In my hands was a big, pink rabbit vibrator. As heat crept up my neck, the room erupted into squeals.

I swallowed. An image of Jenny in a sex-toy shop, examining the toys for sale, holding this one in her hands and inspecting it closely, flashed into my mind.

Blood rushed to my face at the thought, and my hands felt shaky. I hoped it wasn't noticeable. *It's not like she chose it for you. Get a grip, Blake.*

Dragging my eyes away from the vibrator, I looked up at Jenny. Our eyes locked, and my cheeks burned harder. Suddenly paranoid that she could read my mind, that she could tell I'd been thinking of her touching it, I looked away.

I wasn't exactly a prude when it came to toys—I had my own stash in my bedside table and considered myself a sex-positive person—but being accidentally gifted a vibrator by Jenny had completely thrown me. Did Jenny choose it because she liked it?

BLAKE. Whatever you do, do NOT think about Jenny using it.

"You're probably more in need of it, anyway." Amanda's teasing voice thankfully broke my thoughts.

Well, Amanda had a point, since I wasn't the one happily coupled up and about to get married. And while pink wasn't usually my color of choice, I'd make an exception for a vibrator hand-selected by Jenny.

JENNY

I cleared my throat.

"How about we go for a 'promenade around the grounds' to help digest the cakes," I suggested, my voice unnaturally chirpy. I was trying to avoid looking or thinking about Blake, but the air buzzed with her presence, and my whole body was reacting to it, especially my cheeks. At this rate, I'd never have to apply blush again.

I wasn't sure why I felt so embarrassed about Blake getting the vibrator. If it had been anyone else, I wouldn't have cared. But it felt very personal, very intimate, for Blake to be holding it. I'm sure her current outfit didn't help, either. And the idea of Blake potentially using it...*oh boy.* Although, if I'd known I'd been picking out a vibrator for her, I would've chosen one of those expensive, sleek, minimalist ones. *Thinking about vibrator shopping for Blake is not helping matters, Jenny!* I let out a deep breath.

I needed some space. And fresh air. And luckily, we had that in abundance on the other side of the door. Old Cedar Tea Parlor sat on the border of a conservation area, nestled in crimson trees and overlooking a large pond with Monet-esque water lilies.

Everyone seemed receptive to a walk, so we got up and trailed out of the tea parlor. Holding up my dress so it didn't drag on the ground, I fell into step with Maya, who I hadn't had a chance to catch up with yet. Talking about work, family, and life events, combined with the cool air, helped disperse the heat from my cheeks and get my pulse under control.

It was another perfect fall day. The late-afternoon sun was golden and soft, making the leaves of the old oak trees glow. Walter was having the time of his life, racing around sniffing rocks and peeing on tree trunks. Crisp leaves crunched under our feet. And to my relief, Blake was walking behind me. It wasn't quite out of sight, out of mind —I was hyperconscious of Blake's voice, low and warm—but it was far better than being in the same room with her, struggling to keep my eyes off her.

I slowly inhaled the fresh air. Everything was fine. Everything would be fine. Amanda would have an amazing bachelorette night and wedding, and then I wouldn't have to spend any more time with Blake. Everything would be more than fi—

A blur of golden-brown fur raced in front of me toward the pond. The pond was covered in water lilies, providing such a dense green coverage it looked more like a continuation of the grass than a body of water. I had a sinking feeling Walter, who hated getting wet, didn't realize what it was. "Walter!" I yelled. "Come back!"

But it was too late. Walter flew off a rock. With the

athleticism of a long jumper, he landed with an enormous splash in the pond, sending the water lilies wobbling like jelly. When Walter didn't immediately surface, panic shot through my chest. I sprinted down to the water's edge as fast as my too-long period dress would allow. *Shit.*

I desperately scanned the pond for him. After a few seconds, Walter's soaked little head poked up amongst the lilies, his eyes wide with shock and his usually fluffy hair slicked down with water. I let out a deep breath in relief.

"Walter! Come here!" I called, but he just stared at me, panicked. I could see his legs splashing frantically, sending the lilies wobbling but achieving little else. If anything, he was paddling deeper into the pond. Walter started letting out distraught little yelps, and I couldn't stand it any longer.

I jumped into the pond.

Freezing-cold water blasted my skin. I gasped, braced myself, and started wading toward Walter, waist deep in water. This was no easy feat given the amount of excess fabric I was wearing and the water lilies. I'd never thought about what laid under lily pads before, but I soon discovered they had surprisingly thick stems that sunk into the mud at the bottom of the pond.

Focused on reaching Walter, I barely registered that the rest of the bachelorette party had run down to the edge of the pond and was yelling at me.

My lower body slowly adjusted to the frigid water. I was just thinking that this would be an amazing aquarobics class—my thighs were getting a real workout—when my foot caught on a lily stem, and I fell face-first into the water.

In that moment, I fully understood the panic Walter was experiencing. The slimy lily roots felt like tentacles of some murderous octopus, pulling me down into the depths of the murky pond. The icy water sent shockwaves through the upper, unacclimatized, portion of my body. My dress was suddenly as heavy as lead. I flailed about, struggling to lift my head above the water.

I could have sworn the lily roots were curling around my legs. Fear flooded through me. What if...they weren't roots? What if they were eels or...even worse, water snakes?

My flailing increased in intensity, my heart thumping in my chest. I did *not* want to meet my watery grave at Old Cedar Tea Parlor's pond.

And then a hand grabbed my waist, and another grabbed my right arm, and someone hauled me up. I sputtered out pond water and managed to shriek, "Snakes! Snakes on my legs!" as I caught my breath.

"They're just water lilies, not snakes," I heard someone say sternly, holding me with firm hands.

Fumbling, I brushed my hair out of my face so I could check if Walter was okay and see who my savior was. Walter was still paddling desperately amongst the lily pads, and my savior...

My savior was Blake.

Blake. Beautiful Blake, standing next to me, touching me, and looking at me with a furrowed brow. A shiver bolted down my back, and it wasn't from the freezing-cold water. Blake withdrew her hands from my body and took a step backward.

Sensibly, Blake had taken her waistcoat and tailcoat off before she'd jumped in, leaving her in a white shirt. Surrounded by green lily pads, up to her waist in water, her dark eyes intense, her short brown hair falling slightly over her forehead, she looked stunning. My heart, which had already been racing due to my near-death-by-water-lily experience, beat even faster. My eyes, which had been roving over Blake, locked with hers, sending my stomach twisting. The air crackled between us.

"Thank... Thank you," I managed before remembering why I was in the pond to begin with and darting my eyes over to Walter, who was still doggy paddling like a little champ.

"You get back on dry land. I'll get Walter," she directed. Stunned, I obeyed and carefully waded back through the forest of lily pads to the edge of the pond, where Maya and Amanda helped me out, the rest of the party crowding around to check I was okay. I'd never look at another Monet painting in the same light again.

I turned to see how Blake and Walter were faring. Walter, his eyes still wide with panic, clawed at Blake, who clasped him to her chest as she made her way out of the pond. Walter looked about half his normal size with his brown, wet fur plastered to his little body.

A foot from the edge of the pond, Walter leaped out of Blake's arms and onto the grass, where he rolled and shook furiously, spraying the entire bachelorette party with pond water.

I looked back at the pond, and there was Blake, drenched, her white shirt clinging to her.

Oh boy.

It looked like she was reenacting the Mr. Darcy pond scene from the BBC's *Pride and Prejudice*. And while the original scene had never affected me in the same way it affected Amanda (who would swoon each time we watched it, declaring her love of Colin Firth), this scene most definitely did.

Blake was breathtaking. I could make out the lines of a white sports bra underneath her shirt—not that I was staring at her chest or anything. My eyes darted away, noticing some dark lines on her biceps also visible through the wet material. Was that...a tattoo? I blinked.

I forgot everything for a moment and just stared at her. I wanted her arm around my waist again. I wanted to take off her soaking shirt and trace my finger over that mysterious tattoo. I wanted to—

"You guys must be freezing. You should get changed before you get pneumonia." Maya broke my trance. I was suddenly acutely aware that while Blake looked like she'd just stepped out of a queer remake of *Pride and Prejudice*, Walter, rolling around in a pile of fall leaves, looked like a dirty drowned rat, and I'm sure I hadn't fared much better. Heat rushed up my face as I remembered I'd also been shrieking about snakes when Blake had saved me. *She must think I'm a complete idiot.*

"I'm so sorry about the clothes, Maya. I'll get them all dry-cleaned." I looked down at my sodden dress, the bottom quarter covered in mud.

"That's fine. Don't worry about it," she said. "Let's just get you all inside to warm up."

I shivered. "Come on, buddy. Let's find something to dry you off with," I said to Walter, turning my back on the pond and Blake and trying to erase the image of her wading out of the water from my mind.

CHAPTER SIX

JENNY

"Sorry I'm late," Amanda said, looking decidedly worse for wear as she stumbled onto the chair opposite me, still wearing her sunglasses. Her hair was tied into a messy bun on her head. "I don't know why I thought it was a good idea to have brunch with you today."

I put on my best mock-insulted face, my lips twitching. "Geez, thanks. Maybe because I'm your best friend who you haven't seen in months, and who you want to spend some quality, one-on-one time with?"

"You know what I mean. You and Blake did such a great job planning it that I may have had too good a time..." Amanda grimaced. "But seriously, it was great. Thanks again for all your work." Amanda didn't sound quite like her usual self, but I attributed it to a mild hangover.

"That's fine. And I suspected you'd be a bit worse for wear, so I already ordered you a coffee."

I handed Amanda the menu and started packing my laptop away. Not feeling too bad this morning despite the late night, I'd arrived early with my laptop so I could answer a few emails and brainstorm new content ideas. Novel Gossip was the sort of cafe where you didn't feel guilty about staying around for hours, as long as you ordered a coffee every so often. It was warm, inviting, and spacious. As an added bonus, it was also a bookshop, so if you got bored, you could pick a new book from the overstuffed wooden shelves at the back of the shop to read with your coffee.

I looked up as Amanda removed her sunglasses to examine the menu, and did a double-take. Amanda's eyes were red and puffy.

Shit.

This wasn't how Amanda usually looked when she was hungover.

It was how she looked when she'd been crying. Not that Amanda often cried, which was why this was all the more alarming.

"Is everything okay?" I asked gently, possible scenarios racing through my mind. Had she hated the bachelorette party? Or had something happened to her family, or Peter at his bachelor party last night? Images of Peter's night devolving into chaos à la *The Hangover* movies flashed through my mind. Sensible, kind Peter missing after a night of debauchery. *Don't be ridiculous, Jenny.* Quashing my overactive imagination, I focused my attention on Amanda.

Her bottom lip quivered, and my chest tightened. I bounded over to crouch next to her chair, putting my arm around her.

"Hey, what's going on?"

"The wedding..." Amanda's voice trailed off.

What the hell could it be? Peter couldn't have called the

wedding off. He absolutely adored Amanda. Had the venue burned down?

I rubbed Amanda's back and looked at her with my best sympathetic expression. She took in a deep, shaky breath.

"My wedding planner, Miriam, has had pregnancy complications, and she can't attend the wedding. The doctors have put her on bedrest."

"Shit, is she going to be okay?" I didn't know a lot about pregnancy, but bedrest didn't sound good.

Amanda nodded. "Apparently, if she rests up, they think she and the baby will be fine, thank god."

The tension in my chest released. Okay, the situation obviously wasn't great, but it also wasn't as bad as I'd expected. We could deal with an MIA wedding planner. An MIA groom or venue would have been more challenging.

Amanda rubbed her forehead, her frown lines deep. "Miriam sounded super stressed about the wedding. She can still send emails and make calls, but I'm sure stress is the last thing she needs right now, so I told her not to worry about it. That we'd handle it. She's going to email me all the information and said she'd be available if we had any questions. But I'm not sure I will be able to handle it. I stupidly committed to work right up until Friday. Crap!" Amanda's bottom lip quivered again, and she grabbed a napkin and blew her nose.

A tiny flame of excitement sparked in my chest as I had an idea.

"Look, I've got plenty of free time at the moment, and I love this stuff. I did Chris and Sophie's wedding, remember? Let me handle it."

I actually felt energized at the prospect of taking over

Amanda's wedding, throwing myself into something tangible, helping my closest friend celebrate her special day. But Amanda didn't look convinced.

"Seriously, I would love to do it. Pleeeease!" I gave her a pleading grin and fluttered my eyelashes.

"If you're really sure?" Amanda's worried face softened slightly.

"Yes, I'm positive," I stated with conviction.

Amanda stared at me for a few seconds before breaking into a relieved smile. "Thank you so much. You're incredible. I'll email you everything as soon as Miriam sends it to me."

I leaned forward on the table. "Great! So, why don't you tell me about your vision for the wedding? I'm excited to dive in."

"First, let's order." Amanda managed a weak grin, looking slightly more like her usual self. "Do you think it's bad if I order cake for brunch? George's blueberry-lemon cake is amazing."

"Not at all. I'm getting the breakfast burrito, so no judgment here." A waiter came up and took our orders. As soon as he left, Amanda bent forward.

"Before we get into all the wedding stuff, I also want to catch up properly. I feel like we've barely gotten to talk yet. So, what's new with you?"

The excited buzz in my body vanished. Now was my opportunity to tell Amanda about the scandal. I opened my mouth, about to tell her everything, and then snapped it shut. Amanda had enough to deal with at the moment. I didn't want her to worry about me as well.

"Nothing much. It's so nice to get away from LA for a while, have a break from the scene there." At least the last part was the truth. It had only been a few days, but I hadn't been missing it one bit.

Amanda smiled and squeezed my hand. "I'm so glad you could come." She paused for a second. "Any news on the romantic front?"

I shook my head. "I've gone on some dates, but nothing serious. Which, as you know, seems to be the story of my life." I grinned ruefully.

"What about that guy...was it Jeremy? What happened to him?"

I sighed. Jeremy was a tall, blond artist I'd met at a friend's party in January. We'd really hit it off. He was passionate about art, funny, and extremely handsome. "After we'd been seeing each other for a few weeks, I asked him if he was looking for anything long term. The answer was a resounding no, so I broke things off. According to Instagram, he's now engaged."

Amanda winced. "Oh no! What a dick. And that Sarah woman?"

I huffed out a soft laugh. "The same."

"Oh, that's a shame. She sounded really nice."

"Yeah, she was." I'd fallen for Sarah immediately on our first date at my favorite local bar. A gorgeous vet with a great sense of humor.

I realized Amanda was looking at me expectantly, so I continued. "Her dating profile said she was only looking for a serious relationship, so I assumed that's where we were heading. But our relationship never seemed to develop. We'd just go out once or twice a week for drinks and end up in bed afterward. Every time I suggested seeing each other more often, or having brunch on the weekend, or going for a hike, she brushed me off. Eventually, I asked her about it, and she said something like, 'Look, I'm just really enjoying keeping things casual, and I guess, at this stage, I don't see a long-term future for us.' So I broke it off too. I don't want to waste my time on relationships that aren't going anywhere. Two weeks ago, I saw her kissing another woman over brunch." The pain of seeing them together hit me all over again, shooting through my chest. What was it about Sarah's new girlfriend or Jeremy's fiancée that made Sarah and Jeremy want to settle down with them but not me?

And those were just two recent examples. Despite my best intentions, I kept finding myself falling into short-term flings.

"It's hard not to take it personally. I mean, am I just not serious-relationship material?"

In my line of work, I got a lot of people dismissing me as a ditzy blond. Did all my dates see me the same way?

Amanda shook her head. "Of course you are. You're smart, funny, and a genuinely lovely person. But..." Her voice trailed off.

"What?"

Amanda grimaced. "I hope you don't mind me saying this, but I think you're maybe just dating the wrong people. As much as I love your tendency to see the best in everyone —well, everyone except Blake—I think it sometimes means that you, um, overlook red flags. Like I remember you telling me when you first met Jeremy that he had a reputation for being a player, but you dated him anyway..."

I sighed. Amanda had a point. I did have a habit of diving headfirst into relationships without stopping to think whether the person was right for me.

"Look, I'm sure you'll meet someone soon. It's just a numbers game. I know this is a cliché, but seriously, if I wasn't straight and about to get married, I'd date you in a second. I think you're a real catch."

Amanda said it with such earnestness I couldn't help but smile, even though I didn't share her confidence. "Thanks. I hope you're right."

"As you know, I went on a lot of bad dates before I finally met Peter. It sucks, but you just gotta keep putting yourself out there. Like they say, you have to kiss a few frogs to find your prince...or princess."

"But what if I'm the frog everyone kisses?" I grimaced.

"Oh my god, you are not a frog, Jenny!" Amanda laughed. "Hey, on a completely unrelated note, how have you and Blake been getting along the last few days? Are you two still mortal enemies, or did working on my bachelorette party bring you together?"

I studied Amanda's face. Was the "unrelated note" comment genuine, or had she noticed how distracted I was by Blake yesterday?

"Ha ha. Come on, mortal enemies is a bit strong. But don't worry, your claim as my BFF isn't under threat," I responded.

Amanda pinned me with a penetrating stare and I squirmed. "Uh-huh," she said. To my relief, she left it at that. "So, when are you heading back to LA?"

"I'm actually going to stay until January." I kept my voice light, hoping Amanda didn't ask the reason for my extended stay.

"You are?! That's so exciting. Oh, Jenny, excellent!" Amanda exclaimed, her eyes sparkling. Thankfully, before she could ask me any questions, our coffees arrived. Amanda's focus shifted to her mug, which she grabbed and took a deep swig out of. She shut her eyes.

"Oh, thank god," she moaned.

"Okay, now you've got coffee, tell me more about the

wedding," I said, eager to change the subject and throw myself into Amanda's special day.

Given my dating woes, it seemed unlikely I'd ever get to plan my own wedding. But at least I'd be able to help my best friend celebrate hers.

CHAPTER SEVEN

BLAKE

I pushed open the door to Novel Gossip and beelined for the counter. I was a woman on a mission, and that mission was to get caffeine pumping through my veins as soon as possible.

Since moving back to Sapphire Springs, I'd rarely stayed out late—Sapphire Springs wasn't exactly known for its nightlife—so dancing at Frankie's until well past midnight had knocked me around. It also hadn't helped that when I'd finally gotten to bed, I couldn't stop thinking about Jenny—replaying the memory of my hand around Jenny's waist in the pond, the way our eyes had locked, sending electric shocks down my spine. And later, Jenny dancing at Frankie's, her hair swinging, eyes twinkling, a huge smile on her face. Eventually, I'd given in to temptation, pulling the new vibrator out of my side table, and I used it, imagining what might have happened if, in some alternate world, Jenny and I had hooked up. It must have released some of the tension, because I finally drifted off.

I'd gotten about five steps into Novel Gossip when I

spotted Jenny sitting by herself at a table in the corner, bent over her laptop. I froze. *Crap.*

I was wearing gray sweatpants and a hoodie and hadn't looked in the mirror before I left the house. I'd also forgotten to brush my teeth. Not only was I not looking my best, but I was not mentally prepared to see or speak to Jenny. I'd orgasmed eight hours ago thinking about her, for goodness' sake.

My immediate impulse was to turn and hightail it out of Novel Gossip, but the heavenly smell of coffee and the realization Jenny had seen me stopped me—and the fact I owed her a proper apology.

But coffee first, niceties second. I wouldn't be able to string a sentence together without it, and I already had enough difficulty communicating with Jenny. I swallowed, waved at Jenny, and continued heading toward the counter.

When I moved back to Sapphire Springs, I was thrilled to discover a new café-bookstore had opened. I was even more thrilled when I found out the owner, George, was a warm-hearted lesbian with a great sense of humor and a mission to bring good coffee and cake to Sapphire Springs. And thankfully, while George and I got on like a house on fire, there was absolutely zero romantic attraction between us, so she wasn't a threat to the 'no relationship' rule I'd implemented after Grace.

George was standing behind the counter, in her usual uniform of a button-down shirt and chino pants, staring at me with an eyebrow raised so high it nearly reached her brown hair, which was styled in a crew cut.

"The usual?" George asked. I nodded. She looked me up and down and grimaced. "Actually, are you sure you don't need a triple shot this morning?"

That was exactly what I needed. "God, yes. That sounds amazing."

George clearly realized just how pressing my need for caffeine was, because in less than a minute, I had a gigantic latte in my hands. I took a few sips.

"Mmmmm. Have you ever considered going in one of those 'Best Baristas in the World' competitions? I seriously think you might win."

George grinned and rolled her eyes at the compliment. "Amanda was just in here before, looking worse for wear, and your pal over there"—George nodded in Jenny's direction—"also looks tired. You must have had a big night last night."

I followed George's nod over to Jenny. She was chewing on her lip and frowning at her laptop. My eyes lingered on her.

George cleared her throat. "Sorry, Blake, but there's a bit of a line. Can we catch up later, once things quiet down?" I tore my eyes away from Jenny and saw that half of Sapphire Springs had lined up behind me.

Damn. I'd been hoping to get more caffeine into my system before I approached Jenny.

I took a big gulp of coffee, ran a hand through my hair, and started walking toward her table. Jenny was leaning forward over her laptop, her hair falling down the sides of her face like a golden curtain.

"Hi, how are you holding up this morning?" I asked, my heart thudding in my chest as she looked up at me with her dark-blue eyes.

"Surprisingly, I'm not feeling too bad. Amanda, on the other hand..." Jenny shook her head, a wry smile on her face. "We had brunch earlier, but she had to cut it short to go lie down."

"Oh, that's good—I mean about you, not Amanda of course. I...um...hope she feels better soon." *Very smooth, Blake.* There was an awkward pause as Jenny stared up at me, clearly under the impression I had more to say. I swallowed.

"Is everything else okay? I thought you were looking kind of worried."

Jenny shook her head. "Oh, it's nothing serious. Amanda's wedding planner has had to step down, so I'm taking it over. I've just been trying to get my head around all the emails she forwarded me."

My eyes widened. No wonder Jenny was frowning.

"Nothing...nothing serious? Just taking over a wedding? Shit. What happened to her wedding planner?"

Jenny filled me in on Miriam's situation. "So, to be fair to Amanda, her wedding planner canceling is probably the cause of her splitting headache, not her hangover. She's pretty stressed about it."

I shook my head. "Well, let me know if I can do anything to help this week. I'm pretty tied up during the day with work and my niece and nephew who are visiting, but if I can help in the evenings at all, just let me know." Even though it was a Sunday, I was planning to work most of the day so I could get on top of all my admin, especially because I was going to take Tuesday afternoon off to hang out with the twins.

"Thanks, will do." Jenny paused, a thoughtful look flitting across her face. "Actually, while you're here... Would you mind taking a look at the seating plan? Amanda did it a while ago, so it may be a little out of date. A few people can't make it, so I thought I'd check if we need to change it at all. I'm not asking you to breach doctor-patient confidentiality or anything like that, but you probably have a better idea than me of who does and doesn't get along in this town. I've been to a few weddings where booze combined with past hostilities have caused some blow-ups, and I'm keen to avoid that, both as a friend of the bride and in my new role as wedding planner! I'll run all the changes past Amanda, of course."

"Sure." I was privy to a lot of gossip in my role.

Worrying I hadn't brushed my teeth and the coffee wouldn't be helping things, I held my breath and leaned over Jenny's shoulder to look at the screen.

I spotted an immediate issue and stepped away from Jenny, hoping I was a safe distance from her before I opened my mouth.

"Seating Joe Livanidis and Rory Goldsworthy near each other could end badly. They almost came to blows last weekend at Builders Arms arguing about the new fence between their properties. Apparently, Rory was very keen on painting it bright red, but Joe didn't think it would be a complementary backdrop for his red and pink roses and insisted on white. They decided to compromise and paint their side of the fence their preferred color, but Rory was a bit sloppy, and now there are red paint dribbles all down Joe's white fence. According to Joe, it looked like blood stains from people being impaled on his fence, and from what I heard, he was threatening to impale Rory on it as well!" I shook my head, chuckling. I'd heard all about it from the town gossip, Ms. Berry, when she'd been in for her annual physical on Tuesday.

"Oh my god! Well, we don't want anyone being impaled on a candlestick or the like at the wedding, so I'll fix that," Jenny giggled, moving Joe and his wife to another table. "Anything else?"

I don't think I'd ever made Jenny smile before, let alone

laugh, and it felt good. Really good. Warmth washed over me. I stepped closer again, took a deep breath, and then held it again. Damn, I didn't realize the wedding was so big. It looked like hundreds of people were attending. I wouldn't be able to hold my breath long enough to read the seating plan before I passed out. My head started to spin, and my lungs begged to return to their usual rhythm of respiration.

"If it's easier, you can take a seat," Jenny said, looking at me with one eyebrow raised slightly and gesturing at the empty chair opposite her.

I collapsed onto the chair, relieved I could breathe again, my face hot at Jenny's eyebrow raise. She'd clearly caught me acting strangely. Jenny turned the laptop around so it faced me.

I spent the next twenty minutes going through the list, giving Jenny a rundown of Sapphire Springs' latest drama. The caffeine finally worked its way into my bloodstream, and I started to relax in her presence. And in a world record, I hadn't said anything I'd immediately regretted as soon as it left my mouth. In fact, I'd actually strung some intelligible sentences together and even made Jenny laugh a few times.

My eyes alighted on two names next to each other. "Hmmm. Okay, this is a difficult one. So, at the moment, Maya and Jasper, the math teacher at the high school, are seated at the same table but not next to each other. So, apparently, they kissed at Frankie's two weeks ago and are now excruciatingly awkward around each other." Buoyed by the fact that I was not being excruciatingly awkward, I grinned, touching my fingertips together in an evil-scheming gesture.

Jenny giggled, and my heart bounced. "So, what do you suggest, Doc? Should we seat them together in the hope sparks fly, or should we save them from an evening of potential discomfort and move one of them to another table?" Jenny's cheeky grin sent my stomach flipping.

"Hmmm. Given the Jane Austen theme of this weekend, I think we should take a leaf out of *Emma* and impose an evening of awkwardness on them, hopefully culminating in a drunken kiss. It's clear they like each other but are too shy to do anything about it. A wedding, with the booze flowing, could be just the opportunity to get them together for good."

Jenny smiled at me again, and my stomach did a triple backflip. She yanked the laptop back and enthusiastically bashed away at the keyboard for a minute. "Done! Operation *Emma* is underway. Any other comments?"

Jenny pushed the laptop back at me. It all looked... *Goddamnit, Amanda!* She'd seated me and Jenny next to each other, even though she knew full well we didn't get along. And while things had been going well—surprisingly well—for the last twenty minutes, there was no guarantee it would last. But I couldn't exactly say anything to Jenny about it.

I pushed the laptop back to Jenny, plastering a smile on my face. "Nope. The last table looks good."

CHAPTER EIGHT

JENNY

"And I just wanted to confirm there will also be small vases of, um..."—I checked my notes—"cinnamon cloves, dahlias, and fall leaves, for the side tables?"

"Yep, that's right," Olivia confirmed.

"Great, thanks. I'll see you Saturday!"

I hung up and crossed "florist" off my list with a satisfied flourish. Another one down, only another nine to go. I was working my way through the list of the wedding suppliers, introducing myself and confirming the orders. I'd commandeered my parents' dining room table as my wedding-planning headquarters and currently had paper strewn all over it.

Speaking to Olivia reminded me of Blake. Not that I needed a reminder. Images of Blake kept popping into my head with alarming regularity. Blake walking into Novel Gossip, looking adorably scruffy with her tousled hair, gray sweatpants, and hoodie. Blake awkwardly approaching me. Blake behaving like I smelled terribly—I could have sworn she was holding her breath and jumping away from me at the first opportunity. I'd felt so self-conscious I'd suggested she sit opposite me just so she didn't have to inhale whatever offensive scent I was clearly emitting. And then Blake entertaining me with stories about Sapphire Springs. She hadn't struck me as the sort of person who'd have her finger on the pulse of town gossip or be good at comedic retellings, but she had me almost crying with laughter. I'd just been reconsidering my view of her when I'd seen horror flash across her face as she took a final look at the seating chart. It wasn't like I wanted to sit next to her either, but...it'd felt like we were actually getting along, and I couldn't help being a little hurt at Blake's reaction. But now she'd seen it, I couldn't exactly change the seating. That would be too awkward. So we were stuck next to each other for the wedding.

I shook my head to clear it of thoughts of Blake and focused back on my list of suppliers. I'd just picked up my phone to call the photographer when it pinged. I looked down at it with apprehension. Despite the real wedding planner, Miriam, being on bedrest, she'd been calling me and texting me regularly as she thought of other things I needed to do. While I was enjoying myself so far, I hoped there weren't too many more items to add to my to-do list.

But it wasn't the wedding planner. It was Serena. My chest tightened.

> Hi, Jenny, how's country life treating you? I haven't seen a lot of updates on your social media. Does that mean you found a hot lumberjack already? Just remember to post about it! x S

I sighed. I'd been so caught up with wedding planning that I hadn't posted anything for a few days. While the tone of Serena's message was light, I knew it was her way of giving me a kick in the butt. As much as I was tired of social media, if I wanted to have enough money to move back to LA, I needed to keep posting. I couldn't afford to lose any more followers, or the Whamz deal would be off the table.

I looked up at Dad, who was puttering around in the kitchen, making coffee. His Yankees cap covered most of his salt-and-pepper hair, and he was wearing his standard uniform of dad jeans, a long-sleeve shirt, and a fleece vest. A little dorky, very adorable.

"Hey, Dad, I need to do some more posts. Do you have any ideas for picturesque fall scenes around here? I'm seriously lacking inspiration."

Dad carefully poured the coffee into two mugs. "Well, there's Red Tractor Farm. You could do some photos in their pumpkin patch, corn maze...that sort of thing. Why don't you go there?"

"You mean why don't *we* go there?" I asked with my best pleading grin, relief washing over me. I couldn't believe I hadn't thought of that myself. Red Tractor Farm would be a perfect backdrop for a fall photoshoot, and if I got enough content, I could post it gradually over the next week or so, which would take some of the pressure off and allow me to focus on wedding planning.

"I'm not sure. I've got a bit to do around here," Dad said, eyeing the pile of dishes in the sink. Dad worked in the family construction business, but he'd semi-retired the past few years and only helped out with the administrative side of things for a few hours each day. Mom still worked full-time, and I couldn't see her retiring anytime soon. She loved her work too much.

"Come on, it would be a nice father/daughter outing.

Pleeeease." I fluttered my eyelashes dramatically. "And I can do the dishes when we get home."

"Okay, fine. I'll be your photographer for the afternoon. But we need to be back by five. I'm making roast chicken for dinner tonight."

"Thanks, Dad. You're the best." I put my free arm around his waist and squeezed.

———

FORTY-FIVE MINUTES LATER, I was perched on a large orange pumpkin, Walter's little head poking out from behind another smaller one, while Dad took photos. We'd already gotten some great footage of us on a tractor, me pretending to drive it with Walter on my lap, and I was hoping I'd be able to get back to wedding planning soon. Although, with the streaming sunshine and blue skies, it was a perfect day to be outside enjoying some fall activities.

"Let's do the apple cannons next."

On the way over to the apple-shooting range, I ducked into the restrooms to change my red flannel shirt to a blue one so it wasn't obvious all the footage was taken on the same day.

Dad's phone rang just as he was filming me aggressively shooting apples out of a cannon, Walter by my side. It was unexpectedly fun.

"I'm sorry, pumpkin, we've got to go. Your mom needs me to sort out an issue with a subcontractor on the Arnold project. Can we finish this another time?"

Damn. I really wanted to get this over and done with so I could focus on the wedding. "Thanks, Dad, but I really need these shots. I think we might stay, and I'll see if I can sweet-talk a few people into helping me out. Walter and I can walk home."

Dad's face brightened. "That's a good idea. You might even meet a nice young man or woman who'll give you a hand." He winked. I shook my head, smiling. Despite Dad's optimism, I wasn't holding my breath. Given it was a Tuesday, it wasn't particularly busy. The visitors who were here were almost all families with small children—not exactly fertile ground for meeting single people my age.

I waved Dad off and made my way over to a surprisingly attractive scarecrow I'd spotted in a corner of the farm, next to a run-down barn. He was wearing flannel and a cowboy hat. Even if the photos weren't good enough to post, at least I'd be able to send them to Serena and Dad, along with a message letting them know I'd had an encounter with a hot lumberjack/nice young man after all.

"Howdy, handsome. Do you mind if we get a pic?" I looked around for anyone who might be willing to take a photo, but this section of the farm, away from the main attractions, was deserted. I went through the bag of outfit changes I'd brought, and decided, since no one was around, to change into boots, a denim miniskirt, and a green flannel top. The skirt was *not* my style, nor was it really the season for miniskirts, but unfortunately, I'd run some stats on my posts. The more skin I revealed, the better they performed. Given my current situation, now wasn't the time to be prudish.

I quickly changed in the spiderweb-filled barn, balanced my phone on the frame of one of the barn windows, set the timer, and then sprinted over to the scarecrow, wrapped an arm around him, and pretended to land kisses on his face while the camera app clicked. Because no one was around, I really let myself get carried away. If this was one of those fantasy-romance movies, he'd come to life and start kissing me back. While this was not what Serena had in mind when she suggested a fling with a flannel-wearing lumberjack, it was probably as close as I was going to get. I bent one leg up in front of him and was going hard on the kisses when—

"Jenny?"

Shit. My stomach sank. I knew that voice. I turned my head to look behind the scarecrow, still embracing him.

Blake, in flat black ankle boots, black jeans, and red flannel, her dark hair peeking out of a gray beanie. And two small children, staring at me, slack-jawed.

CHAPTER NINE

BLAKE

"Blake! Hi!" Jenny's face was bright pink as she disentangled herself from the scarecrow and smoothed down her short skirt. My eyes lingered on her bare legs. *Eyes up, Blake.*

"Hi. What are you doing?" My lips twitched. The last thing I'd expected on a wholesome visit to Red Tractor Farm was to come across Jenny in a miniskirt, her legs wrapped seductively around a scarecrow like it was a stripper pole—and for me to find it kind of hot. *Good lord, what's wrong with me? Do I have a scarecrow fetish I never knew about? Is that even a thing?*

Jenny tugged her skirt down again and ran a hand through her hair. "I'm just...just getting some content to post." She pointed at her phone perched on one of the barn windows. "Dad was helping to take them, but he had to leave. What are *you* doing?"

I ruffled Liam's hair. "Taking my nephew, Liam, and my niece, Ava, on an excursion while they're in town. Since I won't get to see them much on the weekend with Amanda's wedding, I took the afternoon off to show them around. Say hi to Jenny, guys!"

"Hi, Jenny," the twins responded in unison.

God, they were cute. My brother and his wife loved dressing them in matching outfits, and today, they were both wearing blue jeans, brown rain boots, and red jackets. That, along with their round faces and curly brown hair, was giving off adorable Noddy vibes. I'd been stressed about taking the afternoon off work, but now we were out, I was glad I'd done it, even if looking after them was a little hectic.

"Why were you kissing that scarecrow?" Ava asked, clearly very intrigued. "Did he kiss you back? Can I kiss him?"

"Is that your dog?" Liam asked at the same time, pointing at Walter who was sitting near Jenny. "Can I pet him? Does he eat pumpkin? Does he bite?"

Jenny, still flushed, looked down at them, smiling. "I'm kissing him for a silly photo. No, he didn't kiss me back. And I wouldn't rec—" The kids lost interest in her responses and ran over screaming to the scarecrow, which they proceeded to poke with sticks.

I sighed and sidled up to Jenny. "It's been a constant barrage of questions and activity since my brother dropped them off," I muttered under my breath. "I love them to bits, but it's . . . it's a lot."

Liam and Ava, now bored with the scarecrow, started to jump excitedly on a hay bale next to him. I winced. How on earth did my brother and his wife do this on a daily basis?

My eyes darted to Jenny, who was watching them, chuckling. It dawned on me that, while my heart still beat faster in her presence and her smile sent my stomach twirling, the panicky feeling that made me lose the ability to form sentences around Jenny had disappeared. This was a decided improvement. Maybe our chat at Novel Gossip on Sunday morning had cured me of my painful awkwardness.

A kernel of an idea popped into my mind. Before I had a chance to overthink it, I opened my mouth. "Hey...if you need help with photos, would you be willing to do a trade? I can take the photos, and you could help me look after these two inquisitive Energizer bunnies."

Jenny looked apprehensively at said Energizer bunnies, who were now running in circles around the scarecrow. She was clearly trying to weigh the benefits of me taking her photos versus the cons of hanging out with me and two small, hyperactive children all afternoon.

"I'll throw in some free cinnamon donuts and hot cider," I offered, a pleading edge to my voice.

"Will you throw in an apple fritter as well?" Jenny asked, grinning.

The twins started to throw rotting apples at each other, screaming with laughter. Walter sensibly took shelter behind a hay bale.

"Oh no!" I sprinted over to stop them, pulling them away from the apples and coming back a minute later with a twin in each hand, out of breath and slightly desperate. "I'll buy you all the damn apple fritters you can eat."

Jenny looked at me, her eyes twinkling, and my heart bounced. "It's a deal."

Thank god. "So, what's the next photoshoot location on the list? We've only run around the pumpkin patch shrieking so far, so we're happy to follow your itinerary."

"Well, I was thinking the hayride, the corn maze or—"

"Ponies, ponies, ponies," Liam began chanting, and Ava joined in, tugging at the bottom of my flannel top. "You promised us ponies, Auntie Blake."

I leaned toward Jenny and lowered my voice. "Sorry, I

did say we could do a pony ride. Do you mind if we go there first to get it out of their system?"

"It does seem easier to concede to the demands of these little tyrants, rather than deny them ponies," Jenny whispered, smiling. "But first, I might just quickly change, if that's okay." I looked at her, confused.

"I brought a few changes of clothes, so it didn't look like I took all the footage on the same day," Jenny explained before running into the barn with her backpack, emerging a minute later, her miniskirt replaced with jeans and brown boots.

I clapped my hands. "Okay, kiddos, let's go see some ponies!"

Ave and Liam sprinted to the petting zoo, Jenny and I breaking into a slow jog to keep up with them. Dogs weren't allowed in, so Jenny tied Walter to a post next to a water bowl and then joined us inside.

Once I'd handed over some cash, the kids were given helmets with cowboy hats stuck on them, lifted onto the ponies, and walked around in a circle. Five laps of the yard later, the twins' feet were back on the ground. But then some baby goats caught their attention, and they rushed over to them squealing.

"Sorry, we'll get to your photos soon, I swear," I said, looking at Jenny apologetically. "And the donuts and cider too. I haven't forgotten the terms of our pact."

"And fritters. Don't forget about all those damn fritters," Jenny said, teasing. "But seriously, no rush. They seem to be having a great time." She gestured at the twins, who were now cuddling rabbits, one of whom kept trying to climb on Ava's head, causing her to scream with laughter.

A farm employee, a young woman in baggy jeans and a

warm wool sweater, crouched down next to Ava. "For some reason, Donna always likes to climb on people's heads."

"Maybe 'cause she can see lots from up there," Ava hypothesized. Liam nodded solemnly in agreement.

I elbowed Jenny and nodded my head toward Ava and Donna. "That could be a good photo."

"What?" She looked at me, confused.

"You and Donna...sitting on your head." Before Jenny had a chance to process my suggestion, I turned to the woman next to Ava and gestured at Jenny. "Do you think Donna would sit on my friend's head for a photo?"

"I'm sure Donna would like nothing better. Just sit down here, and we'll get her set up." She pointed to the ground.

"I'm not sure about . . ." Jenny started to protest, but I put a firm hand on her back and steered her toward Donna, taking her phone out of her hand.

Jenny reluctantly sat cross-legged on the dirt and examined Donna closely. She was white and fluffy with long, floppy ears. Jenny gave her a tentative pat. "She's very cute, but are you sure she likes this? And how sharp are her claws?"

"They're paws, not claws. And don't worry, we keep her nails well-trimmed, and she loves it, I'm telling you. Now, if you just sit still, I'll arrange Donna," the farm employee said very matter-of-factly, placing Donna's back feet on her shoulders and gently positioning the rest of her over Jenny's head, Donna's front paws on Jenny's forehead.

"There you go, Donna!" The farm employee looked at us with satisfaction, while Ava and Liam clapped their hands in delight. Donna did look surprisingly relaxed lying on Jenny's head.

I cleared my throat, trying not to laugh. I bit back an

inappropriate joke about face-sitting. "Okay, Jenny, look up at me!"

Jenny plastered a smile on her face and carefully looked up at me, clearly concerned any sudden movement might dislodge Donna. Her smile faltered. "Does...errr...does Donna pee or poop much?"

I snorted, and the farm employee smiled. "You'd be very unlucky if she decided to go while she was sitting on you. And her poops are small and round, so they'd just roll down your back."

The farm employee's response clearly didn't fill Jenny with confidence as her smile transformed into a wide-eyed grimace, but Ava and Liam were very taken by the idea and began chanting, "Poop, poop, poop."

At this rate, I was concerned Donna would lose interest in her perch and hop down before I'd had a chance to capture this moment for posterity.

"Jenny! Stop worrying about Donna's bathroom habits and focus on the photos. The faster we get them, the faster Donna will be off you." Although, Donna was still looking extremely comfortable resting on Jenny's golden waves.

Jenny's chest rose as she took in a deep breath, then she resumed her pose and smile.

I began snapping photos from all angles, doing my best over-the-top-professional-photographer impression to entertain the twins, who'd finished chanting about poop. I knew from past experience that if they weren't engaged, they were likely to cause mischief. "Perfect!" I crouched down low. "Oh yeah, that's good. Give it to me, Donna!"

Jenny started giggling. I shot her a mock stern look. "Jenny, you have to stop laughing. Not only is it ruining the photos, but you're going to make Donna nervous with all that shaking. And you know what happens when you get nervous? You need to pee."

Jenny's eyes widened, and I tried not to laugh.

"I'm sure you've got some good photos now. Do you mind getting Donna down now?" Jenny looked at the farm employee pleadingly.

She nodded, gently disentangling Donna from Jenny's head and placing her on the ground. Donna hopped over to Jenny and gave her an affectionate nudge before bouncing off toward a group of small children eager to shower her with attention.

"Aw, I think you made a new friend," I said, grinning at Jenny.

Jenny stood up, dusting the dirt off her jeans, and walked over to me, shaking her head. "I hope some of those photos worked out, and my humiliation wasn't in vain."

I handed Jenny her phone, and she swiped through the photos as I peered over her shoulder. Thank god I brushed my teeth this morning.

Some of them were absolutely ridiculous—Jenny's face red and lips pressed together as she tried not to laugh while Donna rested nonchalantly on her head, her ears flopping—but there were also some really cute photos I thought her followers would love.

"Are they okay?" I asked.

"They're great. Thank you." She smiled at me, sending my heart soaring. I may have gotten over my nerves, but all my other feelings for Jenny were definitely still there. "Okay, should we go check out that corn maze?"

When we reached the entrance to the maze, Jenny paused. "Do you mind taking a quick photo of me again with the corn? Sorry."

"Don't apologize. Remember, that was part of our deal.

You help me with these two, and I take some photos. Now, get on with it!"

Jenny pulled on a brown plaid jacket and stood in front of the corn, trying to look coolly sophisticated while the twins danced around Walter, just out of the shot, singing a very out-of-tune song about Donna the rabbit and her poops.

Satisfied with the photos, I handed Jenny her phone back. "Here you go. Let me know if you're not happy with them, and I'll take some more. I think you look great, despite the difficult working conditions." Heat crept into my face as the unintentional compliment slipped out of my mouth. Our eyes locked for a moment, and my breath hitched in my throat.

The twins ran up to us and started tugging on my shirt. "Can we go in now, Auntie Blake?"

"I'm sure the photos are fine, thanks," Jenny said, pocketing the phone and calling for Walter, who trundled over, his leash dragging behind him. "Now, let's go explore this maze."

"Can you hold my hand so I don't get lost, Jenny?" Liam held out a small hand to Jenny, melting my heart. How fucking adorable.

"Of course." Jenny smiled down at him, taking his hand in hers.

We began walking through the maze, the corn towering on either side of us. Liam almost immediately dropped Jenny's hand and sprinted ahead, Ava following.

"Liam, Ava! Come back here. We need to stay together." My words seemed to spur them on to run faster. "Damn it," I muttered. "Sorry, I'd better go get them."

"Don't apologize. This was part of our deal, remember?" Jenny shot me a smile as we started to jog after them, sending my heart fluttering. Ava and Liam suddenly turned and ran out of our sight.

"Shit!" I exclaimed, and we picked up our pace. We reached the spot where Ava and Liam had turned and followed in their footsteps, but we couldn't see them. There was a fork in the path up ahead. "Ava! Liam!"

We could hear them faintly but couldn't tell which way they'd gone.

"Should we split up?" Jenny panted, eyes wide with concern.

I nodded, and we ran in opposite directions.

CHAPTER TEN

JENNY

Walter and I took the left turn, running as fast as we could. While I was worrying about the twins, Walter was having the time of his life, his little pink tongue hanging out as he bounded over the dried corn leaves. We reached another fork in the path and stopped. I could hear Ava and Liam yelling faintly over my heavy breathing, but I couldn't tell which direction they were.

"Which way did they go, buddy?" I looked down at Walter. He tugged me to the left and we set off again. We turned a corner, and I saw a flash of red ahead of me, disappearing to the right. *Thank god.*

My lungs were starting to burn, but I pushed myself forward. I turned the corner and almost yelled with relief. The twins were about ten feet up ahead, and they were clearly losing steam. They were no longer running. In fact, they looked like they'd had one too many beers over lunch, stumbling down the path as their little legs tired. Walter and I reached them quickly.

"Stop, stop, you two!" To my relief, they obeyed. I

crouched down next to them. "We have to stick together, okay? Otherwise, I'm worried we won't have time to get donuts. Now, let's find Auntie Blake."

I pulled out my phone and called Blake. She picked up, breathing heavily. "I've got them. Meet you back at the entrance?"

"Oh, thank god. Yep, see you there."

I dropped Walter's leash and took the twins' hands in mine. Out of Walter, Ava, and Liam, Walter won the "most trustworthy and least likely to run away" award by a mile.

We began to slowly retrace our steps with a few wrong turns on the way back. The twins, exhausted, began whining.

"I'm tired. Can you carry me?" Ava asked, looking up at me plaintively.

"Can you carry me too?" Liam tugged at my hand. "Or can I sit on Walter?"

I eyed them. Carrying one of them would be a struggle, two impossible. "I'm afraid I don't think I'm strong enough to carry you both, and neither is Walter. But we should be out soon."

"Well, can we have donuts now, then? I want to sit down." Liam started to squat. Sitting down and eating donuts right now was extremely appealing, but unless UberEats delivered to corn mazes, it wasn't an option. Finally, I understood why they were exploring drone deliveries.

"No, I'm sorry, Liam. We have to get out of this maze first before we can get donuts," I said, channeling my best "fun but firm" mom voice—a voice I'd never needed to use before—and giving his hand a gentle tug.

"But I want donuts!" Liam started wailing, an ear-piercing screech. I flinched. Good lord. I suddenly had a newfound appreciation for my parents raising two children.

"We will get donuts as soon as we're out of this maze," I said firmly.

After a few more painfully slow minutes of walking, I spotted a familiar figure up ahead. *Thank god.* I'd never been so pleased to see Blake in my entire life. She jogged toward us and crouched down next to Liam and Ava, enclosing them in an embrace.

"Thanks so much for finding them," she said, looking up at me, her brown eyes soft.

"No problem. I promised them we could go get donuts now, and I think there may be a small mutiny if we don't follow through with it." I grimaced at her.

Blake stood up, smiling. She stepped forward, and suddenly, unexpectedly, her hand was coming toward my face. *What the...?*

Her eyes firmly fixed on my head, Blake's hand made contact with my hair, tugging something gently. Being this close to Blake, her touching my hair so tenderly, caused a quiver in my belly.

And then she stepped back. "Sorry, you had something in your hair."

"Oh god. It wasn't Donna poop, was it?" I shut my eyes in horror.

Blake burst out laughing. "No, it was a piece of hay." She looked at me, her eyes glinting in the afternoon sun, before quickly looking down to the twins. My heart stuttered.

I was starting to get the distinct impression Blake didn't hate me, after all. And that maybe I'd misjudged her. To top it all off, I was, to my surprise, thoroughly enjoying her company.

TWENTY MINUTES LATER, we were sitting at a rustic wooden bench near the farm stand, devouring cinnamon donuts, apple fritters, and cups of steaming-hot cider.

The twins, exhausted from their exploits and busy licking the sugar off donuts and putting them back on the plate, sat opposite us, blissfully quiet. When Blake realized what they were doing, she'd opened her mouth as if about to tell them off, and then slumped back on the bench, a look of defeat on her face. She caught me smiling at her and muttered, "I might just keep buying them donuts to lick the sugar off if it keeps them entertained and sitting for any period of time." She picked up a pre-licked donut, examined it, shrugged her shoulders, and shoved it in her mouth.

I laughed. "Me too. By the way, have you tried these apple fritters? They're incredible." I took a bite of deep-fried apple-cinnamon deliciousness and then followed it with a swig of the cider.

Blake ate one and then closed her eyes and let out an appreciative moan that sent tingling between my thighs. Cinnamon-sugar dusted her mouth, and her usually pale cheeks were flushed, possibly with exertion from chasing the twins or from the steaming-hot food and drink. I took advantage of her eyes being closed to stare at her shamelessly.

She was so close to me I could see some tiny indentations that looked like chicken pox scars and some light freckles on her cheeks. So close I noticed a few silver hairs poking out from under her beanie. So close that if I just leaned over a few inches, I could tease her soft, pink, juicy-looking earlobe with my teeth. My eyes widened as the image materialized in my mind. *This is Blake, remember, Jenny? Snap out of it.*

She opened her eyes and turned to look at me. *Shit, had she sensed me ogling her?*

If she did, she didn't say anything. Instead, she took off her beanie and handed it to me. "Here, put this on and give me your phone."

"Okay..." Unsure where this was going, I put on the beanie, still warm from Blake's head, and handed my phone over.

Blake took some photos, and then scrolled through them, smiling. "Perfect!"

To say I was surprised at how seriously Blake was taking her duties as my personal photographer was an understatement. I'd assumed Blake, like those teachers at the careers panel, thought my career was a joke. But the way she'd been suggesting photo ops and snapping photos without any hint of judgment had been pleasantly unexpected.

She passed the phone back to me. "Need to make sure I'm holding up my end of the bargain," she said gruffly. I was about to look at the photos, to see what Blake had been so keen on capturing, when a bell rang.

"The last hayride is leaving in five minutes!" a young farm employee yelled.

The twins pulled the donuts away from their tongues, reinvigorated from sugar.

"Can we go on the hayride, Auntie Blake? Please?" asked Ava.

"Pleeeeeeaase!" Liam echoed.

Blake looked at me, an eyebrow raised.

I nodded. "Anything that involves sitting is fine with me. And I should probably stop eating apple fritters, or I may turn into one." I downed the rest of my cider, surprised at how eager I was to extend my time with Blake and the twins.

"Okay, let's do it, then." Blake pulled some baby wipes out of her backpack and attempted to remove the sugar from the twins' faces before grabbing a hand each and walking toward a cart lined with hay bales and attached to another red tractor.

We helped the twins up onto the cart and sat down on the bales. Blake nodded to a bale opposite us. "If you sit over there, I could take a photo of you."

I shook my head. "Thanks, but I think I'm all photo'd out."

"Come on, I think it'll look good," Blake said with a grin.

I just wanted to enjoy the hayride, but Blake was right. The late-afternoon sun was hitting the trees in front of us, and behind them were the mountains and blue sky with a smattering of fluffy clouds. It was picture perfect.

I swapped sides and got Walter to pose beside me, looking out as if the hayride was moving while Blake captured the moment. Then I took my place again next to Ava.

A man with a sleeping baby strapped to his chest and a toddler in tow climbed onto the hay bales, and then the driver secured the gate at the back of the cart, gave us a short spiel about safety, and we were off.

The cart bumped along the dirt track, past the pumpkin patch, apple orchards, and the corn maze. As we went farther out, we passed a field covered in colorful dahlias, zinnias, and snapdragons, and a greenhouse full of more flowers.

"That's where Olivia gets most of her flowers." Blake nodded toward the field and greenhouse.

"Oh wow! I didn't realize she sourced them locally."

The fact the flowers we'd used for Amanda's bachelorette party might have been growing in this field last week gave me a little buzz of warmth.

Behind the flowers was a field of verdant-green pine trees, almost ready for the Christmas tree harvest. The scent of pine lingered in the air, and I inhaled with gusto.

"Is there anything this farm doesn't do?" I asked, only half joking. It certainly made the perfect setting for a content creator. I'd have to come back in December for another holiday-themed photoshoot.

Despite—or perhaps because of—all the sugar the twins had consumed, to my relief, they were content to sit and enjoy the ride. The rhythmic bouncing of the cart and the warm fritters and cider in my belly made me deliciously cozy, while the crisp fall air, blazing red trees, and blue skies made it feel like we were in a fall wonderland.

"How's the wedding planning going?" Blake asked, turning to me.

"Pretty good. I've got a lot to do, but I'm enjoying it. I think it's going to be a really special day."

"Oh great. Well, my offer to help still stands if you need it." She paused. "So, how long are you staying in Sapphire Springs?"

"Probably until January." I studied Blake's face for a reaction, but she just nodded.

"Hey, Auntie Blake, where do babies come from?" Ava piped up as she stared at the sleeping baby sitting across from us, causing me to almost choke from trying to hold back my giggles.

"Let's ask your dad when he picks you up, okay?" Blake said solemnly, her lips twitching.

"No, I wanna know right now." Ava stared at Blake.

Blake's eyes widened, and she shot me a panicked look. I slapped my hand to my mouth to stop laughter escaping.

"Well, babies are made by combining an egg from a woman and sperm from a man. A doctor can do it in a lab or—"

The cart jerked as it drove over a pothole, and Ava shrieked with glee. Much to my disappointment, she forgot about the birds-and-the-bees talk Blake was valiantly attempting just as it was getting interesting. Blake caught my eye and mimed wiping her brow in relief, and I stifled another giggle.

The hayride was over too soon. I could have spent another hour enjoying the views and fresh air, but the farm was closing. We scrambled off the cart and were making our way toward the exit when the twins spotted one of those "put your face in the hole" boards and ran toward it. It was adorned with a painting of cartoon farm animals, their faces cut out so you could poke your head through.

"You go too, and I'll take a photo of the three of you." I shooed Blake with my hand and pulled out my phone.

Liam poked his head through the yellow duck's head, Ava's head appeared on top of the pig's body, and a second later, Blake's head popped through above the cow's shoulders. I'd taken a few photos when the farm employee who'd put Donna on my head approached.

"If you'd like, I can take a photo of your gorgeous family so you can be in it too," she said, smiling.

Blake and I exchanged amused looks. To be honest, it was refreshing. The number of times I'd been out with a woman I was dating, only for people to assume she was just my friend, my sister, or even once—much to my date's horror—my mom, was too many to count. It was nice for once for the assumption to go the other way. Blake and I weren't dating, or even friends, but this woman had thought we were a couple. Well, at least, we hadn't been friends. Now, I wasn't too sure what we were.

"That would be lovely, thank you," I said, handing over my phone.

"C'mon, Jenny! You can be the horse!" Ava yelled.

"Okay. Okay. Coming!" I looked down at Walter. "You can be in the photo too, little guy."

I jogged over to the board, directed Walter to sit next to Liam's duck, and poked my head through the remaining hole.

"One, two, three, say, 'corn cob'!" The woman took some shots, and then we extricated our heads from the holes and thanked her.

"Can you send me those photos?" Blake asked.

"Of course." I smiled and then noticed Blake's bare head, my smile fading. "Oh shit, I forgot to give back your beanie."

Without thinking, I turned to her, taking the beanie off my head and, with both hands, gently placing it on Blake's hair, tugging it down.

I suddenly became conscious of how close I was to Blake again, how intimate this felt. I could smell the sweetness of cinnamon and cider on her breath, feel the softness of her hair on my fingers. If this was one of those Hallmark movies, we'd look intensely into each other's eyes and slowly lean in for a passionate kiss. I yanked my hands away and took a step back at the thought. *What the hell are you doing, Jenny?*

Blake cleared her throat. "Um, do you need a lift home?" Her voice sounded normal, like I hadn't just invaded her personal space and imagined kissing her. *Thank god.*

I paused for only a second before accepting Blake's offer. After overexerting myself in the corn maze, walking home had lost its appeal.

We spent the ride home in comfortable silence, the twins dozing in their car seats behind us. I leaned back in the passenger seat, Walter on my lap, warm and relaxed after the adventures of the day. I hadn't felt this content and peaceful since the scandal happened. Maybe longer. I stole glances at Blake's face in profile as she focused on driving down the dark, winding roads back to Sapphire Springs.

As I got out of the car, Blake cleared her throat. "Thanks for hanging out with us this afternoon. I'm not sure we'd all still be in one piece if it hadn't been for you. And I... I had a really nice time." Her voice was gruff.

"Me too." I hoped my voice didn't sound as surprised as I felt.

CHAPTER ELEVEN

BLAKE

"Shouldn't you be working?" George asked, surprised, as I walked into Novel Gossip.

I huffed. "Yes, thanks for the warm welcome and reminder. I blocked out an hour this afternoon to try to get on top of paperwork, and Dad is waging another battle with the printer that I can't listen to any longer, so I thought I'd give you some business, see how my BFF is doing, and do a bit of work. But if you're not interested, I can go to Dippin' Donuts instead." I raised an eyebrow.

She took a dramatic intake of breath and glared at me. "You wouldn't dare!"

"No, you're right, I wouldn't. You've got me addicted to your double shot lattes, and I'm now a loyal customer, no matter how annoying you are." I grinned at her. "Speaking of..."

"One double shot latte coming right up."

I took a seat near the window and pulled out my laptop to start work. But first, I took my phone from my pocket to look at the photos Jenny sent me from yesterday. For the twelfth time, I zoomed in on Jenny's face poking out from the horse's body, a lock of her wavy blond hair tumbling out of the hole and down the horse's chest. Her cheeks and the tip of her nose were pink, perhaps from the cold or the cider, and she was beaming. I zoomed in closer, the heat in my chest expanding as I remembered how she'd tenderly tugged the beanie onto my head, so close I could feel the warmth of her breath on my face. I'd had to fight the urge to put my hands around her waist and draw her to me. From the moment we'd sat down for donuts, apple fritters, and cider, yesterday afternoon had taken on a magical quality, and I hadn't wanted it to end.

There was a thud as George placed a double shot latte and her delicious lemon-blueberry cake in front of me, and then took a seat opposite me, a mug of coffee in her hand.

"Thought I might join you for a few minutes since it's not busy at the moment, if that's okay?"

"Of course. So, how's business, anyway?"

The chain coffee shop, Dippin' Donuts, had opened in Sapphire Springs a few months ago. George had been very concerned it might affect Novel Gossip's bottom line. From what I could tell, it hadn't impacted the café at all, but she still got very riled up every time I mentioned the "D" word. I'd made a concerted effort to buy coffee from her every day to support her, which was no hardship on my part, given how good her barista skills were. I took a long sip of my latte and relaxed.

"It's fine. I've noticed a slight drop off in coffee and pastry orders, but it's not significant. I'm still planning to diversify the business—hold some paint-and-sip nights here, maybe do a few author events, that type of thing—to keep things fresh. I'd love Novel Gossip to become a real community hub, a place that brings people together," George said earnestly.

I put down my mug and smiled at her. "That sounds great. Although, I think you're underestimating just how much you've already achieved. You've got the book club and game nights. And just look around today." I gestured at the other customers, busy catching up with friends or sitting alone, reading books or typing on their laptops. "Before Novel Gossip opened up, we'd have to drive over to the tea rooms for decent coffee. Having a place we can meet for good food and coffee on Main Street has made a huge difference. And Dippin' Donuts definitely can't match your atmosphere, or food or coffee, for that matter."

George let out a pleased huff. "Well, that's good to hear." She took a sip of her coffee. "So, how did it go with the twins yesterday?"

I'd brought the twins in to meet George a few months ago. Despite them almost knocking over her book displays multiple times and dropping a milkshake on the floor, she'd been very taken with them.

"Well, it was...it was interesting. I had some unexpected help in return for my photography skills." George raised her eyebrows, bemused. I filled her in on yesterday's events.

When I'd finished, George clapped her hands and did a fake swoon. "What a delightful fall date! Hayrides, corn mazes, hot cider, and donuts. It all sounds so romantic."

"Did you just listen to anything I said? Small children singing about poop, getting lost in corn mazes, and generally running wild. It was anything but romantic."

"Well, I heard it on good authority from Amanda that Jenny is single." George grinned, and my heart jumped. I'd wondered what Jenny's relationship status was, but I hadn't wanted to ask Amanda, in case it invited uncomfortable questions.

"Uh-huh. And I don't see how that's relevant. As you know, I am very happily single and intend to stay that way."

George frowned. "Look, Blake. Since there've never been any eligible women in town, I haven't bothered saying this before, but swearing off relationships forever just because of what happened with Grace seems a little drastic. I know it was awful, but it was over three years ago now—"

My chest tightened at Grace's name. "And it still hurts." My words came out shorter and snappier than I intended.

Despite it being over three years since Grace, I wasn't over it. I was over *Grace*, that was for sure, but I hadn't recovered from the absolute devastation I'd experienced after it all happened. The depression. The loss of appetite and weight. The obsessive thoughts. All my hopes and dreams destroyed. It was the worst period of my life, and I never wanted to go back there again. The break-ups with Anna and Hanh had been bad enough, but with Grace it had been a whole different level of pain.

"I'm sorry. I shouldn't have brought her up," George said, grimacing.

My face softened. George was just trying to look out for me.

"Look, I like being single. My life is full. Besides, Jenny is only here for a couple of months, so she's not an option anyway."

I stirred my coffee, watching the miniature whirlpool my spoon created. I firmly believed that not everyone needed a partner and that society put far too much emphasis on marriage and long-term relationships. But if I was being honest with myself, I wasn't sure I was one of those people. I had a history of serious long-term relationships for a reason. While my cat Fred was great, I missed the companionship a partner offered. And seeing Jenny again had reminded me of some other things I'd missed as well, desires I hadn't experienced for a long time. One of the many reasons I'd moved back to Sapphire Springs was the absolute lack of dating options. If there wasn't anyone to date, then there was no risk of getting my heart broken. But now Jenny was back, reminding me what I was missing out on.

My phone pinged, and I looked down immediately, in case it was Dad telling me a patient had unexpectedly turned up. Jenny's name popped up, and my heart skipped a beat.

> It's totally fine if you're not, but I was wondering if you'd be free to meet me tonight at the barn and help make the wedding favor bags?

I was torn. Hanging out with Jenny had significantly more appeal than spending another night working late on the couch with Fred. But at the same time, was it a good idea, given my feelings for her? Maybe not, but the anticipation vibrating through my body at the thought of seeing her was too strong to ignore.

> OK.

I watched the three dots blinking on my phone.

> Awesome, I can lick you up at 7?

I chuckled. The three dots reappeared.

Damn autocorrect, I meant pick. Pick
you up.

I laughed, and George raised her eyebrows. "Who are you texting with?"

"Jenny."

"I knew it! Are you two arranging another date?" She leaned in, waggling her eyebrows suggestively.

I glared at her, suppressing a chuckle. "No, you fool. I'm just going to help her with the wedding favors tonight."

"Uh-huh. That doesn't sound particularly funny." She narrowed her eyes.

I slid my phone across the table.

George picked it up and snort-laughed. "She wants to lick you up? That's definitely a Freudian slip. And then she goes on to say she wants to pick you up. I don't think her intentions could be any clearer."

"Ha ha, very funny. We might be getting along well, but we're not getting along *that* well." The image of Jenny sitting on a hay bale, the soft afternoon sun lighting her face as she enjoyed the hay ride, appeared for a split second.

"You should respond, 'You can lick me anytime.'" I rolled my eyes. "But if you don't mind me giving you some unsolicited advice, you need to work on your text-messaging game. 'OK'? You sound like a teenage boy."

George slumped back in her seat and let her face fall slack. "'OK.' 'Fine.' 'Yes,'" she grunted in her best sullen-teenager impression. "She's going to think you don't want to hang out. I'm used to your texts now, so I know not to take them personally, but she won't know that."

I snatched my phone back. "I just like efficiency. Why type out five words, one exclamation mark, and two emojis when you could use a single word?"

"Because you might unintentionally offend someone or come across as standoffish?" George retorted.

I sighed. It wasn't the first time I'd received that feedback. After Amanda thought I didn't want to come to her viewing of *Sense and Sensibility* a couple of months ago because of my short messages (which was, to be honest, partially true, but I hadn't meant to be that obvious), she'd gently suggested a few extra words or some emojis or exclamation marks might help convey my tone more accurately. It had also been a source of frustration for my exes. But texting didn't come naturally to me. Short, efficient, no-frill messages did.

I typed out

> Sounds good

and let my finger hover over the exclamation mark. Urgh. I pressed it, scrunching my face, and sent the message.

"Done. I used two words instead of one *and* included an exclamation mark. I hope you're happy."

George grinned. "Very." She downed her coffee and stood up. "I'd better get back to it."

"Me too." I sighed, glancing at all the unread emails on my laptop screen. I needed to buckle down to finish all my work before seven p.m.

JENNY PULLED up outside the gorgeous old red barn where Amanda and Peter would be married on Saturday. Not that you could tell it was a gorgeous old red barn in the pitch-black night, but I'd seen it enough times to know exactly what it looked like. We pulled out our phones, turning on the flashlight function to help guide us over to the barn door.

Metal clanged on metal, and I realized Jenny was fumbling with a handful of keys. "Sweet Jesus, how many doors can one barn have?" she muttered, her hair falling over her face. I shone the phone light on the lock so she could see what she was doing.

We finally got in, and I turned on a light switch next to the door. Strings of fairy lights appeared, crisscrossing the barn's rafters and dimly lighting the barn. We searched for the switch for the other, more powerful, lights attached to the rafters, but we couldn't find it.

"I guess we're stuck with mood lighting." Jenny shrugged, smiling.

Since we'd given up on trying to find the light switch, I looked around with interest. I'd driven past the barn since I was a kid, but I'd never been inside. It was now a popular wedding venue—a particular favorite with New York City couples who fancied a rustic vibe. We were standing on what would presumably be the dance floor. The barn was huge with a high, A-shaped, beamed ceiling with wooden rafters. White sheets were draped over tables that covered most of its wooden floor. I was sure when all the lights were on, the tables were set, and the barn was filled with guests, it would be different, but it currently felt extremely eerie.

As if she'd read my mind, Jenny said, "This feels kinda... spooky. It would be the perfect venue for a Halloween party."

It really would be. I didn't have much interest in party-throwing, but George held an annual Halloween party at Novel Gossip, a venue that was too warm and cozy to give off true horror vibes. I made a mental note to keep this barn in mind in case she ever wanted a bigger, scarier venue.

Jenny nodded her head at a stack of boxes in a corner of the barn. "They must have the wedding favors in them. Miriam, the wedding planner, said they'd been delivered here." We opened them and found that they were, indeed, the wedding favors. One of the boxes had small brown paper gift bags, another had heart-shaped chocolates, and the last one had small packets of flower seeds.

"Rooooooooooooooooh." A loud, high-pitched noise outside made us both jump.

My heart rate picked up. "That must be a coyote," I said, more to reassure myself than anything. Coyotes were common in this area and not usually dangerous. "Although, it sounded more like a woman wailing."

"Or a ghost," Jenny helpfully suggested.

"Thanks for that." I didn't believe in ghosts, but the unnerving noise did have an otherworldly quality.

The lights flickered for a second, and we looked at each other, eyes wide. Good lord, this barn was definitely giving me beginning-of-horror-movie vibes. Next, a bloody corpse would probably drop from the rafters. I eyed the ceiling of the barn with trepidation.

"We could always take the boxes back to my parents' house and do it there," Jenny suggested, clearly having similar thoughts.

"Then we'll just have to cart them all back here again. Let's stay here. It'll be fine," I responded as confidently as I could. Blake Mitchell did not believe in ghosts.

We dragged the boxes into the center of the barn and sat down next to them. Jenny checked her phone for instructions. "Okay, so we're supposed to put four chocolates and one packet of seeds in each bag. I'm under strict direction not to eat any of the chocolates because they got exactly the right number, so I brought a few snacks to keep us going, including homemade brownies, courtesy of my dad." She pulled out a bag of salty-and-sweet popcorn, brownies, and a few Bruce Cost sodas and offered them to me.

"Amazing, thank you." I'd made myself a quick sandwich for dinner, which hadn't been terribly filling, and had already been eyeing the chocolates, so I happily took a brownie.

We got to work sorting the chocolates and seeds into the bags.

For a few minutes, as we got into the rhythm of filling the bags, we sat in comfortable silence. Every so often, I'd sneak a glance at Jenny sitting cross-legged on the floor. The glow of the fairy lights gave her a warm, golden radiance. The word angelic came to mind. *Damn.*

"So, how did the twins do after you dropped me off yesterday?" Jenny looked up at me.

I smiled. "Apparently, they slept for thirteen hours last night, which is unheard of. My brother is threatening to drop them off regularly so they can get the 'Auntie Blake treatment,' and he can sleep in the next day. He even suggested I should shut down my practice and open up a childcare center instead. Needless to say, I didn't tell him about losing the twins in the corn maze." I chuckled. "Were you happy with the photos?"

"Some of them were great, some of them were hilariously bad. Like the look of horror on my face when I started stressing about Donna pooping on my head, and some of the scarecrow-kissing you witnessed." Jenny laughed, her head tilted back, her eyes twinkling. "But people often love the terrible photos, so I might do a funny 'outtakes' reel of all the ridiculous ones."

"Do you find it hard thinking of things to post? I feel like I'd run out of ideas almost immediately." I couldn't think of anything worse than doing Jenny's job. I was an intensely private person, and having to constantly put myself out there, be bright and bubbly, would be exhausting.

Jenny's smile faded. "Yeah, I've been finding it tough for a while. Initially, I really loved it. I'd post whenever a funny idea popped into my head, if my boss's dog was being particularly cute, or if I was wearing an outfit I liked. But then I got a lot of followers, started getting sponsorships, and things gradually changed. I know I'm really lucky I can make a living from it, but there's a lot of pressure to post all the time, to come up with something new to catch people's attention. And it's very unpredictable. The algorithms that work out who sees your posts aren't transparent. They can change without warning, and suddenly, you're not getting the views you used to and have no idea why. You also get all sorts of gross messages. And if you fuck up, people can get nasty." Jenny's face clouded.

My chest tightened at the thought. "It's really brave putting yourself out there. I couldn't do it."

Jenny shot me an indecipherable look. "I never made a conscious decision to become an influencer. It just happened. So I'm not sure that makes me brave. Dealing with sick people all the time, giving people difficult news, having peoples' lives in your hands...now *that's* brave. And so is setting up a clinic here by yourself." I was tempted to ask Jenny why she kept doing it since it sounded like she didn't enjoy it anymore, but I didn't want to come across as too nosy.

"It's definitely been a big learning curve. But to be honest, dealing with sick people is what I love about my job.

The part I don't love is all the paperwork and the financial side of things."

I stopped there. I didn't usually complain about my job, but Jenny was looking at me expectantly, so I continued. "Quite a few people in Sapphire Springs don't have health insurance, and some can't access Medicaid. Knowing they'll struggle to pay my fees, let alone any medication or tests I recommend, is tough. I often waive my own fees, and I've been helping some of them apply for financial aid, but it's really time-consuming. Some hospitals seem to go to great lengths to make their application process as complicated as possible. So I'm finding it hard to juggle that with actually seeing patients, doing admin, and having some time off."

Jenny frowned. "That sucks," she said bluntly. "Do you know what other small-town doctors in this area do? They must have similar issues."

"You know, I'm not sure. But that's a good idea." I'd had some limited interactions with the doctors in neighboring towns but hadn't thought to ask them for advice. Some of them had been practicing for over twenty years. Surely by now they would have ironed out these sorts of problems.

As the evening wore on, we created a mini production line. I'd put the chocolates in the bags and then hand them to Jenny to add the seeds and seal the bags.

There were no more disturbing sounds or flickering lights, and we snacked on brownies and popcorn while I filled Jenny in on the latest in the Rory and Joe fence dispute and other Sapphire Springs gossip, our laughter filling the large, empty space with warmth. The barn no longer felt eerie. If anything, with the fairy lights, snacks, and banter, it felt kind of...romantic.

Pausing for another snack break, Jenny giggled. "You know, this reminds me of the midnight feasts that always featured in the girls boarding school stories my mom read to me as a kid. They'd sneak out of their dorms with treats and a picnic blanket and meet in some deserted part of the school. I always wanted to have one, but Mom wouldn't let me."

"Well, I'm glad I could help you live out your fantasy." I grinned. As soon as the words were out of my mouth, I regretted them. Without meaning to, they'd sounded a little —okay, very—flirtatious.

Shit.

Jenny looked at me sharply. Heat rushed up my face. Hopefully she wouldn't notice I was blushing in the dim lighting. Should I say something to make it clear I didn't mean it like that?

But before I could formulate the appropriate words, Jenny held out her hand for the next half-filled bag and smiled. "Next! We'd better keep going, or we'll be here all night."

LYING IN BED THAT NIGHT, indulging in my guilty pleasure of scrolling through Jenny's TikTok page, my phone lit up with a message.

Jenny.

My pulse quickened as I clicked on her text.

> Thanks again for coming out tonight. You were a huge help, and I had a really nice time 😊

Remembering George's and Amanda's urgings to use more emojis, I scrolled through the options available on my phone. Love heart. Nope, that seemed way too romantic.

Smiley face. Nah, that didn't really convey my agreement to her words. And then I spotted the thumbs-up emoji and smiled.

Perfect.

CHAPTER TWELVE

JENNY

It was Friday afternoon, and the welcome dinner for the bridal party and Amanda's and Peter's immediate families was due to start in less than two hours. I should have been focused on placing the name cards on the tables. Instead, holding Blake's name card in my hand, I stared out the floor-to-ceiling windows of River's Edge, Sapphire Springs' fanciest restaurant located on the edge of the Hudson River.

But rather than admiring the spectacular views of the river and the red, orange, and yellow hues of the fall-foliage-covered hills behind it, I was reliving a montage of Blake.

Blake stepping out of the pond, looking like Mr. Darcy incarnate. Blake tenderly pulling hay out of my hair. Blake moaning over the apple fritter. Blake looking at me while I gently tugged the beanie over her hair. Blake laughing as we sat on the floor of the barn, eating way too many brownies.

A warm, trembling sensation appeared between my upper thighs.

Shit. I needed a cold shower or, at the very least, a cold shot of reality, so I opened Blake's last message and stared at it for the umpteenth time.

I'd agonized over the message I'd sent her on Wednesday night for at least twenty minutes. Should I put an x or a 😄 at the end? Should I say I had a *nice* time or a *great* time? Should I delete the message altogether?

And in return, Blake had just sent me a thumbs-up. Not a "Me too 😄" or a "No problem, any time!" Just a thumbs-up. I didn't know how to interpret it. To me, the thumbs-up emoji came across as a little passive-aggressive or sarcastic. Did it mean she didn't have a good time? Or was I just reading too much into it? And why did I care so much anyway?

I scrolled up the messages. There was a definite theme to our correspondence. I'd send a text with a smattering of friendly exclamation marks and smiley faces, and she'd respond in well-punctuated monosyllables seriously lacking in warmth.

I sighed. Blake was such an enigma. I would just start thinking we were getting along really well, and then she'd send me a curt text or say something abruptly that gave me the distinct impression she didn't feel the same way. It wouldn't have been a problem—after the wedding tomorrow, there'd be no reason to see her unless I, god forbid, needed medical attention—except I couldn't get her and that damn montage out of my head.

It had been a mistake inviting her to help with the gift bags on Wednesday night. Since she'd offered to help, she'd been the easiest option. But in retrospect, it had just fueled whatever was going on in my head right now.

I looked down at her name card in my hand. Amanda had placed us together on her seating plan for the welcome dinner as well, and I was struggling with a dilemma. I hadn't shown Blake the seating chart for this dinner, so I *could* easily move us apart without offending her. But I had enjoyed her company the last few times we'd hung out...

The montage started again. I squeezed my eyes shut. *Good god, make it stop.*

I strode down the long table until I spotted Maya's name card and swapped it for Blake's. I let out a long breath. The montage stopped. Yep, that was definitely the right decision.

My phone vibrated. I picked it up, hoping no last-minute wedding issues had arisen. My stomach dropped. It was Serena.

> Loving all the fall content this week! Keep it up. Any luck finding that hot lumberjack?

A vision of Blake in flannel, smirking at me as she caught me making out with the scarecrow, flashed into my mind.

I sent Serena the photo of me kissing the scarecrow instead.

> Yep! We're engaged 😄. Any news on the job front?

I'd been posting one photo a day from the farm, and they'd been doing pretty well. The outtakes video I'd posted on TikTok had actually been my best-performing post in some time. Given its success, I'd created another video featuring photos of me looking ridiculous kissing the scarecrow, which I'd post later tonight in peak time. Yes, I looked absurd, but people liked it, and I didn't mind making fun of myself. I'd even gained a few hundred new followers, much to my relief. I hadn't posted the Donna photos yet, though.

While the farm employee had assured me Donna *loved* sitting on people's heads, and she had looked quite happy perched up there, I was worried someone might claim it was animal cruelty. That was the last thing I needed right now. My phone vibrated again.

> 🌎 What a gorgeous couple. No new offers yet, but I'm sure it's only a matter of time.

I sighed. Hopefully Serena was right. Companies used to ask me to post sponsored content all the time, but no one had approached me for weeks. This did not bode well for my bank balance, especially since I'd cut ties with Ruff after the incident.

Exiting out of Serena's message, I saw I'd received another message earlier that I'd missed. It was from Jeremy, the artist I'd dated in LA earlier this year—the artist who'd recently gotten engaged.

> Hey Jenny! Long time, no see. How are you doing? Let me know if you feel like coming over one night this week. I miss you.

Frowning, I opened Instagram and searched for Jeremy's profile, clicking on the latest photo of him and his fiancée, posted yesterday. They were kissing, and the caption read, *How will I survive a week without this gorgeous human? Have fun in Hawaii, babe.*

My stomach turned. What a jerk. Amanda was right, I really was terrible at ignoring red flags.

"How's my wedding planner extraordinaire?" I jumped and turned to find Amanda standing a few feet from me, holding a tray with two takeout coffees from Novel Gossip.

"Hi! I wasn't expecting you for another hour. How's my

favorite bride to be?" I grabbed the coffee with the J written on it. "Thank you!"

"The principal let me leave early, so I thought I'd see if there was anything I could help with. And I'm good. Nervous, but good." Amanda smiled, brushing her hair behind her ear.

"I think everything's under control. I'm just putting out the name cards as per your seating plan." Usually, I'd tell Amanda all about Jeremy's douchery, but complaining about men being dicks the night before she got married didn't seem like the best move.

"This doesn't look like my seating plan. Why is Blake sitting next to Evie?" Amanda raised an eyebrow.

I squinted at her. "I don't know what you're playing at, but it hasn't slipped my attention that you sat me and Blake together tonight and tomorrow. You know things are strained between us. Blake already saw the wedding seating plan, so I can't change that, but I would actually like to have a nice time tonight, so I took matters into my own hands."

Amanda raised her eyebrows, a mischievous look on her face. "Oh, when did Blake see the wedding seating plan?"

Damn. I could feel my treacherous cheeks warm at Amanda's words. "I ran into her at Novel Gossip on Sunday, and she had a quick look at it. Most of the changes I sent you were at her suggestion. For someone who seems so aloof, she's surprisingly tuned in when it comes to Sapphire Springs' gossip."

A sly grin formed on her face. "Oh, is that right? That's funny. When I was getting these coffees, George just happened to mention that you and Blake had a nice little excursion to Red Tractor Farm on Tuesday and that she helped you with the wedding favor bags. For someone you don't like, you're spending a lot of time with her. Is there anything you'd like to tell me?"

I glared at Amanda, silently cursing George, although I couldn't help but wonder exactly what Blake had said to George about our joint activities. "Excuse me, do you want a wedding planner or not? Just because we've spent some time together to save our mutual friend's wedding, and we both date women, doesn't mean we're into each other. Seriously. Shouldn't you be getting ready for dinner or something?"

Amanda's phone pinged, and she pulled it out of her pocket, frowning as she read the message. "Well, you're in luck. Blake needs to make a house call tonight, so she's sent her apologies for the dinner."

An unexpected wave of disappointment washed over me. Despite moving her name card, I'd apparently still been looking forward to seeing her.

Amanda continued to stare at her phone, a wry smile on her face. "God, Blake is shocking with texts. She reminds me of my dad. Seriously, look at this." Amanda shoved her phone in front of my face.

I took a step back and let my eyes adjust.

> Would you like to grab brunch this Saturday at Novel Gossip? I was thinking maybe 11am? x A

OK.

> Thanks again for planning the bachelorette party with Jenny. It was great!

Urgent house call. Can't make dinner. Sorry.

Amanda shook her head. "I'm sure she probably feels terrible she won't be able to come, but her text really does not give that vibe at all."

I laughed loudly, far too pleased for my liking. Clearly, I shouldn't take Blake's abrupt messages too personally. She was just hopeless at texting.

CHAPTER THIRTEEN

JENNY

I blinked away a tear as Amanda and Peter stood between two gnarled apple trees near the barn, exchanging their vows. The green-gold leaves of the apple trees were glowing in the afternoon sun, and behind them was a gorgeous red maple, its leaves blazing crimson.

They were looking at each other with such adoration my heart hurt with happiness. And also, if I was being honest, with a twinge of envy for what Amanda and Peter had together. I wanted that. So much. But with my dating track record, it felt completely unattainable.

I snuck a glance at Blake. She was two bridesmaids away from me, looking smoking hot in a shirt made of the same fabric as the other bridesmaids' dresses and a blue tailored suit, watching Amanda and Peter with a faint smile on her face. I was glad Amanda had been totally fine with Blake wearing a suit. Some other brides might be less accommodating for their gender-nonconforming friends.

So far, the wedding was going smoothly. I'd sent a few updates to Miriam, letting her know things were under control. I'd never met her, but given how often we'd talked over the past few weeks, she was starting to feel like a friend. The only thing I was waiting on, and that was potentially not under control, was the cake. The lack of cake was the reason for the heavy, unsettled sensation in my stomach.

The baker from a nearby town had promised to deliver the cake over an hour ago, and he still wasn't here. Before the ceremony started, I'd called him multiple times, left a voice message and sent a text, all of which had gone unanswered. When I wasn't tearing up over Amanda and Peter exchanging vows or stealing glances at Blake, I'd been keeping an anxious eye out for him.

As soon as the ceremony was over, I raced back to the barn and grabbed my phone, hoping there'd be a *Sorry, I'll be there in ten minutes* type text waiting for me.

There were no text messages, but there were three missed calls and a voicemail. I clicked on the voicemail, holding my belly with one hand in an attempt to calm its churning.

The message started with a rhythmic *beep, beep, beep*— the sort you heard on hospital medical dramas when the person was on life support.

I took a sharp intake of breath. *Shit.* That was not a promising start.

After a few seconds, a man cleared his throat. "Jenny, it's Charlie. I'm so sorry, but I've been in an accident. I... There was a deer, and I hit a tree trying to miss it. The cake is destroyed, and I'm in the hospital, but I'm fine. I'm so sorry. I feel terrible." There was some muffled talking. "Look, I've got to go. Please tell Amanda I'm sorry." The message cut off.

Trying to keep my panic at bay, I took a few deep breaths and looked around the barn. At one end, there were rows of long tables now covered in crisp, white tablecloths and Olivia's gorgeous fall flower arrangements of red, orange, and yellow dahlias, zinnias, rudbeckia, and snap-dragons. Rustic wooden chairs with white silk bows and matching cushions were tucked under the tables.

It looked fantastic.

Amanda was going to have an amazing wedding, even if she was short a wedding cake. With the canapes and three-course meal, it wasn't like anyone would go hungry. But then the small, round, empty table where the cake was meant to sit caught my eye, and my confidence faltered.

Amanda loved cake, and I knew she and Peter had spent weeks sampling different options before they'd settled on Charlie's coconut-and-lime cake. Should I call Miriam and see if this had ever happened to her before? Or Google, *What to do if your wedding cake gets ruined?*

"This place looks great! No hint of our haunted barn. And the wedding is fantastic so far. Good job," Blake said behind me, causing me to jump. I turned, and she saw my face. "Is everything okay?"

"Yeah... Everything except the cake, which is no longer with us." Blake's eyes widened. "The baker had a car acci-dent on the way here, and the cake didn't make it. It sounds like no one was seriously hurt, thank goodness. But it's obvi-ously not great for the wedding. We don't have any dessert now. They won't be able to do the traditional cake cutting..." I trailed off, tears welling in my eyes. *It will be fine, Jenny. It's just a cake.*

"Shit!" Blake chewed on her lip for a second and then looked at her watch. "What time is the cake scheduled to get cut?"

I examined the schedule. "Eight thirty."

"Great. That gives us plenty of time," Blake said, satisfaction in her voice.

"Plenty of time for what?" I asked Blake as she turned and walked out of the barn, ignoring my question. I shook my head and started to Google.

A few minutes later, Blake walked back in with George, who was looking dapper in a black tuxedo.

"I've spoken to George, and we are going to bake a new wedding cake," Blake announced with authority.

"You...you are?" I looked between them, some of the tension in my chest lifting. "Are you sure? I mean, that would be amazing, but won't it be a lot of trouble?" I was touched Blake and George would be willing to miss half the wedding to bake a new cake. And the fact Blake had thought of it herself and managed to rope George in was surprisingly sweet.

George grinned. "Yep, I can't promise it's going to look super professional—I'm not a cake decorator—but I'll make sure it at least tastes good, which is more than I can say for most wedding cakes. Do you know what sort of cake Amanda ordered?"

"It was a coconut-lime layer cake with lime filling, cream-cheese frosting, and candied limes."

George grimaced. "Hmm, that sounds a little tricky to pull off in less than four hours."

A thought hit me. "What about your lemon-blueberry cake? Amanda mentioned it was incredible. Would that be doable?"

George clapped her hands. "Perfect! Now *that* I can do. I have enough different sized tins that we should be able to make a three-layer version with white lemon frosting."

"That sounds amazing!" My face fell. "Where are you going to bake it, though? The caterers need the kitchen."

Behind the back of the barn was a smaller barn, which housed a commercial kitchen. When I'd peered in the door earlier, it was already a hive of activity. Blake and George could probably bake at the Novel Gossip kitchen, but that would mean they'd miss even more of the wedding. They'd also have to drive all the way back, and I didn't want to lose another cake to the road.

"I know Ms. Levi, the owner," Blake said gruffly. "I just called her. She's happy for us to use the kitchen in her house. We'll drive back into town quickly so we can pick up George's baking supplies, and then we'll get to work."

I breathed out a sigh of relief and fought the urge to throw my arms around them both.

Amanda's wedding was back on track.

CHAPTER FOURTEEN

BLAKE

I stared at all the ingredients, bowls, and spoons spread out on the kitchen table. This was *not* how I was expecting to spend Amanda's wedding. But it was a relief to have something to keep me busy. Watching Amanda and Peter exchange vows, I couldn't help feeling a pang of sadness I'd never have a similar experience. I'd tried my best to push those emotions away and focus on being happy for Amanda, but hadn't been altogether successful. I knew I couldn't risk any more heartbreak, but that didn't extinguish the feeling that I was missing out on something.

"It's like we're on an episode of the *Great British Bake Off*. Okay, what do we do first?" I asked in my best British accent, looking at George.

"First thing's first, stop that atrocious British accent. Next, take off your jacket, roll up your sleeves, and put this on." She threw me an apron. "Then, we need to turn on the oven so it can heat up."

I was closest to the oven, so I walked over to it as I rolled up my sleeves. "Should I put it on 500 so it cooks fast, given we're short on time?"

George stopped what she was doing and shot me a look. "God no. Put it on 350. Um, Blake, have you ever made a cake before?"

"Yeah, of course. But it was a boxed cake mix, not from scratch. Who has the time for that?"

George looked at me aghast, her eyes wide. "Oh dear. And am I correct in understanding that your use of the singular 'boxed cake mix' means you've only ever cooked one cake?"

I grinned, and George grimaced. "Okay. Well, that would have been useful information to have before I committed to cooking a three-tiered wedding cake with you under time pressure. How about you start with washing the blueberries, then?"

George handed me the blueberries and began prepping the other ingredients.

After a few minutes of comfortable silence, George asked, "So, how are things with Jenny?" Her voice was full of meaning. I looked up sharply. She was focused on measuring out the flour, but I could see the corner of her mouth twitching.

"Fine. Why?"

"I caught both of you sneaking glances at each during the ceremony. And then you offered to cook an entire cake for her despite, um...not being a baker."

My chest warmed at the thought of Jenny looking at me. Had she been checking me out too?

But I wasn't about to tell George that.

"I don't know what you're talking about. And we're cooking this cake for Amanda, not Jenny." Denying everything seemed like the best strategy at this point.

There was a knock on the front door and then a creak as it opened.

"Hello?" Jenny called.

Damn. I quickly ran my tongue across the front of my teeth, hoping none of the blueberries I'd sampled were stuck to them.

"We're through here," George called out, as she winked at me.

"Behave," I muttered under my breath just as Jenny appeared at the kitchen door.

While the doctor in me knew it was physically impossible, I could have sworn my heart stopped for a moment.

Jenny looked so damn cute. The pen tucked behind her ear, the clipboard with the schedule under her arm, and her business-like stride were in stark contrast to the flowing, floral bridesmaid dress, silver heels, and cream shawl over her shoulders. Her hair fell in waves over the shawl. And between her hair, the shawl, and the V-neck of the dress, there was more than a hint of her cleavage, which I tried to ignore. In her hands were two glasses of champagne.

"How are my favorite bakers doing? I feel terrible you two are stuck in here while the rest of us are sipping on champagne and eating vol-au-vents, so I brought you both a glass. Sorry, I didn't have enough hands to bring you food as well, so I had to prioritize." She grinned.

George grabbed one of the glasses and took a swig. "Thanks. I'm glad to see you've got your priorities straight!"

Ms. Levi walked into the kitchen just as Jenny handed me the other glass, our fingers narrowly missing each other. "Hi, Jenny! I thought I heard you. I was just coming in to see how the cooks were doing. Please shout out if you need anything at all."

"Hi, Ms. Levi. I'm just dropping off some drinks. Sorry,

I didn't bring one for you too. Thanks so much for lending us your kitchen."

"Call me Leah, Jenny. And it's no problem. In fact, it's the least I can do." She smiled at me and then turned to Jenny. "I don't know if Blake mentioned it, but we had a scare with Zelda last night, and Blake dropped everything to come out and check on her. She's feeling much better today, thank goodness." Zelda was Ms. Levi's daughter, who had some ongoing health issues.

Jenny looked at me, and I flushed, dropping my gaze to the lemon I was zesting. I don't know why I felt embarrassed about doing my job, but I did. I sensed Jenny's eyes on me for a few moments but didn't dare look up.

"I'm sorry to hear that. That must have been stressful. I'm glad she's doing okay." Jenny glanced at her watch. "Well, I guess I'd better be getting back to the barn to make sure nothing else has fallen apart in my absence. Thanks again for saving the wedding!"

AN HOUR AND A HALF LATER, I took a seat next to Jenny. I took a deep breath, hyperaware of Jenny's proximity to me. My eyes darted over to her face, confirming that, yes, she still looked gorgeous, and then away again before I was distracted by her V-neck.

According to the schedule she'd shared with us, the first course was due to be served any minute.

Jenny turned to me, a smile on her face that made my heart hiccup. "How's the cake doing?"

"It's currently cooling on Ms. Levi—I mean, Leah's—kitchen counter. We'll go back and assemble the tiers and frost them during the speeches."

Jenny sighed in relief. "Thank god. I'm so impressed you and George have been able to pull this off." She dropped her gaze from mine, staring lower on my face. Was she...was she looking at my lips? Without thinking, I rolled my lower lip in and bit it, wetting it in the process.

She leaned in, still staring at my face, and my heart jolted. *What is she doing?*

"Oh, you've got a little flour on your cheek." *Of course she wasn't going to kiss you, you idiot!*

I sat still in my chair as Jenny leaned over and did a slow, gentle swipe across my right cheek with her thumb, igniting sparks in my chest. She looked up at my hair and grinned. "And in your hair."

"Are you sure that's not just my gray hair?" I smiled. I wasn't self-conscious about having some gray hairs in my early thirties. In fact, I kind of liked it. Being a young, female doctor, I often faced skepticism, especially from older men, and I thought it gave me a bit of gravitas.

"Yes, I'm sure," Jenny said, her lips twitching as she carefully dusted my hair with her hand, causing a small cloud of flour to drift down in front of me, settling on the tablecloth.

"Mmmmh," she hummed, sending a warm tingle down my spine. "If this cake tastes anywhere near as good as you smell, Amanda will be thrilled."

After Jenny was done, she nudged me. "Looks like our scheming is paying off." I followed her gaze to Maya and Jasper, who were engaged in deep conversation, smiling at each other with their eyes sparkling.

"Oh, excellent. Operation *Emma* is underway. Have you told the caterers to keep their glasses full?" I said jokingly.

"Ha! No, but by the looks of it, I don't think we

need to."

We both stared unashamedly at Maya and Jasper. "Imagine how horrified we'd have been as teenagers if we'd seen two of our teachers get together."

Jenny giggled. "Oh my god, can you imagine? Like Mrs. Harding and Mr. Peck, or Mrs. Bingham and Mr. Reynolds?"

We both burst into laughter at the thought of those unlikely pairings.

I shook my head. "It's actually quite scary to think that when we were in high school, they were probably our age. At the time, they just seemed so old!"

"Ancient, at the ripe old age of thirty-two." Jenny grinned at me, and for a second, I thought I spotted the same look in Jenny's eyes as I'd just observed in Maya's and Jasper's. But that was ridiculous... Wasn't it?

AS SPEECHES BEGAN, George and I snuck back to the house to assemble, frost, and decorate the cake with fresh blueberries and candied lemon peel.

George usually opted for flavor over form, so we pulled up some YouTube videos on how to frost wedding cakes. After a nail-biting forty minutes, we stood back to admire our work.

"Despite not having all the utensils YouTube recommended and never having iced a wedding cake before, I think it looks pretty good," I said, looking at George for confirmation.

She nodded. "I think the overall effect is delightfully rustic. Perfect for a barn wedding in the country."

I hoped Amanda agreed.

CHAPTER FIFTEEN

JENNY

"This is incredible, Blake!" I mumbled through a mouthful of cake. To my relief, Amanda had taken the news of her original cake's demise and its more rustic-looking— but absolutely delicious—replacement remarkably well.

Blake grinned at me. "I'm glad you like it, but I can't take any credit. If anything, the cake got made *despite* me. If I'd been left to my own devices, it would've been an over-cooked rock. But I will take praise for the very clean blueberries and perfectly zested lemon."

I swallowed the remaining cake and smiled back at her. "I do love a well-washed blueberry. But you deserve a round of applause for getting George involved. We'd be cakeless if it wasn't for that spark of brilliance." I also wouldn't have seen Blake hard at work in Ms. Levi's kitchen, wearing an apron and looking completely out of her comfort zone in the cutest way possible.

I surveyed the barn. Most people were still seated at their tables, devouring cake. A few eager guests were already on the dance floor. And Amanda was doing the rounds, making sure she said hello to everyone. She looked stunning and, more importantly, happy.

I let out a deep breath. Now the cake situation had been satisfactorily resolved and all the food and speeches were over, I could relax and enjoy the rest of the evening.

Leaning forward, I pulled the bottle of champagne out of the ice bucket on the table. I'd limited myself to one glass so I was clear-headed enough to deal with any disasters that might unfold, but now most of my responsibilities were over, I refilled my glass to the brim.

"Champagne?" I looked at Blake with an eyebrow raised, holding the bottle.

"Yes, please! Baking is stressful." She held up her glass, tilting it so the bubbles didn't overflow.

Once it was full, she held out her glass, gazing steadily at me. "Cheers!"

"Cheers! To successful baking and weddings." I held her gaze as we clinked glasses and took a long sip. I wasn't sure if it was the champagne or the look we were exchanging, or both, that was causing my insides to fizz and heat to rise in my cheeks.

Blake broke eye contact, looking over my shoulder in the direction of the dance floor.

"And cheers to Operation *Emma* too. We're on a roll tonight!" She nodded her head behind me, and I turned to see Maya and Jasper dancing close together.

We clinked our glasses again, both taking another big swig, and again looked at each other, smiling and slightly flushed. *It's the champagne*, I told myself. But the giddy awkwardness between us that was sending my heart racing and my stomach fluttering felt less like alcohol-induced sensations and more like...sexual tension. *Oh boy*.

If I was being honest with myself, I was very attracted

to Blake right now. She'd saved the day with her cake, she hadn't insulted me once—in fact, I'd really been enjoying her company—and she looked...well, she looked incredible. The faint pink in her cheeks accentuated her warm, brown eyes, dark lashes, and naturally red lips. She was leaning forward, causing her hair to fall in a swoosh on her forehead. And that damn suit fit her perfectly.

I'd been gazing at Blake for more than a beat too long when Maya came up to us. "Amanda's doing the bouquet toss now. Come on, ladies. Tonight might be your lucky night!"

Blake let out a cynical huff at the same time I rolled my eyes. But we downed our champagne and made our way over to the gathering of women standing in front of Amanda.

"Oh god, this is looking a bit intense," I muttered to Blake, surveying the crowd. Maya was crouching in a sumo stance, shifting her weight between her feet as if ready to wrestle anyone who got between her and the bouquet. Another woman had taken off her heels, presumably for enhanced speed and coordination.

"So, I take it you're not going to bulldoze through the crowd to secure a prime bouquet-catching position?" she murmured.

"Ha! No thanks."

Blake grinned, grabbing my hand. "Well, in that case, let's skip it. Come with me. I've got something to show you."

Acutely aware of Blake's soft, warm hand grasping mine, I followed her lead.

We walked over the dance floor to our table, where she handed me my shawl. My body buzzed with intrigue. *Where the hell is she taking me?*

Buoyed by that second glass of champagne, I grabbed a

whole bottle from the table and looked at Blake with a raised eyebrow. "Should I bring this?"

"Great idea!"

Walking briskly, Blake led me through the back door of the barn, out into the cold night air, still firmly holding my hand. This felt...nice. Very nice. Hmmm.

"Where are we going?" I asked, giggling. "I hope Amanda doesn't notice we ran away from the toss."

"You'll see soon enough," Blake said mysteriously.

It was a clear night. In the moonlight, I could make out a small wooden barn a few hundred feet in front of us. Still giddy from the champagne, or Blake, or perhaps both, I took in a deep breath of cool air. It smelled of woodsmoke and fall.

We reached the barn, and Blake stopped, turning to me. "Zelda told me about this last night when I was doing the house call, and I popped my head in earlier to check it out. When I saw it, I thought of you." *She thought of me? What on earth in this barn made Blake think of me? Another scarecrow she thought I might fancy? More cute rabbits?*

She pulled the door open with her free hand, her other hand still holding mine, and then tugged me into the dark barn.

"Are you ready?"

"Yes!" I said too loudly. The suspense was killing me.

Blake flicked a light switch, bathing the barn in a warm glow.

I blinked, taking the scene in with awe.

It looked like an ordinary, working barn—sheltering a green tractor, rusty farm equipment, and hay bales from the elements—except for the walls.

The wooden walls were covered, floor to ceiling, in stunning, colorful murals depicting the Levis's property in every season. In fall, with the apple trees blazing red. In winter, with the barns and ground blanketed in snow, a white-tailed deer in the foreground. In spring, covered in wild geranium, violets, hepatica, and other local flowers. And in summer, fields of tall golden grass being mowed for hay, bluebirds perched on the apple trees laden with apples. Each scene was captured in meticulous detail and had clearly been a labor of love. The juxtaposition between the colorful, intricate murals and the otherwise normal barn made the whole thing even more striking.

"Wow! This is incredible, Blake," I said, breathless.

"I know. The Levis had a farm laborer who was also an artist stay with them a couple of years ago, and he painted this all himself." Blake looked at me, her cheeks slightly pink. "I...uh, I thought it might make a cool post, if you want?"

"That's an awesome idea!" I'd almost run out of Red Tractor Farm content, and I'd been too focused on Amanda's wedding the past few days to spend time coming up with new ideas. But this...this would be perfect.

Blake held out her hand. "Well, give me your phone."

I handed it over, took a swig out of the champagne bottle before putting it on the ground, and ran over to the summer scene, posing on a hay bale in front of it. Blake took photos of me in front of each wall, and then I filmed the entire scene.

"I think that'll do, thanks!" I walked back to Blake, who'd sat down on a hay bale, leaning back on another one behind her. I picked up the champagne bottle on the way.

"Champagne?" I asked, holding out the bottle as I sat down next to her.

"Sure." She tipped her head back and took a gulp. I watched her, admiring her face in profile. The sharp angle of her jaw, her straight nose, those dark, long eyelashes most people would kill to have naturally.

I must have been too obvious, because Blake put the bottle down and turned to look at me, her gaze lingering on my lips. *Oh god.* Did she want to...?

We stared at each other in silence, the air crackling around us with tension.

I leaned toward her, tentatively, to see if my move was reciprocated.

It was. She leaned toward me, my heart picking up pace.

Do it. Kiss her, my body urged.

It's probably all in your head. It'll be so embarrassing if she rejects you. DO NOT KISS HER, my mind implored.

"Jenny?" Blake's voice was lower than usual, husky. *Oh shit.* She was looking intensely into my eyes now, her gaze burning right through me.

A strangled, "Mmmm?" was all I could manage. *Is this really happening? Is she about to ask me what I think she is?*

Blake took a deep breath, holding my gaze. "Can I kiss you?"

Oh my god. I can't believe this is happening.

It felt like a kaleidoscope of butterflies had been released in my stomach, sending my whole body vibrating with nervous anticipation, and excitement, and want.

I nodded, leaning in further and shutting my eyes as Blake's soft lips touched mine.

She tasted like champagne and lemon-blueberry cake.

Blake placed her hand on my hip bone, and I swiveled my body toward her so I could wrap my arm around her back.

My mind cleared of thoughts, leaving me only with all-consuming feelings and sensations. Blake's teeth gently biting my lower lip, my tongue teasing hers, the warm swell of her breasts against mine, blood pulsing through my veins, a giddy sensation in my stomach. Fuck. This kiss was going to be my undoing.

I grabbed the hair on the back of her head, which was just long enough to grasp, causing Blake to moan. I untucked her shirt with my other hand and slipped my hand underneath so I could feel the warm, smooth skin of her back.

Blake moved her mouth away from mine and began kissing along my jawline, stopping at my ear where she began lightly pulling it with her mouth, sending shivers down my spine. This time, it was my turn to moan.

I gripped Blake's hair tighter, caressing her back with my other hand. Blake's lips made their way down my neck to my collarbone as I nuzzled my nose in her hair, breathing in the faint sandalwood scent of her shampoo.

Suddenly, we heard a loud bang.

Startled, we flung ourselves apart, spinning to see what caused the noise. It was the barn door swinging open. And there, in the middle of the doorway, stood Maya and Jasper, in a passionate embrace.

I didn't know whether to laugh or cry that Maya and Jasper were responsible for breaking up our make-out session. We really only had ourselves to blame, given our *Emma*-like meddling.

I wiped my mouth on the back of my hand and ran my other hand through my hair, hoping I didn't look as hot and bothered as I felt. Out of the corner of my eye, I saw Blake tucking her shirt back into her pants. *Goddamnit.*

We exchanged glances, and I nodded toward the door, raising an eyebrow in a silent question. Blake nodded, and we rose to our feet, walking toward the barn's entrance until we were only a few feet from Maya and Jasper.

We stopped, standing there awkwardly while Maya and Jasper, completely oblivious to our presence, continued to make out in the doorway, blocking our escape.

After what felt like an interminable length of time but was probably only a few seconds, I coughed to get their attention.

Nothing.

Maya and Jasper were in the throes of passion and clearly only had eyes, and ears, for each other. *Had Blake and I looked like that a minute earlier?*

I coughed again, louder, at the exact same time Blake also did a loud, fake cough.

The combined effect of Blake and me fake-coughing loudly was alarming, reminiscent of a room full of pneumonia patients. *Surely that will do it.*

Maya and Jasper jumped back, their arms falling to their sides, eyes wide.

"Blake? Jenny?" If surprise hadn't been written all over Maya's face, it would have been clear from her voice alone. I saw her eyes flit briefly over the champagne bottle in my hand.

"We were... I was just showing Jenny the amazing murals." Blake gestured to the walls. "Anyway, we should be going now. Leave you two...in peace." The corners of Blake's mouth twitched, and both Maya and Jasper blushed.

"Uh, yes, thanks..." Jasper's voice trailed off.

Blake and I escaped the barn, suppressing laughter that burst from our mouths as soon as the door shut firmly behind us.

"It seems like our matchmaking efforts were a little too successful!" I said through my laughter.

"Yeah." Blake chuckled.

But as a cloud moved across the moon, blocking the light, I could have sworn Blake's expression also darkened.

And then the reality of what we'd just done sunk in. *Shit.*

I just kissed Blake Mitchell. And I liked it.

CHAPTER SIXTEEN

BLAKE

"George, it's me." I pulled up my mask, smiling at George who stared at me blankly. She looked quite adorable as *Where's Waldo*, in a striped red-and-white beanie, matching sweater, and large, round, black-rimmed glasses.

"Good lord, you are terrifying. You definitely aren't into the sexy Halloween costume, are you?" George grinned as she eyed my *Scream*-inspired Ghostface mask and black hooded robe.

"Excuse me, you're one to talk. I wouldn't exactly class Waldo as sexy."

"Hey, who doesn't love a cute guy in a beanie?" George ran her hand over her beanie and ushered me into Novel Gossip, which was buzzing with laughter and conversation. All the costumed guests looked like they were enjoying themselves—a lot.

George must have read my mind. "I may have made the punch a little strong." She half-smiled, half-grimaced.

George had removed most of the tables and chairs from the cafe section of Novel Gossip to make plenty of room for people to mingle. She'd also gone all out on the Halloween decorations. Fake spiderwebs, the sort that looked like stretched cotton balls, hung from the windows and bookcases. Cut-out cardboard spiders, pumpkins, and skeletons were stuck to the walls. Orange and black balloons floated above a table full of Halloween-themed cupcakes, donuts decorated with orange and black icing, deviled eggs transformed into bloodshot eyeballs using pimento olives and red mayonnaise, mini pizzas with cheese spiderwebs melted onto them, jack-o'-lantern pastries and bowls of standard Halloween candy. Bottles of wine and spirits, a punch, mixers and red plastic cups covered another table nearby. The warm air smelled of cinnamon, sugar and mulled wine.

I tugged my mask back over my face. "I'm not really into Halloween costumes, so this seemed like the easiest option. No makeup, no fuss."

But it wasn't just the no-fuss nature of my outfit that had appealed to me. After George had delightedly warned me Jenny would be at the party, it had occurred to me that a horrifying Halloween costume might act as a chastity belt to stop anything further happening between us.

But now, as I scanned the room, looking for Jenny, butterflies fluttering at the thought of seeing her for the first time after the wedding last weekend, I started second-guessing my outfit choice. I should have worn something more flattering. And also more breathable. George was clearly keeping the room well-heated for all the skimpy Halloween costume wearers, and I was uncomfortably warm.

"Well, you aren't the only one. There's actually another *Scream* costume here."

I couldn't see any sign of another Ghostface, or Jenny, for that matter. "Oh, I can't see anyone wearing it. Who?"

"Jasper," George said, eyes twinkling. I'd told her about the barn incident on Saturday night, including Jasper and Maya's appearance.

"Ah, I see. Maybe he's off with Maya, then," I said, still looking around. I spotted Olivia in a cute Rosie-the-Riveter outfit consisting of a denim shirt and jeans with a red-and-white polka-dot bandana, deep in conversation with a Batman I didn't recognize, and smiled. My sister was the lucky recipient of fashion genes that had skipped me.

"Jenny's not here yet, in case you're wondering. Are you going to talk to her about the kiss?" George asked.

I'd told George the whole story on Sunday morning, hungover and stressed. It wasn't that I hadn't enjoyed our kiss. I had. A lot. But now I'd finally satisfied my teenage fantasy, the question of "*What next?*" kept swirling around in my head.

I didn't want a relationship.

Jenny was leaving in three months.

There should be no more kissing...or any of the other things I'd been dreaming about.

But I hadn't been able to stop thinking about her—flash-backs to her warm, soft lips pressed against mine, her hand under my shirt, tugging my hair. I started sweating under my black robe just thinking about it.

"Blake, you guys need to talk about it."

"I know. I know. It's just super awkward. I don't have a clue how she feels about the whole thing. I don't want to be presumptuous and assume she's interested in something more, so I...I don't know what to say. I suck at these conversations."

"I don't think you do. You have difficult conversations as a doctor all the time, and based on what I overhear here"—it wasn't called Novel Gossip for nothing—"you do an excellent job of it. You just need to channel some of those skills for this situation."

"Yeah, but it's different. With my patients, I can keep my composure and go into professional "Dr. Blake" mode. But when it's personal, when it's about my feelings, it's not so easy."

"Well, maybe you should try to harness some of that Dr. Blake energy, because look who just walked in."

I followed George's gaze to the front door, where Wednesday Addams, AKA Jenny Lynton, was taking off her coat.

My heart sputtered, and the rest of my body froze.

Unlike me, Jenny had actually made an effort with her costume.

Her blond hair was covered by a jet-black wig with two long pigtails that fell down her front. An oversized, sharp-edged white collar poked over her long-sleeved, knee-length, black dress. Black stockings, chunky black loafers, dark eye makeup and white foundation completed the look. It was a complete contrast to her usual laidback, colorful, warm style. And yet she still looked incredible.

I was suddenly thankful for my mask. Perhaps this outfit wasn't such a bad idea after all, and I could just spend the evening ogling Jenny without her knowing. But unfortunately, my anonymity was short-lived. George caught Jenny's attention and waved her over to us.

"Jenny! You look fantastic!" George leaned down and hugged her.

Jenny broke into a very un-Wednesday Addams smile. "Thank you! I love the stripes, and the decorations are incredible. Thanks so much for having me. And thanks again for saving the wedding with your cake-baking skills."

I stood silently next to George, hoping Jenny wouldn't notice me.

"Well, I couldn't have done it without my sous-chef," George said fondly, patting me on the back. I silently cursed her for giving me away.

"Blake?" Jenny turned to stare at me, her voice full of surprise. I thought I saw a faint blush of pink under her white make-up.

"Yeah, hi." I kept my mask on to hide the heat on my own cheeks. *Be cool, Blake.*

I frantically tried to think of something intelligent to say to the woman I'd been fantasizing about for the last five days—well, the last seventeen years, more like it—but my mind was blank. *Shit. Not again. I thought I'd gotten over this.*

It suddenly felt like it was 110 degrees in my outfit.

"Sorry, I'm...er, feeling a little hot. Think I need some fresh air," I mumbled and hurried to the front door, wincing at my ineptitude.

Shit, shit, shit.

That was the opposite of cool.

CHAPTER SEVENTEEN

JENNY

"Um, is she okay?" I watched Blake walk out of Novel Gossip, bewildered.

Was she regretting the kiss so much she didn't want to talk to me? I'd hoped we'd be able to behave like adults. Even if it was a mistake, things didn't need to get awkward between us.

And it *was* definitely a mistake. A mistake I'd thought a lot about since it happened, reliving the sensation of Blake's lips against mine, trailing my jaw, teasing my ear. A delicious shiver ran down my spine at the memory, even now.

But things weren't going any further. They couldn't. First of all, it was Blake Mitchell, who, despite me warming to her somewhat—okay, a lot—was someone I'd disliked for well over a decade. That was a major red flag, and not one I was going to overlook. Second, I was only looking for a serious, long-term relationship. Getting involved with Blake while I was in Sapphire Springs temporarily was not going to assist that cause. It could only create more awkwardness between us, which would haunt me every time I visited Sapphire Springs and ran into her.

No thank you.

And in any event, I was sure Blake regretted the kiss. We'd gotten carried away on champagne and the high of pulling off the cake replacement. But in the cold light of day, Blake would have realized it was a mistake. She was probably horrified at what had happened.

"Yes, I'm sure she's fine." George tugged at the collar of her red-and-white-striped sweater. "I should probably turn down the heating. It's getting a little warm in here."

"Okay," I responded, unconvinced.

I'd been buzzing with nervous excitement all day at the thought of seeing Blake tonight, but it'd been a complete letdown. Not only was her face and body completely obscured by her awful *Scream* outfit, but she appeared to have reverted back to rude, abrupt Blake. I couldn't help feeling disappointed.

Dwelling on Blake was doing strange things to my insides, so I changed the subject. "Hey, I was thinking... How would you feel if I posted a photo of the two of us and all your fantastic decorations on Instagram and tagged Novel Gossip? We could even do a short "Where's Waldo" video for TikTok?"

While I was getting a coffee the other day, George had not so subtly suggested I was more than welcome to use Novel Gossip in any content. She was clearly keen for some publicity, so this posting would kill two birds with one stone. I winced as the very non-animal-friendly phrase appeared in my mind.

George's eyes lit up. "Sure! That sounds fun. We'll just need to find someone sober enough to take a decent photo." She surveyed the raucous crowd, and her smile wavered slightly. "Hmmm. Look, why don't I go grab Blake? She just arrived, so unless she pre-gamed, we should be able to trust her."

I paused. I knew from experience that Blake could take a great photo. However, our brief interaction didn't give me the impression Blake wanted to spend any more time with me.

"Okay, if she's feeling up for it, then that works," I said hesitantly.

George disappeared out the front door. I stood, waiting, for a couple of minutes. After deciding that either Blake had run away or was embroiled in an argument with George about helping, I walked over to the table of food and helped myself to a spider-web-covered cupcake, which turned out to be a delicious caramel-pumpkin flavor with walnuts. Good lord, George could bake.

I looked around the room for familiar faces. Most of my high school cohort had, like me, fled Sapphire Springs after graduating. And in the past few years, there'd been an influx of people fleeing city life. Those factors, combined with the Halloween outfits, meant I didn't recognize most of the guests. I wished Amanda was here so I could confide in her about the whole Blake situation, but she was currently gallivanting around Mexico on her honeymoon. Relieved, I spotted Olivia in a Rosie-the-Riveter costume and made my way over to her.

"Hi! I love your outfit! I just wanted to thank you again for the gorgeous flowers. Amanda loved them."

Olivia smiled, lifting up an arm and pretending to flex her bicep, recreating the classic pose. "Thanks! I love doing weddings, even though I don't get to do a lot of them. I'm so glad she liked them."

"I'll definitely let Miriam know what a great job you

did. Hopefully, she can recommend you to some other clients."

"That would be awesome, thank you!" Olivia grinned, and then turned slightly as something caught her eye. "And here's my favorite ghoulish sister and the host of this amazing party!"

George and Blake materialized out of nowhere, George gripping Blake's arm like she was a flight risk.

"Okay, I've found our photographer. Let's get started before things get too rowdy..." A loud crash, caused by Spiderman tripping over Wonder Woman's handbag, made us all jump. "Um, I mean even more rowdy."

I handed my phone over to Blake. It was disconcerting not being able to see her face. Despite my thick white Wednesday Addams face paint and dark eye makeup, my face could still betray my feelings. Blake, on the other hand, was a closed book.

George led us to a corner adorned with fake spiderwebs, where we posed in front of a large black tarantula.

Next, we did a video of George "hiding" behind a bookshelf, a bunch of balloons, the table of food, always with her head poking up, and me asking "Where's Waldo?" A few guests who'd been enjoying George's punch a little too much ruined a couple of shots, but we got enough footage for me to edit down to what I hoped would be a cute video.

I was just about to take my phone back from Blake when George jumped in front of us and put her hand out. "Why don't I take a photo of you two, over there."

Grinning, she ushered us away from the party and down one of the aisles of books. George pulled a book off the shelf, handing it to me as we reached the back of the shop. Apart from the three of us, it was deserted.

"Okay, now you pretend you're reading this." George

handed me a copy of *The Shining*, grabbed my shoulders, and turned me slightly. "Really channel Wednesday."

I adopted my best surly look.

"And then Blake, you lean menacingly out from the bookshelf behind her."

Blake followed her directions, and George stepped back, grinning at us. "Perfect!"

George took a few photos, and then, before I knew it, she was handing my phone back and scuttling back toward the other guests.

"I'd better check on the party!" she yelled halfway down the aisle, leaving Blake and me alone. I had a sneaking suspicion that might have been her plan all along.

What had Blake told her about Saturday night? Given the way George's eyes darted between the two of us just before she ran off, I suspected a lot.

I took a deep breath and looked directly at Blake. I could just make out the gleam of her eyes through the holes in her mask. "So, I guess we should probably talk about Saturday night?"

There was a pause, and then Blake cleared her throat. "Yeah."

"So, um, I'm not sure how you're feeling about it. I had a really nice time," I said. "But as you know, I'm leaving in January, so it probably isn't a great idea to, you know, do anything like that again." Ghostface stared at me blankly, giving no indication of how Blake was reacting to my words.

"Not that I'm assuming you want to or anything, but it..." I added, frowning. "I'm sorry. It's quite disconcerting having this conversation without being able to see your face. Would you mind taking the mask off?"

I watched as Blake reluctantly pulled up the mask and hood.

Goddamn.

I was expecting Blake to look at least slightly disheveled and sweaty. But no. How did she manage to look hot, even wearing a shapeless black serial killer robe? I'd thought the mask was distracting, but this was just as bad, if not worse.

Those gorgeous brown eyes framed by long lashes were staring at me expectantly.

"Thanks. So, what do you think?" I asked, eager to get this conversation over and done with.

"Sorry?" Blake blinked.

Good lord, this was painful. "About Saturday night... Are we... Are we on the same page?"

"Yeah, I think you're right," Blake said. "I also had a nice time, but yeah, I don't think it makes sense to, er...keep doing it. I don't... I'm not looking for a relationship or anything right now."

There was an awkward pause.

We stood there, looking at each other, not moving, while sparks zapped around my nervous system.

Shit.

It wasn't just my body that was electrified. The air between us was wired as well. Charged with attraction, crackling with tension. My breath hitched.

It was the same, full-body vibrating sensation I'd experienced at the barn on Saturday night.

We both stepped forward, and then I was lost in the sensation of Blake's lips on mine, the heat of her body pressing against me. Blake cupped my jaw in her hand, her thumb brushing my cheek. Our eager mouths explored each other, while our hands roamed over each other's bodies. I felt drunk, out of control. This was *not* what I needed, but it was exactly what I wanted.

Eventually, I gently disentangled myself, breathless and dazed.

Well, so much for not doing that again.

Goddamnit. Now I had no idea where we stood, and I couldn't bring myself to raise the topic again. I needed to regroup.

"We should get back to the party," I said, slightly panicked.

We walked back down the aisle in silence, Blake pulling her mask and hood back over her face while I reapplied my lipstick, which had almost certainly all been removed by Blake's mouth. Blake's soft lips, her inquisitive tongue... *Stop it, Jenny!*

I cleared my throat. "Would you like a drink? I think I'll try some of the punch."

"I'm all good, thanks." Blake's voice was hoarse.

I stared at the mask, which didn't give me anything back. "Okay, then...well, I'll just go grab some."

Relieved to have some space from Blake, I made my way over to the drinks table. The enormous punch bowl was nearly empty, but I managed to fill a red plastic cup. Looking around the lively room, I wished again that Amanda was here to confide in.

I couldn't see Blake anymore. Maybe she'd run out the front door again. I wouldn't blame her.

Not feeling my usual social self, I walked over to a display of books, pretending to admire them while I tried to get a handle on my feelings. There was no denying there was a strong attraction between us. Or that my plan for Saturday night's kiss to be a one-off hadn't gone so well.

Maybe after tonight things would get easier. With Amanda's wedding over and the Halloween party almost done, there wouldn't be any reason to see Blake. But who was I kidding? I'd inevitably run into Blake at Novel Gossip, at the general store, or walking down Main Street. And if I was being honest with myself, I didn't love the idea of not seeing Blake. In fact, I wanted to see her. To touch her. To kiss her...

I slammed the book I was holding shut, trying to break my line of thought. I picked up another book and stared blankly at its blurb.

Maybe I'd been too hasty in dismissing the whole casual-relationship option.

I'd sworn off casual relationships because I wanted a serious one. I didn't want to be distracted from that goal by relationships that had no future. But it wasn't like I'd be missing out on the love of my life if I dated Blake during my short stay here. The chances of finding any eligible candidates in Sapphire Springs who'd be willing to move to LA with me was extremely low, if not zero.

I also hated getting hurt. The number of times I had ended up falling way too quickly was getting ridiculous, and the recent disappointments with Jeremy and Sarah made me even more cautious about putting myself out there. But I couldn't see that happening here. Yes, Blake was extremely hot. And yes, Blake and I had been getting along better in the past week. But surely with our history, with the red flags I was all too aware of, I'd never be head over heels for her.

While all this rationalizing was going on, I kept remembering the way Blake looked at me just before she kissed me. Her soft lips, her body pressed against mine, and the feel of her firm hands on my waist.

Maybe exploring our attraction would help us get it out of our system. Surely sleeping with Blake couldn't be as good as I'd fantasized about, right? And if it wasn't, well, that would pour cold water all over my horny mind, and I could return to focusing on reviving my career. And things were already going to be awkward between us, so did we really have anything to lose?

Decision made, I took a big gulp of punch, placed the book back on the table, and looked around to see if Blake had reappeared. I spotted her sitting on one of the chairs George had pushed against the wall and walked over to join her.

Taking a seat, I took a deep breath and turned to her. I didn't ask her to remove her mask this time. I'd learned my lesson. I opened my mouth, and then shut it again, and then swallowed.

"So, I was thinking... We're clearly attracted to each other. Maybe we should just enjoy each other's company and see where this attraction takes us while I'm here?" I paused, but Blake didn't say anything. Maybe I hadn't been clear? "You know, like date casually, knowing there's an expiration date on this whole thing?"

There was a long pause. What the hell was going on behind that mask of hers?

"Well, um...look, I'm flattered, Jenny, but I'm actually seeing someone at the moment," said someone in a deep voice. Someone who was most definitely not Blake.

Heat rushed up my face.

Oh god.

Who have I just accidentally propositioned for casual sex?

"Here you go, babe." Maya appeared in front of me, holding two glasses of wine, one of which she handed to the Ghostface-who-was-not-Blake sitting next to me. Ghostface pulled down his mask, revealing a pink-cheeked Jasper.

Maya registered that it was me sitting in her seat. "Oh! Hi, Jenny. Cute outfit!"

I scrambled to my feet, hoping the white make-up was hiding the blush burning my face. "Oh shit, I thought you were someone else. Sorry about that, Jasper! And sorry for stealing your seat, Maya. Enjoy your evening!"

Now was probably a good time to call it a night before I embarrassed myself any further. Even if Blake did reappear, after the Jasper incident, I'd lost motivation to repeat the awkward conversation all over again. It was probably better I sleep on it before making any rash decisions, anyway, especially given I'd drunk George's potent punch.

I wove my way through the crowd of increasingly tipsy, happy guests, grabbed my coat from the coat rack, and walked up to George, who was chatting to Harley Quinn and Batman.

"I'm going to head out. Thanks for having me!" I gave George a quick hug, waved goodbye to Olivia, and beelined for the front door.

The cold night air hit me in the face, cooling my flushed cheeks and calming me slightly.

I'd taken three steps along the sidewalk, my eyes still adjusting to the dark, when I walked right into a hooded figure and nearly screamed.

It was another Ghostface. *Good lord, how many* Scream *aficionados are there at this damn party?*

"Jenny?" a voice, low but distinctly feminine, asked.

The pit of my stomach jolted.

Blake.

CHAPTER EIGHTEEN

BLAKE

"Oh, hi. Sorry. I was just heading out." The side of Jenny's face closest to Novel Gossip glowed with light, but it was difficult to make out her expression.

"Oh." I paused, pulling off my mask. "Can I...can I walk with you?" I'd been heading back to find Jenny. As difficult as I found it to talk about my feelings, I had to stop running outside each time something awkward happened between us and have an adult conversation with her instead. The only problem was, I still wasn't sure what to say. I'd been hoping inspiration would hit when I saw her.

It had not.

"Yes, of course."

We started walking down Main Street in silence. I kept my hands firmly in the pockets of the black wool coat I was wearing over my robe. I did *not* trust myself around Jenny.

"Well, George knows how to throw a great party," Jenny said.

I exhaled, relieved Jenny's small talk would buy me time to work out what to say. "She sure does. I know some folks like to complain about out-of-towners moving here, but Novel Gossip has become an indispensable part of the community. I don't know what I'd do without her coffee—or her company, for that matter. She's been a good friend to me since I moved back."

"That's great. It must have been so strange moving back to Sapphire Springs after living in New York for so long. At least it's improved a lot since we were teenagers."

"Would you ever consider moving back?" I tried keeping my voice nonchalant. Jenny living in Sapphire Springs permanently would make my life a lot more complicated, but my heart beat faster as I waited for her response.

Jenny shook her head. "Nope, there's no work for me here. My agent was hoping I might attract some different sponsors by posting more rural content, but no one has shown any interest so far. And none of the local stores would have the budget to pay an influencer. But it's nice to be back for a couple of months. Spending more time with Mom and Dad, seeing Amanda and Maya, and enjoying the new-and-improved Sapphire Springs 2.0."

A ripple of disappointment washed over me, but I knew it was for the best. When Jenny left, I'd hopefully no longer be tormented by my attraction to her.

"This wig is making my head really itchy," Jenny said as she pulled it off her head, stuffing it in her bag and shaking out her hair, transforming herself from Wednesday Addams into a very pale but still beautiful Jenny.

A gust of warm air and rowdy laughter escaped Builders Arms as a patron exited the pub, and I suddenly realized where we were.

"Shit, we've passed the turn to your parents' house. Should we head back?"

Jenny shrugged. "Since we're nearly there, do you want to walk down to the water?"

"Sure," I said, relieved Jenny didn't want to rush off before I'd gathered my thoughts. Not that walking with Jenny was helping that process. It was difficult to focus on what to do about the woman I found incredibly attractive and kept accidentally kissing when she was only a foot away from me.

A block away from the water, Jenny inhaled a sharp breath. My eyes darted to her face with concern, which quickly vanished. In the faint light of the cast-iron lamps that lined Main Street, I could see she was smiling.

"Look!" Jenny pointed. "They've already decorated the bandstand for the holidays!"

The bandstand, a hexagonal pavilion next to the river, was glowing from the strings of fairy lights adorning it.

"Good lord, it's not even November yet!"

"Well, I'm not complaining. It looks gorgeous. In fact, they should leave them up all year round. Why limit fairy lights to the holiday season?"

"Energy conservation?" I replied, a teasing tone to my voice.

Jenny frowned, but I was almost certain her lips were twitching. "I'm sure they could purchase some energy-efficient lights, or even install solar panels on top of the bandstand to power them."

"I'm not sure they'll put solar panels on a historic 1920's bandstand, but feel free to raise the issue at the next town hall meeting."

"Maybe I will." Jenny grinned, and my heart leaped.

Damn, I liked spending time with her. And kissing her. And the more time I spent with her, the more into her I got. The sensible thing to do would be to cut off contact for the remainder of her stay. That would eliminate the risk of accidental kisses and hopefully reduce my current levels of pining. But that option sounded very unappealing right now.

We walked past the bandstand and down the pier until we reached the railings. The moon peeked out behind clouds, faintly reflected on the river. Across the river, a few lights twinkled.

I leaned against the railing, listening to the water lap against the side of the pier, and tried to gather my thoughts. If cutting off contact with Jenny wasn't the answer, what was? I sighed, and it came out louder than expected.

"Are you okay?" Jenny turned to look at me.

I'd never been great at communicating my feelings, and it was even harder when I was unsure what those feelings were, but I had to say something. It might as well be the truth.

"Yeah, sorry. I'm finding this whole thing—us—a little confusing."

"Well, that makes two of us." Jenny gave a wry smile. "Kissing about thirty seconds after agreeing to keep things platonic didn't exactly clarify where we stand."

I chuckled. "No, not exactly."

"Since platonic doesn't seem to be working for us, what do you think about—"

Oh shit. Is she going to suggest cutting off contact?

But Jenny didn't finish that thought. Instead, she looked at the sky. "Did you feel a raindrop?"

"No," I replied quickly, hoping she'd continue what she'd been saying.

"Hmmm. I'm sure I felt one." Jenny grabbed my hand, the soft warmth of her skin against mine sending my nerve endings tingling. "Let's go to the bandstand, just in case."

She tugged me toward the bandstand. I still hadn't felt a drop of rain. "You know you don't need an excuse to take a closer look at the fairy lights, right? You could've just asked," I teased.

Jenny laughed. "Hey, I'm not making it up. I swear I felt a raindrop."

"Uh-huh."

As we got closer, I had to admit that the fairy lights were a nice touch. They gave the bandstand an ethereal charm, like it was a floating portal to another, magical world.

We walked up the stairs onto the bandstand floor, where Jenny let go of my hand and twirled around, smiling. "This is gorgeous!"

I couldn't help grinning at her enthusiasm. Or thinking just how gorgeous she was as well.

She stopped suddenly, her smile fading. "Although, if it starts raining, the fairy lights won't electrocute us, right?"

I snorted. "Oh my god, Jenny. They would not cover an outdoor pavilion in wires that could electrocute us."

Jenny giggled. "Good point. I'm blaming that comment on George's punch."

Jenny walked toward me, and my heart started thumping.

I cleared my throat. We needed to finish the conversation we'd started before we got carried away again. "So, before the alleged raindrop, I got the impression you were about to say something, perhaps about us?"

Jenny stopped a foot in front of me, looking at me directly. "Alleged?" Jenny asked, mock outrage in her voice. "But yes, I was going to suggest that..." She swallowed. "Look, I don't know if this is a good idea, since I'd promised myself I wouldn't do it anymore but..."

My heart beat faster. Where the hell was she going with this?

"I was thinking, since we're clearly attracted to each other, perhaps we could just, um, have fun until I go back to LA. You know, we could be un-platonic, but keep things casual."

My mind started racing. I'd only ever had serious relationships before. I'd never even considered having a friends-with-benefits arrangement, which is what Jenny seemed to be suggesting. I could never see the point. Either I liked someone enough to want to date them seriously, or I didn't. Period. But this time, it didn't feel so clear-cut.

A buzz of excitement grew in my chest. Perhaps this was the solution. I'd be able to do all the things with Jenny that I'd been fantasizing about for years, get it all out of my system, and then return to my normal, comfortable life as a spinster in January. I'd banned relationships so I didn't have to go through the agony of getting my heart broken again. But if I went into a relationship with Jenny knowing it was just a short-term thing, then surely I'd be able to protect myself from heartbreak. The clear expiration date would give me certainty.

"Blake? What do you think?"

I realized Jenny was standing in front of me, fidgeting with her hands while I left her hanging. *Stop overthinking this, and make a decision.*

I stepped forward, brushing a stray hair from her face.

"I would love nothing more than to be casually un-platonic with you, Jenny Lynton."

And with that, I leaned in and kissed her.

CHAPTER NINETEEN

JENNY

"Is it this steep all the way up?" I paused to catch my breath, looking at the rocky path with trepidation. Blake stopped a few feet ahead of me and turned.

"It gets steeper right near the end." Her voice betrayed no signs of exertion.

"Steeper?" I yelped.

Blake smiled at me, and my heart bounced, despite being exhausted. "I promise you, the view is worth it. Especially at this time of year."

Based on past experience, I'd assumed our casual relationship would consist primarily of drinks and booty calls. So, when Blake texted me the day after the party and suggested we go for a hike up Breakback Ridge on Saturday before the fall foliage disappeared, I'd been a little surprised. To be honest, I'd been surprised she hadn't suggested we go back to her house after the Halloween party. But she hadn't, and I wasn't exactly keen to invite her back to my parents' house with its thin walls.

I'd agreed to Blake's suggestion, thinking it would at

least compensate for the amount of Halloween candy I'd consumed and hopefully provide content for my social media accounts.

But now we were halfway up the mountain, I was starting to think this hadn't been the best idea for our first date—or any date, period. It was now very clear to me why the mountain had been named Breakback Ridge. I was already tired, sweaty, and a little hangry. I hadn't thought to wear hiking boots, and my worn sneakers weren't giving me the support I needed over the uneven ground.

We could have been enjoying a glass of wine while overlooking the Hudson River, or going back to Red Tractor Farm for hot donuts, apple fritters, and steaming cider— activities much more conducive to making out than hiking.

To make matters worse, Blake was a *lot* fitter than I was. While I kept suggesting we "enjoy the view" as an excuse to catch my breath, Blake bounced along the path, barely breaking a sweat.

The only good thing about constantly falling behind Blake, and this hike in general, was getting a very nice view of Blake's butt. Her navy hiking pants clung to it in an extremely flattering way, accentuating how round and firm it was. Like a dog having a treat dangled in front of it, Blake's butt kept me going, reminding me why I was on this damn hike in the first place.

I took a deep breath in and continued up the stony path, hoping I didn't fall over and break my leg. Which reminded me...

"Hey, did you ever speak to the other local doctors about how they manage uninsured patients?" I asked, trying not to sound too winded and failing miserably.

"I did." Blake slowed to walk beside me. "Some of them offer payment plans for their fees, but none of them are helping patients try to get funding for their hospital bills or other costs. Apparently, some towns have funds to help pay for uninsured people's medical costs, which are usually run by non-profits or the city council." Blake sighed. "But we don't have anything like that in Sapphire Springs."

"Hmmm. Would it be worthwhile talking to the mayor about why we don't have a fund like that? Perhaps the village board could run it. And if they raised enough money, they could potentially pay for someone to help out with all the applications?"

Blake shot me a glance. "That would be great. But it would be heaps of work for them to set it up, and I think they're pretty stretched as it is. It would also involve fundraising, which is really not my thing." Blake grimaced. "I hate asking people for favors and don't love public speaking either."

An unexpected rush of energy shot through my body. "I could look into it. I think the mayor could be interested in something like that. I remember Dad saying she was thrilled when you opened your practice in Sapphire Springs because healthcare is one of her passions. And if she says yes, I could do a fundraiser. I like that kind of thing—you know, planning bachelorette parties, weddings, fundraisers. And I don't have a lot to do, apart from coming up with more content. In LA, I was always busy going to events and schmoozing, but there's not so much of that here." Now the wedding was over, I'd been feeling restless. There was only so much content I could produce.

Blake chuckled. "Oh, what? The Sapphire Springs social scene isn't up to your liking? I thought George's Halloween party would have been up there with the parties at Chateau Marmont?"

I snorted. "Honestly, I liked George's party a lot more

than most of the LA ones, but it wasn't exactly great for schmoozing, and my social calendar is looking quite empty for November."

"I thought we schmoozed quite well." Blake raised an eyebrow, her lips twitching.

Giggling, I shook my head. "I don't know what you think I'm getting up to at these parties, but I wouldn't exactly call our, um, interactions 'schmoozing'?"

Blake waved her hand dismissively. "Potato, potahto. Schmoozing, smooching."

The giggles turned into full-blown laughter. Laughing while out of breath was surprisingly difficult, and I stopped for a moment to regulate my breathing. "But in all serious-ness, I'd be happy to talk to the mayor and see if I can help get a fund set up," I said once I was breathing normally.

Blake shot me a skeptical look. "Are you sure this is something you'd actually like to do?"

"Yes, I'm sure." I picked up my step at the prospect. "We could do a raffle. Perhaps see if George could cater. We could ask Amanda and Maya if the students could provide entertainment and get a few people to give speeches. I'm sure the mayor would be willing to say a few words. If we did it around the end of November, we could have a Thanksgiving theme, which would be in keeping with trying to get people to donate money." That wouldn't give me a lot of time to organize, but I had plenty of time on my hands at the moment. And while, in the big cities, people often cleared out to go back home for Thanksgiving, Sapphire Springs was "back home" for a lot of people, so our population actually increased. More people to donate.

Blake hesitated. "Well, if you're sure, that would be incredible. Thank you." Her voice was gruff, but I thought I heard genuine gratitude.

We hit a steep, rocky section of the hike and stopped talking so we could focus on keeping our balance as we scrambled over boulders.

"WELL, WHAT DO YOU THINK?" Blake grinned at me, still barely breaking a sweat, as we reached a rocky outcrop showcasing sweeping views of the Hudson River and the sepia and golden hues of the Hudson Highlands Mountains.

"This is incredible!" I took in a deep breath and then breathed out slowly, trying to get my heart rate back to its normal speed as I took in the spectacular surroundings.

"Yeah, I love coming up here in fall."

"Do you mind taking a photo of me so we can get it over and done with?"

I quickly wiped down my face and checked my hair in selfie mode on my phone, and then got Blake to take a photo of me posing in front of the view.

"Now, are you hungry?" Blake asked as she handed my phone back, taking off her backpack. The last hour of intense hiking had made me forget my empty stomach. As soon as the words left her mouth, my stomach rumbled.

I eyed Blake's backpack in eager anticipation as she began to unpack. She pulled out a light tartan picnic blanket and laid it on the ground. And then she unpacked an assortment of bagels from a cooler bag, a bowl of berries, four massive cookies, and a thermos. Okay, this definitely felt more date-like than I was expecting. And I kind of liked it. I couldn't remember the last time someone I was with had gone to this much trouble.

"Help yourself. The bagels and cookies are from Novel

Gossip. I wasn't sure what fillings you liked, so I got a few. There's smoked salmon and dill, BLT, pastrami, and an avocado and sundried tomato one."

My heart warmed at the thought of Blake lugging excess bagels up Breakback Ridge just to make sure I had options.

Blake sat on the blanket, her back against a boulder, facing the view. I lowered myself next to her, reaching forward for the smoked salmon bagel, which I began to devour.

"This. Is. Amazing." I shut my eyes, savoring the dense, chewy, everything bagel.

I opened my eyes to find Blake grinning at me, and my pulse stuttered. How did she manage to look so goddamn good after hiking up practically a cliff face for hours? The only obvious sign of any physical exertion was slightly pink cheeks. I wondered if Blake's cheeks went red after all forms of physical exertion... My cheeks, already warm, started blazing at the thought. Blake's grin widened, as if she'd read my mind.

"What?" I asked, narrowing my eyes at her.

"Nothing. I'm just glad you're enjoying the bagel so much." She bit into the pastrami bagel, looking very pleased with herself.

We ate our bagels in companionable silence, watching boats putter down the Hudson and a smattering of white fluffy clouds slowly move across the otherwise blue sky.

"Coffee?" Blake lifted up the thermos. I nodded. After filling a camping mug, she passed it to me and then offered me a cookie.

"This cookie is to die for." I tried to keep my face less orgasmic this time, but it was a challenge. The crunch of the walnuts and the crispy outer layer of the cookie perfectly complemented the rich, gooey interior. It was so rich I only got halfway through before I had to set it aside. I leaned back onto the boulder, groaning slightly.

"That was so satisfying. Thanks for bringing everything. You're very welcome to the squished granola bars I packed if you'd like."

Blake, also leaning back on the boulder, turned to me and smiled, sending butterflies fluttering low in my belly. "No problem. And I think I'll pass on the granola bar, but I appreciate the thought."

We held each other's gaze, and a shiver ran down my spine. "Come here, you," Blake said, her voice low and warm.

I shifted to be closer to her, but then panic swept over me, and I froze.

"What's wrong?"

"I'm gross, and sweaty, and probably smell like fish." I grimaced at her.

"I don't care." Blake leaned over and kissed me softly on the lips before pulling back and looking at me. "I can't smell anything. But I get it. You know the day I ran into you at Novel Gossip, the day after the bachelorette party? I was so paranoid I had terrible coffee breath because I hadn't brushed my teeth I was literally trying to hold my breath every time I got near you."

I laughed. "Are you serious? I thought I must have smelled bad." I shook my head. "That's hilarious. God, it's so weird to think the bachelorette party was only two weeks ago. Things have changed a lot since then."

"Oh, like what?" Blake asked, a little too innocently.

I narrowed my eyes at her teasingly and then leaned forward and kissed her, gently biting her lower lip.

"Like that."

"May I remind you that two weeks ago, you gifted me a

lovely, pink vibrator? Perhaps things haven't changed as much as you think." Blake grinned before leaning in to kiss me again, this time with a hint of tongue.

As much as I was enjoying the kiss, I couldn't help responding. "Oh, really? Well, first of all, that vibrator was for Amanda. Not you."

"Ouch." Blake pouted.

"And second, until very recently, I thought you hated me. So, I would say that a lot has changed since then."

Blake's eyes widened. "Hated you? I thought you didn't like me, but I never hated you. You always... Well, I always felt super awkward around you, but I never hated you."

Her words took a few moments to sink in. When they did, I did a double-take. Blake Mitchell felt awkward around me? That was...unexpected.

"Why did you get awkward around me?"

Blake's gaze increased in intensity. "Why do you think?"

The world suddenly felt off kilter as I reassessed our previous interactions in light of this new information. All those times I thought Blake was standoffish or abrupt with me, she was actually just awkward because she *liked* me?

"Do you still feel awkward around me?"

"Well, I haven't today. I think... I think the more I get to know you, the more comfortable I feel."

"I'm glad to hear. Well, I think you should lie back and get even more comfortable." I leaned forward, pushing Blake gently down on the picnic blanket and straddling her before bending down to kiss her again.

IT WAS ONLY when Blake flipped me onto my back and I happened to look up at the sky during a short breather from our very enjoyable make-out session that I noticed the clouds were closing in.

"Um, do you know what the time is? I didn't think it was meant to rain today, but the sky is looking a little threatening."

"Is this like the raindrop from the other night, or are you being serious?" Blake grinned at me.

I rolled my eyes. "I was serious then, and I'm being serious now."

Blake looked up at the sky, and her grin disappeared. "Okay. That doesn't look good." She looked at the smartwatch on her wrist. "My watch says there's a 50% chance of rain. And somehow, it's already after two. We should probably get moving."

We readjusted our clothes and packed up the picnic. Before long, we were heading back down the mountain.

Halfway down, it started to rain. My sneakers were well-worn and had lost their grip. Their condition, combined with the rain, forced me to slow my pace as I navigated the rocky terrain. It took all my focus to keep my balance. Blake stopped to help me down the larger boulders, adjusting her pace to suit mine. I felt bad I was slowing her down.

"Just a second." Blake spotted something just off the track. She walked over to it, and picked up a tall, sturdy stick.

"I'm sorry. I should have warned you about how rocky it is. Would this help?" Blake held out the stick, which I grasped gratefully.

We'd almost reached the end of the trail when the sky opened up, pelting us with rain. My feet squelched in my shoes, and the jacket I'd put on was not waterproof. The ground had flattened out, so I started jogging, hoping to get back to the car before I got completely drenched.

"How are you doing? We're almost there!" Blake yelled.

"Yep, just a bit we—"

My stomach flew into my chest as my left foot slipped on a rock. My ankle twisted, and I lost my balance. I stuck out the stick, hoping it would support me, but it hit another wet rock and slid off.

For a sickening moment, I was falling, and then I hit the ground.

I struggled to sit up, registering the thick mud covering most of my front and a shooting pain in my ankle.

"Shit! Are you okay?" Blake rushed over to me.

"Yeah, I'm fine," I said a little curtly due to the pain. I stood unsteadily, wincing as I put weight on my left foot.

"Where does it hurt? Any numbness or tingling?" Blake crouched next to me, carefully tugged my sock down, and inspected my ankle, frowning.

"It's just painful here." I pointed to the tender spot. "But no numbness or tingling."

"Okay, good. The fact you can stand on it and don't have any other symptoms is promising. Hopefully it's a mild sprain rather than a fracture." Blake looked up at me, her eyes soft with concern, her wet hair slick against her forehead, and any residual irritation vanished.

I resisted the urge to lean over and sweep her hair away from her eyes with my hands, to tug her up and kiss her until the worry in her eyes disappeared. But given my ankle was throbbing and the rain was pouring down, a kiss was not the most practical course of action.

"Do you think you'll be able to walk the rest of the way

back? I think we're probably about ten minutes away from the car. You could use me as support."

I tentatively stepped forward. It was painful, but not agonizingly so.

Blake stepped closer to me. "Here, put your arm around my shoulder." I followed her instructions, and she wrapped her arm around my waist. We slowly hobbled back to the parking lot, the rain now a light drizzle.

When we reached Blake's car, she opened the passenger side door.

"Sit."

I looked down at my clothes. "But I'm all muddy. I'll ruin your car."

"No, you won't. Now let me look at your ankle again." Blake's voice was so firm I obeyed.

I carefully lowered myself onto the seat, sitting sideways so my legs were hanging out the side of the car. Blake crouched down and inspected my ankle again, touching it gently. "I can't see any swelling or bruising yet." Blake took off her backpack, rustled around in it, and pulled out an ice pack from the cooler bag that had held our bagels.

"Hold this on your ankle." Blake was frowning again, her voice stern and authoritative. A delicious chill ran down my back. Bossy Doctor Mitchell was kind of hot. *I wonder how Blake feels about role play...*

Just then, Blake looked up at me, and her mouth twitched, ruining my doctor fantasies.

"What?"

"You, uh, just have a little bit of mud on your face." Blake's mouth twitched again and then broke into a wide grin.

I yanked down the sun visor to examine myself in the mirror and burst out laughing.

"Oh my god! A *little* bit? Here's hoping this mud has rejuvenating properties, because it's giving me a full-blown facial." Mud caked my nose, cheeks, and forehead. The rain must have dislodged some of it, because dirty dribbles ran down my lower face and neck. I looked like an absolute disaster.

Blake grabbed some tissues from the glove department and was about to hand them to me when she stopped. "Wait! We should take a photo of this for one of your funny posts."

"One of my funny posts? Have you been looking at my social media accounts?" I asked in a teasing tone, secretly thrilled Blake had been engaging in some light internet stalking.

Pink crept up Blake's cheeks. "No comment. Now hand me your phone."

CHAPTER TWENTY

JENNY

By the time Blake pulled up at my parents' house, I'd managed to clean most of the mud off my face.

I undid my seatbelt and leaned over to push open the door.

"Wait! Let me help you out." Blake yanked off her seatbelt.

"I think I'm fine, really. It's already feeling a lot better," I protested.

Ignoring me, Blake jumped out of the car and walked around to the passenger side, offering me her arm. Once I started walking, I was grateful for Blake's support. Like contestants in a very slow three-legged race, we made our way to my parents' front door.

On entry, we were immediately assaulted by Walter leaping on me, his eyes wide with excitement.

"Ow, Walter! Calm down." I turned to Blake. "My parents are out this afternoon, so he's furious he's been left home alone. Do you want to come in?" Butterflies took flight in my stomach as soon as the words were out of my mouth.

"Sure."

We hobbled down the hallway, Walter still dancing around us, his little tongue hanging out and his golden-brown ears bouncing.

When we reached the living room, I stopped. "Do you mind if I take a quick shower to get all the remaining mud off?"

"Not at all. I might do the same after you."

The idea of showering together flitted through my mind, but I quickly shook it off. My ankle was not in any state to support me getting intimate with Blake in the shower. That required both balance and strength.

"I'll use my parents' ensuite so we can shower at the same time."

Blake insisted on helping me to my parents' room before heading to the other bathroom, holding the towel and clean clothes I'd given her.

Once I saw how much mud came off me in the shower, I was even more relieved I hadn't invited Blake to join me. *This is not sexy.* In fact, it was quite horrifying.

I reemerged fifteen minutes later, much cleaner and more comfortable in fresh, dry clothes. I found Blake lying on the couch, in my white *The Eras Tour* t-shirt and navy sweatpants, petting Walter. Under the sleeve of the t-shirt, I could see a hint of the tattoo I'd noticed at the bachelorette party. I itched to pull the sleeve up to examine it.

Blake jumped up when she saw me and helped me over to the couch, sitting down next to me.

"You should keep your weight off your foot and ice it every few hours. Elevating it will help reduce swelling," Blake said with authority. She put a cushion on her lap and patted it, clearly expecting me to lie down on the sofa and place my feet on the cushion. I did not comply. I had other plans.

"Thanks for looking after me, but seriously, I'm fine. It really doesn't hurt that much at all."

"Hmmm." Blake looked unconvinced and adorably concerned, her brow furrowed. "I can't help feeling responsible for it. I should have warned you how rocky it was and that you'd need hiking boots."

"Don't be silly. I should have known better than to wear my old sneakers." Still finding Blake's doctor persona quite the turn-on, I decided to take advantage of the fact we were home alone. I just hoped Blake wouldn't react badly to what I was about to say. I swallowed.

"Although, Doctor, there is something else I need your medical opinion on." I fluttered my eyelashes, doing my best sincere, innocent expression, and then bit my lip.

Blake stared at me blankly for a second before her eyes widened with realization. *Please let her be into this.* I could see her trying to suppress a smile as she leaned toward me, her voice low and slightly hoarse. "Of course, how can I help?" My stomach swooped. *Thank god.*

"I keep having these...urges. I'm worried they are getting out of hand."

Blake nodded, pursing her lips. "Hmmm. That sounds serious. I'm glad you're seeking medical advice. On a scale of one to ten, how would you rate the severity?"

"An eight."

"Okay. And where are you feeling these urges?"

I bit my lip again. "Mainly my...my mouth." Okay, I was not the best at role play, but thankfully, Blake didn't seem to care.

"I see. I'm afraid I will need to inspect it, then." Blake

ran her thumb gently over my lower lip and then leaned forward and kissed me softly before pulling back to look into my eyes. "How did that feel?"

"Mmmh, good. But the urges haven't gone away. In fact, I think they're worse. It's maybe a ten now?"

Okay, I was really bad at role play, but I was enjoying it too much to back out. I was so close to Blake I could smell my sandalwood soap on her.

Blake frowned. "I'm afraid that means I will need to increase the intensity of the treatment, then. Please lie down." I lay lengthways down the couch, and Blake straddled me before leaning down and kissing me more passionately than before. I returned her kisses, running my hands under the t-shirt she was wearing, enjoying the sensation of the soft, warm skin of her back.

After a few minutes, Blake pulled her head back to look at me, her lips red and her cheeks flushed. "Has there been any improvement in your condition since the treatment began?"

"My mouth has definitely improved, but now the feeling has spread to, um, other parts of my body." My cheeks burned with heat.

"Oh really?" Blake's eyes sparkled, but she retained the serious expression.

"Well, then...I'd better inspect your ears," she murmured, her breath warm against my cheek. Blake trailed her mouth across my cheek to my left earlobe, gently teasing it with her teeth, sending my core aching. I moaned.

After Blake had given my right ear the same electrifying treatment, she moved her hand to my breasts, caressing them. "Do you feel it here?"

"Yesss," I managed to murmur, giddy with desire.

"I'm afraid my hands alone won't be sufficient to cure you. Do you consent to me using my mouth?"

I nodded.

Blake deftly undid my bra, tugging it off and lifting my t-shirt up. She bent down and took one of my nipples in her mouth, teasing it with her tongue. I shut my eyes, focusing on the sensation. *Oh god, that feels so good.* I started moaning again.

Blake's hand slowly made its way down my stomach to my crotch. "Do you feel it here as well?"

"Uh-huh." She continued to tease my nipples as she slipped her hand under my sweatpants, touching me through my underwear. *Fuck.* The urges I was feeling were off the charts.

Over my moans, I heard a faint whimper. It didn't sound like Blake. I opened my eyes and flinched.

"What's wrong? Is everything okay?" Blake pulled back.

I started giggling. "Yes, sorry. That was amazing. It's just...Walter." I nodded behind Blake, where Walter had jumped up on the couch. He was panting heavily, his pink tongue hanging out, while he maintained intense, concerned eye contact with me.

Blake turned, breaking into laughter when she saw his expression. "Oh my god. Does he think I'm hurting you or something? The poor little guy."

"Maybe. It could have been my moans or the fact we're occupying his favorite spot in the house. Or because he was left alone all day, and now we're not paying him any attention. Whatever it is, he's clearly not happy!"

Blake shook her head, chuckling. "Walter, the sex-police dog."

"Walter, get down. Come on, puppo." I gestured for

him to jump off the couch, but he wouldn't budge. "Walter, get down!"

"Let's just ignore him. He'll probably lose interest soon. Now, where was I..." Blake leaned back down to my breasts, and I tried to focus on enjoying the sensations. But each time I opened my eyes, Walter was still standing behind Blake, staring at me intently. It was unsettling, to say the least. Even with my eyes shut, I could still sense his gaze boring into me.

"I'm so sorry. I can't do this with him looking at me like that. It's too creepy. Maybe we should move to my bedroom so we can lock Walter ou—"

A rattle of keys made me stop mid-word and sent my stomach sinking.

"Shit, Mom and Dad must be home early."

We scrambled to our feet, readjusting our clothes. There wasn't time to put my bra back on, so I stuffed it under a cushion. When Mom and Dad walked in thirty seconds later, we were both sitting awkwardly on the couch, hoping it wasn't obvious what we'd just been up to. *Good lord, it's like I'm back in high school, trying to hide the fact I'm hooking up with Johnny Butler from my parents.*

My parents, both wearing jeans, puffer jackets and beanies, stopped as soon as they saw us. Despite the unwelcome interruption, I couldn't help but smile. They were so damn cute. Thirty-five years married, over twenty years working together, and they still absolutely adored each other. While I was enjoying spending time with Blake, *that* was what I wanted.

"Hello, Blake," Mom said, a note of surprise in her voice. Mom was aware that I hadn't been Blake's biggest fan in the past, and I hadn't told her about the recent developments in our relationship.

"Hi, Mrs. and Mr. Lynton," Blake responded, her cheeks a faint shade of pink.

Mom pulled her beanie off her short blond hair, which was slowly fading to gray, and sat down next to Blake while Dad put on a pot of coffee.

While my parents and Blake made small talk, I vowed that, next time, we'd go to Blake's house. No Walter or parents to interrupt us. And next time better happen soon, before I exploded with sexual frustration.

CHAPTER TWENTY-ONE

BLAKE

George put a slice of lemon-blueberry cake with two forks in the middle of the table.

"Hopefully you're not sick of this after the wedding."

"God, no." I took one of the forks and stabbed a piece of cake, shoving it in my mouth. "It still tastes incredible despite the fact I played no part in its baking."

"Despite or because?" George asked, grinning.

"Rude." I glared at her. "Amanda's cake also tasted incredible, thank you."

George ignored my retort, taking a sip of her coffee and then leaning forward. "So, how did your date with your gal pal go?" She winked.

"Gal pal? Seriously, George?" I raised an eyebrow.

"Well, I don't know what to call her. You said she wasn't your girlfriend." She had a point. I wasn't exactly sure what the correct label was either.

"Well, your bagels and cookies were a hit, thanks. But it rained, and Jenny twisted her ankle." I sighed, still annoyed at myself for getting carried away making out with Jenny and losing all sense of time and place. If I hadn't lost control like that, I would've noticed it was getting late and the clouds were coming in, and Jenny wouldn't have gotten injured. "Luckily it happened right near the end of the trail, so we got ice on it quickly and could rest it. Jenny texted me this morning to say it was feeling a lot better, which is a relief."

"At least Doctor Mitchell was there to ensure the correct medical treatment was applied."

Heat rushed to my cheeks. Flashbacks to Saturday afternoon had been torturing me for the last two days. I never thought I'd be into role playing, but I'd found it incredibly hot with Jenny. Although, to be honest, I'd find anything involving Jenny incredibly hot, especially if it involved teasing her nipple with my mouth or making her moan with pleasure.

"Why are you all red and awkward-looking all of a sudden? Did you two...?" George leaned forward and wiggled her eyebrows.

"No comment," I said firmly, my face still burning.

"Sorry, I was being nosy. I'm just really excited for you." George sat back in her chair. "But things are going well? You're happy?"

"Yeah, maybe too well." I grimaced.

George snorted. "Come on, there's no such thing as 'too well.'"

"I'm just worried I'm setting myself up for failure. This is meant to be a casual, fun fling, but I'm not sure I know how to do flings."

"Hmmm. I guess going on a strenuous hike with a romantic picnic doesn't scream casual fling."

I sighed. "Yeah, maybe that wasn't the best idea. Until Grace, I was a serious-relationship person, and since her,

I've been a *no*-relationship person. I've never dated someone knowing there was an end date on it. What if I start getting really attached to her?" I chewed on my lip. *What if I'm already attached to her?* The whole point of my 'no relationships' policy was to avoid the heartache I'd experienced after multiple breakups. "I think I got a bit carried away on Halloween and rushed into things without thinking it through properly. This can only end badly, right?"

"Well, a lot of people just go on a couple of dates, realize the other person isn't for them, and part ways amicably. That's not exactly ending badly. Maybe that's what will happen with you two?"

"Hmmm." I stabbed at the cake with my fork absentmindedly. "It just doesn't feel like that's where we are heading." I looked around to check no one was within earshot and lowered my voice. "I really like her, George. I can't stop thinking about her, wondering what she's doing... We're getting along so well I just can't see us going on another one or two dates and breaking up. This feels *real*. Bizarre and totally unexpected, but real."

"That's exciting!" George looked genuinely thrilled. "Well, maybe you won't break up. Maybe Jenny will extend her stay, or you guys could do long distance until you work something out."

I pressed my mouth together, shaking my head. "I've invested so much time, effort, and money in setting up the clinic, and I love it here. I can't imagine living in Los Angeles, dealing with all the traffic, pollution, not being able to see my family whenever I wanted... And Jenny couldn't move here. There's not exactly a lot of work for an influencer in Sapphire Springs."

George studied me intently, leaning over her coffee on

the table. "Well, it seems to me you have two choices. You can either break things off now, or you can keep going and see where it takes you. The benefit of option one is that you won't get any more attached to her, but from what you're saying, that ship may already have sailed. The con is that you may miss out on a lot of hot sex and always wonder what might have been. With option two, of course there's the risk you'll get even more attached to her and find it tough when she moves back to LA, but at least you'll enjoy her company in the meantime. Or you both might realize that things aren't going to work out and break up amicably."

I sighed. I already liked Jenny too much to just end things and move on with my life without some serious pining.

"When you put it like that, it seems like a no-brainer. You're right. The ship has already sailed, and if I don't pursue this, I'll probably always wonder how it would have ended."

George's eyes brightened, and she sat up straight. "Excellent. Well, in that case, can you please ask your unlabeled beau to drop in so I can personally thank her and give her a coffee on the house?"

I narrowed my eyes. "What are you thanking her for?"

George grinned. "I got a call yesterday from *TimeOut New York*. They're planning an article on winter weekends away in the Hudson Valley and want to feature Novel Gossip. Apparently, Jenny's posts on Halloween caught their attention."

"That's awesome! Just don't get so popular you have no time to chat with me when I drop in, okay?"

"Blake, I promise I'll never get too busy to see you."

I took a final bite of cake and sat back in my chair. "Jenny's specialty appears to be helping other people out.

Saving Amanda's bachelorette party and wedding, helping get you a write-up in *TimeOut*, and now she's also offered to talk to the mayor and do a fundraising event for my uninsured patients."

"Oh, that's a great idea! I know how much that's been stressing you out. You know, you two are a great match, what with you helping sick people and all Jenny's good work. Maybe you can become famous lesbian philanthropists." George's eyes twinkled.

I snorted. "Have you been listening at all? Jenny's leaving in three months. And she's not a lesbian; she's bi. And also, to be a philanthropist I'm pretty sure you need to actually be rich."

"Details!" George waved her hand dismissively. "But on a serious note, I'm glad you're letting her help you."

I studied George's face. I'd never spoken to George about it, but she'd clearly picked up that I didn't usually feel comfortable with people helping me. I was the one who helped others, not vice versa. I didn't want to owe someone a favor or surrender my control or independence to someone else. I'd been like that my entire life, but it had gotten significantly worse since Grace. Since I discovered just how devastating it could be when someone let you down.

But with Jenny, it was different. She wasn't doing it for me. She was doing it for Sapphire Springs. And I couldn't imagine her expecting anything in return. Although, I wouldn't mind if she did, because I liked helping her too.

"So, do you have another date arranged with her?"

"We talked about doing something tomorrow night, but we haven't arranged anything yet. I'm thinking maybe a drink at Frankie's or dinner at Builders Arms might be the safest bet."

"You don't want to invite her over and cook for her?" George's mouth twitched, and I had a sneaking suspicion she was teasing me.

"Umm, I don't think that's a good idea. You've tasted my cooking." I'd lost interest in cooking since Grace. It was difficult to motivate myself to cook anything particularly creative or interesting when I was the only person who would enjoy it. My specialty was bland and healthy. Chicken breast with steamed vegetables, omelet with salad, salmon with salad. Not exactly dinner-party-worthy dishes. The lack of practice cooking anything remotely challenging had undermined my confidence and any skills I did have.

"I could send you the recipe for the duck ragu I made you last year. It tastes fancy but it's surprisingly easy."

My mouth watered at the memory of George's rich duck ragu, which she'd served with handmade pasta.

"That's what you said last time you sent me the recipe for that beef Wellington I cooked for Dad's birthday, which was an absolute disaster. But at least he unconditionally loves me. Jenny on the other hand..." My voice trailed off. "Anyway, I think I need to slow things down. While the ship may have already sailed on getting attached to her, I do have some control over how attached I get, and sleeping together always makes me more involved. I know it's not usual "fling" behavior, but I want to spend a bit more time with her to make sure things feel right first. So, I think I should avoid inviting her over to my house for now, with easy access to my couch...and bed...and all that privacy." My desire for self-protection was kicking in. If Jenny's parents hadn't come home, I was confident one thing would have led to another.

"Do you want me to be your chaperone? I could sit directly behind you at the bar or pub, staring at you two like a creep while I munch on popcorn or perhaps really loud chips?" George mimed pulling popcorn out of a large bucket and chewing vigorously, her eyes wide open.

I laughed. "No, thanks. I think I'll pass."

"Actually, if it's tomorrow night, I can't chaperone anyway because we're holding our first paint-and-sip event here."

"That's tomorrow night?" I asked. I'd been planning to go, but I hadn't realized it was so soon. "You know, that would be the perfect date. You'll essentially be chaperoning, just without the popcorn-slash-chip eating and creepy-eyes part. And we'll be in public, so we won't be able to get too carried away."

"Look, I don't want to lose any customers, but paint and sip seems like more of a date-date activity than a casual-fling activity..." George looked at me skeptically. "But I'm probably not the best person to take dating advice from."

George had been single as long as I'd known her and was decidedly vague about her relationship history. I figured if she wanted to tell me about them, she would, so I hadn't pried, but I had to admit I was a little curious.

"I think it's perfect. I'll text her now." I pulled out my phone and shot off a text to Jenny before turning back to George.

CHAPTER TWENTY-TWO

JENNY

"I'm hoping this wine gets my artistic juices flowing. I haven't painted anything since high school, and I got a D in art." I looked at Blake, who was sitting next to me in a matching apron over her black jeans and red flannel shirt, swiping through photos on her phone. She looked up at me, her face breaking into a smile, and my heart skipped.

God, she's hot.

"Thankfully, no one is getting graded tonight, which is probably for the best, given they've already polished off one bottle of wine and haven't started painting yet." Blake nodded over at three women in their forties who were laughing so hard they almost drowned out the background music.

I chuckled. When Blake had suggested paint and sip for our date, I'd been slightly disappointed. I'd been hoping she'd invite me over to her place, and we could pick up where we'd left off on Saturday—without unwelcome interruptions from parents or dogs. But now we were here, I was glad we'd come out. And unlike some of the people I'd dated in LA, it was nice to know she didn't want to keep our relationship quiet, even if it wasn't serious. I'd still optimistically cut my fingernails this afternoon, hoping the night might end at Blake's.

"It looks like we're starting," Blake said, interrupting my train of thought.

The theme of the night was "Paint Your Pet." For those who didn't have pets but still wanted to participate, George had put a blown-up photo of her golden retriever, Maximus, on an easel at the front of the room. Maximus was also snoozing in a corner, in case anyone wanted to do some life-painting. My phone was propped up on the table next to my easel, displaying a particularly cute photo of Walter with his pink tongue poking out.

"Now, everyone, I recommend you first sketch out your pet to get the composition right before you start painting. I'll show you how I'd sketch out Maximus. Just yell out if you need any help." The art instructor, a woman in a long, flowing rainbow dress with long, wavy, pink hair to match, picked up a pencil and began outlining Maximus.

"Here goes." I picked up my pencil and spent the next few minutes deep in concentration as I tried, unsuccessfully, to capture Walter's essence.

I glanced over to Blake, who was already finished. My jaw dropped when I saw her sketch of her cat. "Wow! That's really good." Of course Blake was good at art too. Previously, I would have felt a twinge of jealousy at Blake's talent, but now I just felt...proud? These new feelings were strange but definitely not unwelcome.

"Okay, everyone! Now, we're going to start painting. Everyone come up and get the paint you need for your background." The instructor gestured at a table near the front, which had a row of paints in large pump bottles.

"Shit! I still haven't gotten Walter sketched properly. I'm really struggling with the proportions. Help!"

Blake looked at me. "Do you really want me to help?"

"Yes, that would be amazing." If I didn't get the initial sketch right, my whole painting would be a disaster. I started to get out of my chair, but Blake bent down next to me instead, taking my hand in hers and leaning forward over my shoulder. She was so close I could feel her body emanating heat and smell the faintly sweet scent of her shampoo. A strong urge to pull her around so she straddled me and so I could bite her full lower lip rushed over me. *Wait, Jenny. Be patient. Do NOT make a scene by PDAing at a paint and sip.*

Patience was not one of my virtues, so to distract myself, I focused on her long, slender fingers holding my hand, guiding the pencil as she deftly sketched Walter's outline. But then I immediately imagined those fingers cupping my jaw, scraping down my back, unbuttoning my jeans, and—

"There you go!" Blake let go of my hand and stepped back. Hot and flustered, the space she'd been inhabiting suddenly felt extremely empty. I wanted her close to me again.

After a moment collecting myself, I took in the canvas in front of me and blinked. Blake had somehow managed to transform my sketch from tragic Frankenstein-dog to Walter.

"That's incredible! It actually looks like Walter. Thank you."

"No problem. Do you want me to get your paints so you can rest your ankle?"

"It's fine, seriously." My ankle was still slightly tender, but I was more than capable of getting my own paint.

Despite that, I was touched Blake was so concerned about it.

We went up to the front to get paint, and then, as per the instructor's directions, used the larger paint brush to fill in the background. I tried copying the instructor's approach of quick, broad brushstrokes. Out of the corner of my eye, Blake appeared to be using the same technique. But when I sat back and looked at both our canvases, Blake's background was a smooth sky blue, whereas mine was an uneven, lumpy-looking light green. My brushstrokes were clearly visible, but not in a nice, impressionist way—more like a "look at what my toddler painted" kind of way.

"Luckily, Fred is pretty good with dogs, so he and Walter will hopefully get along," Blake said, putting down her brush. "Walter seems like a pretty relaxed dog—except when his owner is making out, of course." She grinned.

Oh shit. Walter and cats. "Unfortunately, Walter had a run-in with a cat a few months ago, so I'm not sure... We may need to keep them apart, but that shouldn't be too difficult." My words lingered in the air uncomfortably, a reminder that this relationship had an expiration date.

A look I couldn't read flashed across Blake's face. "Yeah, of course. There shouldn't be any reason for them to meet. Um, I might grab another drink. Would you like one?"

"Sure, I'll come up too." We walked up to the counter where George was serving and chatted with her before returning to our seats, wine glasses refilled, just in time for the instructor to clap her hands for attention.

"Okay, everyone, your background should have dried, so it's now time to paint the star of the evening, your pet."

After the instructor gave some practical advice, we picked up our brushes and started to paint. I kept looking over at Blake, who was engrossed in capturing Fred. Brow furrowed, lips pursed, there was a look of intense concentration on her face as she applied deft brushstrokes to the canvas.

It reminded me of the way she'd looked at my ankle after I'd hurt it on the weekend, and that reminded me of the way she'd looked at me on the couch at my parents', the way her lips felt on mine, the way her lips felt teasing my nipple. The yearning ache that'd been torturing me each time I had a flashback—which had been a frequent occurrence—reappeared, and I squirmed in my chair. I forced my attention back to the canvas in front of me. Hopefully, painting Walter would have the same effect as Walter had had in real life on Saturday—the dog equivalent of a cold shower.

An hour later, I put down my brush and sighed loudly, staring at my creation. It was bad. Very bad. The wine had not unleashed my creative juices one iota.

As I took in what I'd done, a strong desire to laugh spread from my belly to my chest, until I couldn't hold it in. "Oh my god," I said, my voice shaking with laughter. "Poor Walter, what have I done to you?"

Blake, who'd been absorbed with putting the finishing touches on Fred, looked at me, and then at the painting, and then back at me, before howling with laughter.

Struggling to speak, she eventually managed a strangled, "His face...the other day...sex police..." before bursting out laughing again. Her laughter pushed me to the verge of hysterics, tears running down my face as I gasped for air.

I don't how I'd managed it, but Walter was glaring at us with intense disapproval. Not only that, but he also had one eye that was significantly bigger than the other, and the way I'd painted the hair on his face made it look like he was walking through a wind tunnel. He looked absolutely terrifying.

"I don't think I'll be hanging this one up at home," I gasped through giggles.

George, who'd been strolling around the cafe, admiring everyone's work, walked over to us. Her eyes widened as she saw my painting. "Oh my," she managed, clearly lost for words.

Luckily for her, the art instructor joined her, peering over my shoulder. "Very impressive. You know, it reminds me of some of Picasso's more surrealist works. I love how you've played with proportions and angles and created a powerful, unnerving work. Very clever."

"Thank you." I sat back in my chair, soaking in the praise and ignoring the fact everything the instructor liked about my work was extremely unintentional.

George and the instructor then turned their attention to Blake's painting, which was actually incredible. I'd never met Fred, but based on the photo displayed on Blake's phone, she'd skillfully captured him. It was so realistic it looked like he might jump off the canvas at any minute.

Once they finished showering Blake with compliments, I turned to her.

"Would you mind taking a photo of me next to my masterpiece?" The photo of me post-hike, with a mud facial, had performed surprisingly well, so perhaps this one would too. Although, it wasn't clear whether unflattering mud facials and hilariously terrible art would help me find new sponsorship deals. There had been radio silence from Serena, and my bank balance was starting to look rather sad.

Shaking off my worries, I handed my phone over to Blake and plastered a smile on my face.

Thirty minutes later, we'd finished our wine, and our paintings were dry enough to be transported home.

"Do you need a lift?" Blake asked as she picked up her artwork from the easel.

It sounded like Blake's offer was to drive me back to my parents' house, not hers. My chest tightened. Was she having second thoughts about us? *She might just be tired, or not be feeling one hundred percent. Don't overthink it.* But it was hard not to overthink it when you were so used to rejection. You began anticipating it.

I realized Blake was staring at me, and I still hadn't answered her question.

"That would be great, thanks." I had to get home somehow, and a ride was more appealing than stumbling home in the cold, dark night.

As Blake drove through the side streets to my parents' house, she asked, "So, what are you going to do with your painting, if you're not going to hang it up at home?"

"Well, since it's a surrealistic masterpiece, I think it deserves to be displayed publicly so it can be enjoyed by the masses. Perhaps at your clinic? If not that, I'll approach MOMA and Dia Beacon, and see if they are interested."

Blake snorted. "I'm flattered you thought of me first. But while I've been meaning to decorate the clinic—and my house, for that matter—I'm not sure your, um, masterpiece is quite the look I'm going for. Patients want a calming, soothing environment. Maybe some watercolor landscapes or cheerful geometric paintings? Not the stuff of nightmares."

"Fine." I huffed. "It's your loss, though."

We joked the rest of the way home, me proposing horrific paintings I could create for Blake's clinic and Blake rejecting them all emphatically.

As Blake pulled up outside my parents' house and turned off the engine, nervous anticipation began to build inside me, giving me the same jittery sensation I experienced when I drank too much coffee.

I took a deep breath and turned to her. "Thanks for suggesting this. I had a really great time. Would you...would you like to come in?" My desires and impatience overpowered my discomfort at the prospect of another Walter sex-police incident and potentially sleeping with Blake with my parents down the hallway.

Blake paused, and that jittery sensation skyrocketed while I waited for her response. "I'd better not, sorry. My first appointment is at eight tomorrow."

A surge of disappointment washed over me. In the dark, I couldn't make out Blake's facial expression. Was that just an excuse?

"Of course, no problem." I unbuckled my seatbelt and was about to open the car door when Blake leaned forward and put a hand on my thigh, sending my nerve endings tingling and the disappointment tumbling away.

"Hey," she said, her voice soft and low. "Would you like—"

She didn't need to finish. I shifted my body to face her. Before I knew it, we were kissing like we were back on the couch. I couldn't get enough of her mouth, teasing her lower lip with my teeth, stroking her tongue with mine. I wanted to get closer, to feel the pressure of her body against me, to explore her body with my hands, but the damn center console of the car was between us.

"Beeeeeeeep!" We both jumped. Blake's arm or some other body part must have hit the car horn. A light switched on in my parents' house. *Shit.*

"Oops. I should probably go before they come out here

in their pajamas to see what's going on!" It wasn't like it was a big deal if my parents caught us kissing, I was an adult, for god's sake, but I felt bad about disturbing them. And I was also getting incredibly turned on making out with Blake, which was only going to make me more frustrated when she drove off alone in a few minutes.

"Okay," Blake muttered, pulling me back for one final kiss.

"Remember to get your painting out of the trunk," Blake called with a little too much desperation in her voice. I stumbled out of the car, smiling at her words, our kiss still reverberating through my body.

CHAPTER TWENTY-THREE

BLAKE

"We're having a very arty week. First paint and sip, and now this!" Jenny gestured at the massive steel sculpture six times her height, which appeared to be defying gravity by balancing precariously in the middle of a grassy field in the sculpture park. "We may need to balance it out by watching some trashy holiday rom-coms."

I chuckled. "Isn't it a bit early for holiday rom-coms? It's only November."

Jenny assumed a mock horrified face, her eyes wide and mouth gaping. "It's never too early for cheesy, so-bad-they're-good, holiday rom-coms. But if you don't want to snuggle up on the couch with me and watch some, I'm sure Walter will happily oblige." She looked down at Walter with a smile, who was furiously sniffing the base of the sculpture.

I wanted nothing more than to cozy up on the couch with Jenny. My plan to take things slow hadn't exactly been satisfying, and my resolve to move slowly was wavering. The more I thought about it, the more it seemed like a stupid idea. This was meant to be a casual relationship, which meant it was all about sex, right? Casual relationships weren't for taking things slow. So what the hell was I waiting for?

"Poor Walter. First, he's traumatized by seeing his mom being mauled by a strange woman on the couch, and now he's being subjected to holiday rom-coms in November. The little guy's been through a lot already. I think I'll have to take one for the team here and offer myself up in sacrifice."

"I promise you won't regret it," Jenny said teasingly. A buzz of anticipation vibrated low in my belly.

Jenny's smile faded. "Would you mind re-assuming your role as my official photographer while we're here? I'm woefully behind on my social media posts. I've been really lacking in motivation, especially when I've got more exciting things to do, like..." She looked at me, and her voice trailed off. She bit her lip, and a shot of electricity ran down my spine. "Like your fundraising event." Yes, of course, the fundraising event.

Jenny had, much to my amazement, already written a proposal for a Sapphire Springs health fund. We'd reviewed it over lunch at Novel Gossip on Wednesday, and then she'd somehow managed to present it at the monthly village board meeting on Thursday night. The board had thought it was a great idea, and provided Jenny could raise enough money, they'd given it a green light. Everything was moving incredibly fast. The least I could do was flex my photography skills.

"Yes, of course, that's fine. I could take one of you pretending to be holding up the sculpture so it doesn't fall on Walter?" I grinned.

"Oh, I like that! You know, if you ever get sick of doctoring, a career as a content creator awaits."

Jenny handed me her phone and walked over to the sculpture, calling Walter to sit directly under the section that would hit the ground first if it was to capsize. She pretended to push the massive steel structure, groaning dramatically. A flashback to me straddling Jenny on the couch, teasing her nipple in my lips while she moaned, appeared in my mind, distracting me from the task at hand. *Focus, Blake.*

"Um, I've just been taking photos. Was I meant to be capturing your sound effects on videos?"

Jenny shook her head, smiling. "Nah, that's okay. They were just for your benefit."

"Thank you?" I laughed and then looked down at the phone and flicked through the photos. "They worked out really well." I looked up, surveying the sculpture park for other photogenic options. "Why don't I take a photo of you next to that red sculpture?"

"Sounds good."

We made our way over to a monumental sculpture featuring vibrant interlocking red banana-shaped pieces of metal which looked striking contrasted against the bright-blue sky.

Jenny also looked striking standing in front of it, smiling at me. Her blond hair, green coat, blue jeans, and black boots offered another stunning contrast against the vibrant red of the sculpture.

My breath hitched as I looked at her through the camera app on her phone. I could not believe she was here, with me. This gorgeous, funny, kind woman who'd saved Amanda's bachelorette party and wedding and who was now going out of her way to help me. This gorgeous, funny, kind woman I'd had a crush on for well over a decade. It hit me like a ton of bricks. *Fuck. I really like her.*

As soon as I was happy with the photos, I strode straight over to her.

"Is everything okay?" Jenny asked as I reached her.

"Yes, why?"

"You just look like a woman on a mission."

"I guess that makes sense." I stepped closer to Jenny so I was only inches away from her.

"And what's your mission?" Jenny's eyes were twinkling now.

"My mission, if you choose to accept, is to kiss you." I grinned, so close to Jenny now I could smell her faint, floral scent. I wet my lips in anticipation.

Jenny rolled her eyes and giggled. "Talking about cheesy rom-coms...but I accept."

My hands on her waist, I gently walked Jenny back so she was leaning against the sculpture. She looked up at me, her lips parted, her eyes locking with mine, and then my lips were against hers, my hands scrambling under her coat and top. Jenny wrapped her arms around my waist, pulling me closer. Fuck. As amazing as the kiss was, I was desperate for more. More than we could do at a public sculpture park. I wanted to be naked with her, in private, now. I must have intensified my kissing, or somehow telekinetically trans-ferred the image to Jenny, because she moaned loudly. The moan further increased the pulsing ache between my thighs.

A sharp pain stabbed in my leg.

I pulled back from Jenny's kiss-swollen lips, flushed and breathless.

"Ouch! My leg. What the...?"

I looked down to see Walter glaring up at me. He was furious.

"What's wrong?" Jenny peered over my shoulder.

"It's fine. Walter just scratched me. Now, where were we..."

I turned back to Jenny, and Walter scratched me again. "Okay, okay, I get it, buddy." I stepped back. "Um, has he done this with other people, or should I be taking it personally?"

Jenny laughed. "This is a new thing. But have you noticed he only reacts after I moan? So you should take it as a compliment. Clearly no one has made me moan quite the way you do." Jenny's voice was teasing, but I couldn't help the surge of pride that welled up inside me.

"Well, in that case, I prescribe a course of exposure therapy to cure Walter." I leaned back in, moistening my lips, intent on making Jenny moan again.

"BY THE WAY, how is your ankle?" I asked as we walked back to the car. "I signed up for the Thanksgiving Turkey Trot this morning. If your ankle is feeling better, let me know if you're interested in doing it with me. It's only three miles."

"Only?" Jenny said, raising an eyebrow. "My ankle is fine, but I'm not really a runner. I'd just slow you down. I'll cheer you on from the sidelines, though."

Jenny's cheers would definitely power me up Main Street, but her company would be even better. "If you're not into it, that's totally fine. But if you're just worried about slowing me down, that's not an issue. I'm not trying to win it or anything, and having you there would make the whole thing way more fun. We could do a couple of practice jogs together to prepare."

Jenny looked at me for a second, her face serious before

breaking into a smile. "Okay, let's do it. But if you want to abandon me in a quest for glory, you have to promise me you will. I don't want to hold you back."

Chuckling, I shook my head. "I am not going to leave you behind."

We reached my car, and my heart dropped at the thought of driving Jenny back to her parents' house.

"Hey, do you have any plans for dinner tonight?" I asked on impulse, not wanting the day with Jenny to end. I didn't want to go home alone to an empty house. *Screw taking things slow.*

"Nope. Wanna watch a holiday rom-com and give Walter some more exposure therapy?" Jenny's eyes twinkled.

I laughed. "Well, I was thinking maybe you could come over to my place, and we could drop off Walter at your parents' on the way. In my medical opinion, we don't want to go overboard on the therapy, especially given Walter would also have Fred to deal with. It might all be too much for him."

Jenny nodded, grinning. "Good point. What were you thinking for dinner?"

"Would you be okay if we just picked up pizza from Michael's?" I didn't want to scare Jenny off with my cooking.

"Done."

TWO HOURS LATER, we were in my living room, watching *Single All the Way*.

Fred, who took a while to warm up to strangers, had

taken himself to the armchair next to the window as soon as we appeared in the living room.

I was debating whether to have another slice of the capricciosa pizza, which was displayed in the open pizza box on the coffee table in front of us. *I really shouldn't...but it was so delicious.*

Jenny, perhaps sensing I was in inner turmoil but mistaking the cause, looked at me with concern. "How are you coping with watching a holiday movie in November? Are you experiencing any side effects? Maybe a sudden desire to go caroling, eat gingerbread cookies, or drink eggnog?"

I laughed, turning to her. "Not yet, but I'll continue to monitor myself. Perhaps it's because I'm not getting the full experience. I distinctly remember the offer was to snuggle on the couch." I raised my eyebrows.

"Eating pizza and snuggling aren't exactly compatible, but if you've finished...?" Jenny shuffled over to make room for me on the chaise section of the couch, grinning.

I immediately lost interest in the pizza and bounced over to Jenny, bringing a throw blanket with me.

"Now this is more like it." I faked a yawn, moving my arms above my head and then putting my right arm around Jenny's shoulders.

"Very smooth." We looked at each other, smiling, and then Jenny rested her head on my shoulder. I let out a breath, enjoying Jenny's warm body pressed against mine. I could definitely get used to this.

We spent the rest of the movie snuggling. As the credits rolled, Jenny looked up at me. "So, are you a convert?"

"While I still believe, on principle, that holiday movies shouldn't be watched outside of December, I'll grudgingly admit I'm supportive of anything involving pizza and snuggling up on the couch with you, even if it involves season-ally inappropriate films."

"I'm glad to hear it." Jenny stretched her neck out and kissed me on the cheek. I turned to catch her kiss on my mouth, shifting my body to get in a more comfortable position.

Our kisses, which started out tender, quickly morphed into something more fiery.

"Do you want to do the doctor thing again?" I asked between gasps.

"No, if it's okay with you, I'd rather just do...you."

"That is absolutely fine," I said, kissing her again.

I pulled back, looking deep into her eyes and seeing the same desire I was experiencing reflected back at me. I traced my thumb over her lower lip, tugging it down slightly, and then kissed her again.

"Do you want to go to my bedroom?"

Jenny nodded. I grabbed her hand and led the way out of the living room and down the hallway to my bedroom, my heart slamming against my chest in excitement.

"Now, where were we?" I asked as we reached the side of my bed.

"I think you were about to take off all your clothes," Jenny responded with a gleam in her eye.

"Oh, was I? I don't remember discussing that." I unbut-toned my shirt, my hands shaking with nerves, as Jenny pulled her top over her head, revealing a black, lacy bra and delicious curves. *Goddamn.*

I tugged my jeans and socks off in an extremely uncoor-dinated fashion, almost falling over in my desperation to be rid of them. When I looked back up, Jenny had also removed her jeans and socks and was standing in front of me in matching black underwear, her hair tumbling down her front. The smile lighting up her face suggested she'd witnessed my bumbling clothes removal, but I was too turned on to care.

"You are so fucking sexy," I murmured, my voice husky.

I stepped forward, putting my hands around her waist, and pulled her toward me for another kiss, trailing my fingers over her back as I did so. Our bodies pressed together, our kisses passionate, verging on frantic, but it wasn't enough. The two layers of fabric between her breasts and mine had to go. Continuing to kiss, I reached behind myself and undid my plain, black cotton bra with one hand and then did the same to Jenny's. The sensation of her warm, soft breasts against mine only increased the heat pulsing between my thighs.

"Fuck. You drive me wild," I gasped between kisses.

Still wanting more, I shifted us around so Jenny's back was to the bed and pushed her gently onto it, before tugging her panties down. For a moment, I paused to take her all in. The soft curves of her stomach, her breasts, her gorgeous face.

Keen to eliminate the space between us, I lowered myself on top of her, trailing kisses from her mouth down her neck to her collarbone. Jenny tipped her head back, whimpering with pleasure and grabbing my hair in one hand while her other hand ran up and down my back. The smell of her skin, floral and fresh, was intoxicating. Remembering the sounds she'd made when I'd teased her earlobe after the hike, I moved back up to her ear, softly biting it. Jenny's whimpers turned to moans, and for a fleeting second, I was glad Walter wasn't here, and Fred, who'd probably reclaimed his favorite spot on the couch, couldn't care less.

After giving her ear some attention, I slowly made my

way down Jenny's body. My tongue circled around one of her hard nipples before taking it in my mouth, sucking it and gently flicking it with my tongue. I caressed her other breast with my hand. Jenny grabbed my hair tighter, and her moans got even louder, sending a thrill down my spine. Damn, I loved that sound. I stayed there for a while, kissing, licking, sucking, and caressing, until Jenny's moans got so loud I was worried she'd orgasm before I'd had a chance to go down on her. Hell, at this rate, I might orgasm just from the sounds she was making.

"That feels so good," she managed to gasp.

I left her nipples and went lower, kissing the soft skin of her stomach, my hands running over faint silver stretch marks and a birthmark just above her belly button. My mouth followed, kissing the soft skin of her lower belly.

Jenny let out a loud, needy sound.

I gently ran my fingers between her legs. She was hot, wet, and ready for me.

"Can I go down on you?" I asked, my voice hoarse with desire.

"Fuck, yes!" Jenny yelped.

I gradually kissed and licked my way between her legs, paying special attention to her inner thighs. Reaching one arm up, I began teasing her left nipple again with my hand as I did a long, slow lick from her entrance to her clit. I repeated that a few times, reveling in her taste and her whimpers, before I moved my focus to swirling my tongue over her clit. I stayed there for a while, experimenting with different techniques to see what would elicit the biggest sounds, all the while teasing her nipple. Every so often, I'd dip my tongue lower, pressing into her and curling before moving back up to her clit.

Jenny's hips began to move, and her breathing became ragged.

"I want you inside of me," Jenny gasped.

While I liked to take things slow, to tease, even I was starting to get impatient with my self-control.

Keeping my mouth on her clit, I pulled my hand away from her nipple and gently ran my fingers over her wetness, circling around her entrance, Jenny's hips moving with desire.

I slipped two fingers inside her and began slowly, very slowly, moving them in and out. Each time they went deep, I curved them, and Jenny moaned with pleasure.

"Mmmm, that feels good," Jenny gasped.

Gradually, my mouth and my hand picked up pace, but each time Jenny felt close to coming, I'd reduce the intensity for a minute or two before increasing it again.

After a few rounds of edging, Jenny groaned. "Oh my god, you are such a tease. Can you just let me come already?"

I lifted my head, taking in the swell of her breasts and her smiling, flushed face looking down at me. Good lord, she was hot.

"You need to learn patience," I said, grinning, before returning my focus to her clit. I wanted to give Jenny a mind-blowing orgasm—and take my time getting there. I mean, I'd waited seventeen years to do this. I wanted to revel in her moans, whimpers, wetness, impatient hip thrusting, and her naked glory.

I took her to the edge one more time for good measure, slowing my hand and tongue, before picking up again.

This time, I didn't reduce the intensity. I kept going. I sucked her little bundle of nerves in my mouth, flicking it with my tongue, and added another finger at her direction.

Giddy with desire, I increased the intensity of my tongue on her clit and moved my hand faster. I wanted her to come so bad, so hard. I'd always enjoyed pleasuring my partners, but the gratification I was getting from going down on Jenny was next level. *So this is what seventeen years of pent-up lust finally being released feels like.*

Jenny grabbed my hair, and again, I thought I might come just from her heat and wetness, her sounds, and the knowledge she was almost at the edge.

And then her thighs were trembling, and she was arching her back and spasming on my fingers, and yelling, "Fuck, yes!" I kept going, riding out her orgasm, not wanting it to end, until she batted my head away, still shuddering from aftershocks.

"Enough!" Jenny said, laughing.

I disentangled myself from her legs, suddenly aware the arm I'd propped myself up on was aching, and peered up at her, sweaty and breathless.

She looked down at me, pink-cheeked and smiling.

"Come up here, you. That was incredible."

Chest expanding at Jenny's glowing review, I clambered up to her, and she pulled me in for a gentle kiss before pushing me on my back and straddling me.

"Well, hello." I grinned up at her.

"Hello, gorgeous," Jenny responded, smiling back, before leaning down for a kiss.

"I'm so turned on right now," I murmured, hoping Jenny would get the hint I didn't need a lot of foreplay.

"You need to learn patience, remember?" Jenny said, smirking.

Jenny took her time, teasing my neck and breasts with kisses, licks, and gentle bites, until I was squirming with need. She placed one of her legs between mine so at least I had something to grind against. Which I did. It was both thoroughly enjoyable and also thoroughly frustrating.

Just when I thought I couldn't take it any longer, that I might need to beg and plead with Jenny to make me come, Jenny shifted her weight onto her left arm. Watching my expression, her face only inches from mine, she trailed her right hand down my body and between my legs, her fingers gently circling over my clit, dipping down to my entrance, and back again. Jenny, her eyes now locked on mine, seemed to be staring into my soul. Good lord, I'd forgotten just how intimate sex could be. In between kissing her, I ran my hands over the smooth curves of her back and side, reaching down a few times to grab her butt. *Damn, I love touching her.*

"I want to go down on you. Is that okay?" Jenny murmured near my ear, sending nerve endings firing.

"Yes," I gasped.

Without stopping the magic her fingers were working, Jenny made her way down my body, stopping every so often for a kiss or a lick, before settling between my legs. She paused for a moment, and then her fingers circling my clit were replaced with her tongue, and seconds later, those fingers were sliding in me. I let out a deep breath, relieved she hadn't made me wait like I'd done.

"That feels so fucking good," I managed, closing my eyes to focus on the sensations.

Jenny hummed into my clit, dispatching vibrations that made my sensitive nerves tingle, before doing something mysterious with her mouth that felt incredible. My sex-addled brain made a mental note to ask her later so I could try it on her.

Jenny gradually increased the intensity of her move-ments, pleasure spreading out from the thousands of nerves in my clit across my entire body. Tension coiled within me, and my breath became ragged. *Fuck.* I was so close.

My body was on fire, about to explode.

Jenny pushed her fingers into me again, and suddenly, fireworks were shooting through me, intense waves of euphoria overwhelming my body. *Christ, this has to be one of—if not the best orgasm of my life.*

As I recovered, Jenny slowly made her way back up to me, trailing kisses as she went.

"That was amazing, thank you," I murmured as she reached eye level, pulling her in for a kiss.

She lowered her head, hair a mess, onto my chest and enveloped me in a hug, a happy sigh escaping her mouth. I pulled the duvet up to cover her and wrapped my arms around her.

Deliciously relaxed and cozy, we lay silently, snuggled up against each other. I'd forgotten how much I'd missed this. Vibrators didn't offer warm, blissful cuddles or make you feel emotionally connected and safe.

"Hey, would you like to stay the night?" I asked softly, a while later, not wanting the day to end.

"That would be nice." Jenny nestled up against my chest. "I don't want to leave."

I didn't want her to leave either. But I knew she would eventually. Not tonight, but sometime soon. If she didn't get sick of me before then.

I pulled my arms tighter around her, trying to commit this moment to memory. Jenny shifted against me, sparking something low in my belly, and my mind turned back to more physical matters. I ran my fingers lightly up and down Jenny's back, testing to see if she was interested. She moved her hand down to the location of that spark, and we were off.

CHAPTER TWENTY-FOUR

JENNY

Light infiltrated the slits between my eyelids, waking me.

Opening my eyes, I looked around the room, disoriented. A plain wooden dresser, full-length mirror, and a built-in closet all looked unfamiliar. My chest tightened. *Where the hell...?*

Suddenly, the memories of last night rushed back to me, and I let out a deep breath of relief, relaxing back into the bed. I was at Blake's. And the reason the room looked so unfamiliar was because I'd been deeply distracted by Blake last night. To be honest, I wasn't sure how I'd forgotten our mind-blowing sex for even a second.

It wasn't just that the orgasms were mind-blowing— although they had been incredible. It was also the emotional connection, the feeling of closeness, of sleeping with someone I liked and who actually seemed to like me back, that had blown me away. Yes, there'd been mutual attraction in the relationships I'd had in the past few years, but this had...this had felt different. When I'd looked into Blake's eyes, my heart had somersaulted as I saw something —something deeper than lust or attraction—reflected back at me. It had felt amazing last night, but this morning, the memories knotted my stomach. *This can only end badly.*

I rolled over, hoping the sight of Blake next to me would reassure me this was a casual fling that could end without heartbreak, but I found rumpled white sheets and a pillow where Blake should have been.

Clambering out of bed, I searched the room for my clothes, spotting my jeans and socks in the far corner of the room, my bra half under the dresser, and the rest of my clothes on the floor right next to Blake's side of the bed. I dressed and went looking for Blake.

Blake's house was an adorable cottage. Well, it was adorable from the outside at least, with its white weather-boards with blue trimmings and a blue door, nestled in a slightly overgrown English country-style garden. The inside had a lot of potential—gorgeous wooden floors, a fireplace in the living room, and large windows—but it was noticeably bare. Like Blake had moved in and never gotten around to properly decorating the place, which was almost certainly what had happened. It was in stark contrast to my vibrant, rather cluttered apartment in LA.

I heard a door bang and followed the noise down the hallway to the kitchen, pausing at the door to take in the scene in front of me. Blake, hair mussed, wearing gray sweatpants and a "Columbia University" navy hoodie, stood over a pan on the stove, an intense look of concentration on her face. Fred was sitting on a bar stool on the other side of the counter, observing her. A blast of warmth hit my chest at the sight of them. I leaned against the door frame, keen to enjoy this charming domestic scene unnoticed for as long as possible. The movement must have caught Blake's attention because she looked up.

Her face broke into a smile at the sight of me. "Good morning. I thought I'd make us pancakes."

"Yum! I love pancakes." The warm feeling in my chest intensified. I couldn't remember the last time someone I was dating had cooked for me. And Blake's smile was also doing things to me. Warm, gooey things.

Her smile faltered. "I've never actually made pancakes before. Hopefully they'll be okay."

It was kind of adorable seeing Blake, who was usually so competent and confident, looking concerned about cooking. I walked up behind her, wrapping my arms around her waist. "I'm sure they will be delicious. Can I help?"

Blake hummed, clearly enjoying my embrace. "No, I've got everything under control, thanks. They should be ready any minute. Would you like coffee?"

"Coffee would be amazing," I said, suddenly desperate for a caffeine hit.

I disentangled my arms from Blake and joined Fred on the bar stool next to him, watching Blake make coffee.

Fred didn't appear concerned by my presence this morning, so I tentatively gave him a gentle pat. He started purring, so I kept going, pushing away guilty thoughts of Walter who would almost certainly be outraged at this scene. But Fred was so damn cute, with his flawless silver-gray coat of hair, green eyes, and adorable little nose. He jumped over onto my thighs and nuzzled into my stomach.

"Looks like you've made a friend." Blake grinned, handing me a coffee, and then turned back to the pancakes.

"Shit!" Blake exclaimed just as a burning smell reached

me. I looked up to find Blake looking flustered, holding the pan off the stove with one hand and swatting smoke away with the other.

"I got distracted making the coffee. Well, at least I have more batter," Blake said as she deposited a blackened disc into the trash.

Ten minutes later, Blake placed a large pancake in front of me on the dining room table. My stomach rumbled in anticipation. Last night's activities must have used a lot of energy.

"Okay, they look a little strange, but at least they're not burned," Blake said as she took a seat next to me.

They did look a little strange. Like they'd risen very high, and then...collapsed. But it didn't matter what they looked like, what mattered was the taste.

I smothered them in maple syrup and took a bite.

Oh god.

They tasted disgusting.

Chalky, salty, and bitter, despite my generous pour of maple syrup. I forced myself to swallow it without grimacing.

Blake looked at me expectantly, so I managed a weak, "Mmmmmm." I looked down at the giant pancake and nearly threw up thinking about trying to eat the rest of it.

Blake's brow dipped at my unconvincing noise. I was about to force down another mouthful when Blake took a bite.

I watched her facial expression as she chewed on the pancake, her eyes widening and her lips pressing together. It was verging on comical. My mouth began to twitch.

Swallowing the mouthful with difficulty, she looked at me, horrified.

"Good lord, what have I done? They taste revolting."

My lips twitched again as I tried to suppress my giggles. "Hey, it's okay. It's the thought that counts. Did you, um, possibly drop a whole tin of baking soda in the mixture by mistake?"

"Not a whole tin. I couldn't find a teaspoon, so I just tipped some in. I must have misjudged it. And I did the same with the salt as well," Blake said ruefully.

We locked eyes, Blake's lips also twitched, and then I couldn't hold in my giggles any longer. We both burst out laughing.

"All I can say is, I hope you're more precise when administering medication, or I may need to report to you the authorities," I said, still giggling.

"Why don't we go to Novel Gossip for breakfast instead? And I'll buy some pancake mix for the next time you come over, to avoid a repeat of this morning," Blake said once we'd calmed down, a sheepish look on her face.

While my heart jumped at Blake's assumption there'd be a next time, I made a mental note to take over pancake-making duties. Cooking appeared to be one of the few things Blake did not excel at. It was a miracle Amanda's cake had turned out so well.

It suddenly dawned on me that I hadn't looked at my phone since dinner last night, more than twelve hours ago, which had to be a world record for me. Anxiety spiked in my chest. As much as I didn't feel like it, I should check how the content I'd post yesterday was performing and try to engage with some of my followers. Unfortunately, in my job, I couldn't just switch off on the weekend.

"Novel Gossip sounds like a great idea. But do you mind if I check my phone for a few minutes before we head out?" Guilt that I was delaying our morning flooded over me, but I knew if I didn't check, I'd be distracted throughout breakfast.

"Of course. I'll go take a quick shower and change into something more presentable."

Blake stood up and gave me a kiss, and I walked over to the couch where I'd left my phone charging last night.

As soon as I opened TikTok, I knew something was wrong. My inbox was full of new messages. And judging from the preview text I saw as I scrolled, my stomach sinking, they were from furious animal lovers.

Jen D
You should be banned from owning animals

Marylovesdogs43
Walter deserves better than you

User48372
I'm unfollowing you as soon as I finish writing this message

Some of the other messages were a lot more vicious. Panic rising in my chest, I tried to work out what had sparked this new wave of ire from my followers. I found the answer in the "activity" tab. Melanie93 had posted a video mentioning me ten hours ago. And the thumbnail of the video was a photo of me smiling, a big red circle with a diagonal line through it overlaid on top with the word *CANCELED* on top. *Fuck, fuck, fuck.*

Slightly shaky, I hovered my finger over the thumbnail,

took a deep breath, and clicked on it. It already had 7,000 likes.

The photo was there for a few seconds before an attractive brunette, presumably Melanie, started talking. "Y'all might remember Jenny Lynton was almost canceled last month after it was revealed one of her sponsors, Ruff Dog Food, had made a number of false claims to be environmentally sustainable when it was actually full of the rainforest-destroying palm oil, which can also be bad for dogs. Well, last night, another product Jenny has been recommending, Bark4Treats, was recalled by the FDA for potential salmonella contamination. Once might be a mistake . . . but twice? I know I don't want to follow people who are making money off shady companies putting the health of our dogs, and our rainforests, at risk, so..." The photo of me with a red circle and *Canceled* overlaid on top reappeared.

Sick to my stomach, I stared at my phone blankly. *Fuck.*

I checked my follower numbers. They'd dropped by over a thousand since yesterday. *Shit.*

"What was that all about?" I startled at the sound of Blake's voice, turning to find her standing at the door, brows furrowed, her hair wet, and a towel wrapped around her. She clearly wasn't into long showers.

At the sight of Blake's concerned face, tears welled in my eyes.

"Urgh, nothing." I swallowed, digging my fingernails into the palm of my hand in an attempt to ward off the tears.

Blake walked over and sat down next to me on the couch. "It didn't sound like nothing," she said gently. "Do you want to talk about it?"

I made the mistake of looking deep into Blake's soft brown eyes, and a tear escaped my eye and ran down my cheek. *Get it together, Jenny.*

I took a breath. "Walter and I were brand ambassadors for Ruff Dog Food, which basically means they paid me to do posts featuring their product. You know, like Walter dressed up in a cute outfit, eating a bowl of their food, with the packet clearly showing in the background?"

Blake nodded.

"Well, anyway. I'd been happy to partner with them because Walter really liked their food, and it was meant to be a good-quality, eco-friendly product. I actually made a big deal out of the eco-friendly side of things in a couple of my posts because a lot of dog food actually isn't very environmentally sustainable."

I paused to wipe my eyes, and Blake looked at me expectantly.

"Well, to cut to the chase, it turns out that a lot of the Ruff Dog Food products don't live up to their claim, meaning my posts were wrong. A few people posted videos criticizing me for lying and advertising shady products. One of them went viral on TikTok, which resulted in me losing a lot of followers and being on the receiving end of a lot of nasty comments and messages. I lost a few sponsorship deals as well."

Blake put her hand on my thigh and squeezed. "Shit, I'm sorry. That sounds really stressful, but it doesn't seem like it was your fault. You couldn't have known they were lying to you. You were duped too."

"Unfortunately, not everyone sees it that way. They think I should have done more to confirm Ruff was credible before I took their money and recommended their products. And maybe they were right. I took them at face value." I sighed, guilt washing over me again. I loved dogs so much. The thought I'd been endorsing unhealthy products and letting Walter—and the dogs at the shelter I'd donated excess food to—eat them gutted me.

"Short of sending their food off for testing or tracking down their supply chain, I don't see what you could have done. And surely no one would expect an influencer to go to those lengths."

I shrugged. "Yeah. Anyway, things were just starting to die down. And then Melanie93 posted this."

I handed my phone over to Blake, who watched the video in silence, wincing as Melane93's words replayed.

"Shit. I'm sorry, Jenny," she said once the video ended.

"It's not even true. I've never had any relationship with, or even heard of, Bark4Treats before, but it doesn't matter. Now my inbox is full of angry messages, and I've lost even more followers."

Blake frowned. "If it's not true, can't you get her to take it down, or sue her for defamation or something?"

I sighed. "Serena, my agent, usually says just not to engage. When the Ruff thing blew up, I did an Instagram story apologizing to my fans and stating I was no longer associated with Ruff. She might want me to do something similar this time, but it's unlikely to achieve much. And taking any kind of legal action would be insanely expensive and might actually make things worse. Suing ordinary people who are passionate about the environment and dogs probably isn't a good look, even if what they're saying is completely wrong."

"Fuck, that's really hard. Let me know if there is anything I can do to help."

My chest felt like it was being squashed by a few giant bags of Ruff dog food.

"Thanks. I'll call Serena, but I think I'll just need to wait for it to blow over."

Blake shook her head. "I don't know how you do it. I'd be permanently stressed about saying something wrong. You must really love it to keep going."

I felt a twinge of annoyance at Blake's words. "I don't exactly have a choice. I'd be broke and stuck living with Mom and Dad in Sapphire Springs forever if I didn't keep doing this." I winced at the way that had come out. Once, I'd thought remaining in Sapphire Springs would be terrible. But now...now I could see its appeal.

"Sorry, I know it's your job. But you have lots of skills, and you're smart. I'm sure you could do something different if you wanted to. I mean, you were incredible stepping in to do Amanda's wedding and—"

Annoyance bubbled up inside, and I cut her off. "Unlike you, I don't have a medical degree from an Ivy League college. I don't exactly have a lot of qualifications. I have limited options, Blake."

Blake pressed her lips together, hurt, and guilt engulfed me.

"I'm sorry. I didn't mean to snap. I know you're just trying to help. I'm super anxious about the whole thing, and I'm taking it out on you. I may also be a little hangry..." I put my arm around her and gently squeezed, giving her a little smile. "How about we head to Novel Gossip and get some food into us?"

Some of the tension in Blake's face released, and she managed a weak smile.

"Sounds good. Do you know what you want to order? Maybe I should call ahead so it's waiting for us, to put both of us out of our hanger as soon as possible." To my relief, there was a twinkle in Blake's eyes.

"If George could do that, that would be incredible. And I'm 100% getting pancakes." I grinned, already feeling a little better. Blake and I had our first, very small, disagreement—if you could even call it that—and everything was fine. We'd soon be eating delicious pancakes. And hopefully, the algorithm would stop favoring Melanie93's video, and it would fade into obscurity.

CHAPTER TWENTY-FIVE

BLAKE

"Ohhh! Look at these prints. They're gorgeous. They'd look nice at your place." Jenny raised her eyebrows, a half-joking, half-hopeful look on her face, as she grabbed my hand. She tugged me over to visit a booth featuring stylized prints of local landmarks.

I followed, smiling. When Jenny had come over last weekend, I'd caught a flicker of an expression—possibly judgment or disappointment—cross her face as she looked around the blank walls.

I'd written off holiday markets years ago as sanctuaries for tacky, overpriced trinkets and overwhelming crowds, so I hadn't expected to find anything I liked at the Hudson Highlands Holiday Market. But I'd already picked up a nice serving platter for my parents' Christmas present and, to my surprise, was actually enjoying browsing the booths run by local artisans. Although, how much of my enjoyment was due to the markets and how much was due to my company was unclear. Based on the past few weeks, Jenny's company improved...well, everything, and her general positivity was infectious. That was one of the reasons her revelation last weekend had come as such a shock.

I'd wondered why she'd decided to stay in Sapphire Springs for so long, but I'd never expected it to be something like that. It killed me that I'd had no idea what she was going through. Despite following her on social media, I'd completely missed the story she'd posted a few weeks ago, refuting the allegations, and had stopped reading the comments on her posts some time ago after getting too riled up by the leering ones, so I'd missed the whole scandal.

Jenny picked up one of the prints. "Look, it's Main Street! It's a shame your clinic is just out of the picture, but there's Novel Gossip and Builders Arms."

I peered over her shoulder at it. The artist had perfectly captured Main Street's essence.

"Wow, that is really nice."

I examined the other prints, spotting the sculpture park we'd visited last weekend and the view from the top of Breakback Ridge, amongst many others. The colors were bright and bold, the designs were eye-catching, and they weren't too expensive either.

The thought of having something on my walls that Jenny had chosen, especially of places we'd been together, filled my chest with warmth. They'd not only be reminders of the experiences we'd shared, but also of this moment. Of standing next to Jenny who, as usual, was looking gorgeous in a green coat, black jeans, and boots, intently examining the prints one by one and exclaiming as she spotted familiar locations. So many times recently, I'd wished I could commit moments with Jenny to my memory like film footage. Unfortunately, my mind didn't work like that. But maybe these prints would help.

"I'm definitely better at appreciating art than doing it

myself," Jenny said, grinning at me, before turning back to the prints.

I chuckled. "Hey, you're a surrealist master, remember? Up there with Picasso."

Jenny elbowed me gently, shaking her head and giving me a smile that I wanted to see over and over again—but in real life, not on replay in my memory.

"You know what, I think I'll get a few for the living room."

Jenny's face broke into an even bigger smile at my announcement, and my heart swelled with happiness. We spent the next few minutes picking out our favorites. Main Street, Breakback Ridge, the sculpture park, and Red Tractor Farm. All of them held memories strongly tied to Jenny.

However, as I paid, negative thoughts crept up, whispering warnings and sucking the warmth from my chest, leaving it tight and empty.

Choosing artwork for your living room together doesn't exactly scream casual relationship, Blake. It's more screeching, "Let's call a U-Haul!"

Is it really a good idea to decorate your home with memories of a relationship that is doomed to fail?

How will you feel when she's back in LA, and you're on the couch, miserable and alone, surrounded by prints reminding you of Jenny?

With effort, I pushed the thoughts away. The prints didn't *need* to be painful. What was that quote again? *'Tis better to have loved and lost than never to have loved at all.* With "love" switched out for "liked a lot," of course. Liked. Definitely not loved.

As we left the booth, I put my arm around Jenny, taking

comfort in the curves of her body, which were already so familiar and reassuring, and her faintly floral scent.

Just live in the moment and enjoy this time you have with her.

"Do you want to grab a drink before we keep going? All this browsing is making me thirsty," Jenny said, nodding at a stand selling hot donuts and drinks.

A hot drink sounded like the perfect way to stave off whispered warnings. We grabbed steaming cups of cider, sitting down on wooden crates they'd turned into makeshift seats.

"Olivia should have a booth here next year for her candles. They'd make perfect holiday gifts." Jenny took a big sip of her cider.

I frowned, confused. "Candles?"

"You know, the candles she's been making? The ones she sells in her store."

Shit. I realized I hadn't been to Olivia's store for months. I'd been so preoccupied with work that I probably hadn't been the best sister, friend, or daughter recently.

I nodded, not wanting Jenny to know what a terrible sister I was. "I've been meaning to ask. Any updates on the Bark4Treats thing?" I asked, keen to change the subject.

Since Jenny had told me what happened, I'd kept a close eye on her social media accounts, scrolling through the comments. To my relief, Jenny had posted a story on Monday night explaining that she didn't have any association with Bark4Treats. It came across genuine and heartfelt, and based on the comments, it appeared to have been generally well received. However, to my immense frustration, Melanie93's video was still up. I'd gotten the impression it hadn't gained a lot of traction after the initial post, but who knew what kind of messages Jenny was receiving. Nausea rocked my stomach at the thought.

I'd asked Jenny how it was going on Wednesday night when she'd come over, bringing Thai takeout and a list of holiday rom-coms. She'd sounded cautiously optimistic that it wouldn't inflict too much damage, but I'd held off asking about it again until now.

Jenny's smile flickered, and I immediately wished I hadn't reminded her about it. But when she spoke, she sounded upbeat. "It looks like it has died down. TikTok has stopped pushing the video, and it definitely didn't take off in the same way the posts about my association with Ruff did. I spoke to Serena again yesterday, and she isn't too worried."

My chest suddenly felt lighter. "I'm so glad to hear that. What a relief."

"Yeah, it really is. I was worried it was going to be the nail in my influencing-career coffin for a hot second."

I shook my head. "It still amazes me that one person can make a baseless allegation and you could lose your whole career over it."

Jenny looked down at her cider. "Yeah. Look, I definitely think cancel culture has its place, but it can be very unpredictable, and the consequences aren't always very proportional. People can lose their livelihood over genuine mistakes, while some rich, famous, white guy who has sexually harassed a number of women can avoid censor or bounce back quickly. And, unlike in court, your accusers can inflict damage without needing to prove anything beyond reasonable doubt or provide any evidence at all. Don't get me wrong. I think most who are canceled probably deserve it, but there is scope for mistakes to be made."

Jenny's smile faded completely. Keen to change the topic, I threw my empty cup into the trash can nearby.

"Should we keep browsing? Maybe we'll find something to hang in my practice's waiting room as well."

"Well, there's always my surrealistic masterpiece. Surprisingly, neither MOMA nor Dia Beacon have snapped it up yet, so it's still available." Jenny grinned, taking my hand in hers and squeezing it.

"Oh, what?" I feigned surprise. "Surely they could get rid of a few Dalis or Warhols to make room for your pièce de résistance?"

Jenny laughed, and my heart felt full to exploding.

This. Joking around but also being able to discuss things that mattered. Being together in public, holding hands. This was *really* nice.

I squeezed her hand back as we walked toward the booths.

To my delight, she didn't let go.

CHAPTER TWENTY-SIX

BLAKE

"That looks great!" Jenny exclaimed as we stood back and admired our handiwork.

The four prints we'd bought at the holiday market hung on the walls of my living room. I had to admit, it made a world of difference to the room. It now felt warm, lived in. Like a home.

"It really does. Thanks, babe." I wrapped my arm around Jenny and pulled her to me, and then I realized what I'd just said.

I froze. *Babe?*

"Babe" was what I'd called Grace, probably around the six-month mark. It was a term I associated with serious relationships, a term I associated with Grace, with Anna, with Hanh. A term I hadn't used since Grace. But it had just fallen out of my mouth so naturally.

In some ways, it wasn't surprising. The last few weeks, we'd spent so much time together it felt like our relationship was on fast-forward. I mean, Jenny had already peed with the door open, chatting to me as she did. And the fact we'd grown up together, even if we hadn't been close, gave us this shared foundation, a shared understanding. It *felt,* in a good way, like we'd already been dating six months, perhaps even more. Although...was it good? By the time January came around, would Jenny's departure feel more like the dissolution of a twelve-month relationship rather than a two-and-a-half-month one? Surely that would make it more painful.

"What were you thinking for dinner?" Jenny asked, interrupting my thoughts.

"I thought I could make a roast chicken with vegetables. Are you okay with that?" When I'd been brainstorming simple dinners I could make for Jenny with George, roast chicken had sounded relatively foolproof—and a lot healthier than the takeout we'd been sticking to for safety after the pancake incident.

"Why don't we make it together?" Jenny suggested, a little too adamantly. Not that I could blame her.

Ten minutes later, supporting my theory that Jenny's company made everything better, I was actually enjoying being back in the kitchen. I liked chatting while I rhythmically chopped potatoes, butternut squash, and fennel to roast. Once finished, I tossed the vegetables with olive oil and thyme and seasoned them. When I turned around, Jenny was bending over and shoving an entire lemon into the chicken's cavity. The fact I found that image kind of hot said something about just how into Jenny I was right now.

"Done!" Jenny said triumphantly, a lock of blond hair falling over her face as she stood.

She brushed the hair away with the back of her hand— the only part of her hand that wasn't covered in raw chicken —but it immediately fell again.

I stepped over to her, reaching my hand out. "Here, let me do it."

I gently swept the hair back behind her ear, tracing my fingertips over her cheek, our eyes locking in the process. A small thrill dashed down my spine as we bit our lower lip in unison. Grabbing her waist with both hands, I pulled her in for a kiss, sending a surge of electricity pulsing through me. The physical side of our dating still felt white-hot in its intensity. I couldn't get enough.

But this time, something didn't feel quite right. Jenny's lips were telling me she was into this kiss, but the rest of her body...not so much. She felt stiff, restrained. My stomach dipped. Was something wrong?

I pulled back. "Hey, is everything okay?"

Jenny's face broke into a grin, and relief washed over me, settling my stomach.

"Yes. But my hands were just up the butt of a raw chicken, so I'm just trying to avoid touching you. Although, of course I want to touch you, which is driving me a little wild."

"Oh, really?" I let out an evil chuckle before leaning in and ensnaring Jenny's earlobe between my teeth while I grabbed Jenny's butt, pulling her even closer to me. "It's driving you wild, is it?" I murmured near her ear.

Jenny moaned. "Oh my god, that's *so* unfair."

I slowly kissed down her neck, enjoying Jenny's whimpers of pleasure.

Jenny pulled back, giggling, as I reached her collar bone. "Okay, okay! Why don't we put this all in the oven and give me a chance to wash my hands before I accidentally smear raw chicken juice all over you in a fit of passion!"

"Mmmm, raw chicken juice! Very sexy," I said, laughing as I reluctantly disentangled myself from Jenny. As much fun as I was having, Jenny's suggestion was sensible.

"Now, where were we?" Jenny asked, stepping toward

me after she'd washed her hands and I'd put the food in the oven.

"I think you were about to sexily rub raw chicken all over me." I wiggled my eyebrows suggestively.

Jenny pretended to glare at me, her lips twitching. "Hilarious. Actually, I have an idea. Come with me."

Jenny grabbed my hand and led me toward the bedroom, my heart picking up pace with anticipation.

When we reached our destination, she beelined for the drawer in my side table, where I kept a stash of sex toys, and rummaged around.

"Aha! I thought I'd spotted this in here." Jenny triumphantly pulled out the plastic handcuffs I'd received at Amanda's bachelorette party and walked over to me, a wicked grin on her face. "Given you just took advantage of me while I was incapacitated, I think it's only fair you get a taste of your own medicine..."

Jenny dangled the handcuffs in front of me, raising an eyebrow in question. I eyed them.

I liked being in control in most, if not all, facets of my life, including in the bedroom.

But, to my surprise, the idea of letting Jenny take control wasn't a turn-off. In fact, the warm, tingling sensation between my legs suggested that maybe, just maybe, it could be a turn-*on*. Quite a turn-on. I trusted Jenny enough to be vulnerable with her, to try something out of my comfort zone. I'd never felt this way with Grace, despite the years we were together.

"Okay," I said, hoping I didn't live to regret it.

Jenny's eyes and grin widened with delight. "Okay? Well, in that case, let's get you naked."

Five minutes later, we were both naked, and I was handcuffed to the headboard of the bed. It was a slightly uncomfortable but titillating experience. It was also strangely liberating. All I could do was lie back and enjoy Jenny's kisses and caresses, which felt inexplicably more intense. All my senses were heightened as she made her way slowly down my body. The sensation of her breasts grazing my chest and then stomach, the warm wetness of her mouth as her tongue circled my nipples and then trailed kisses and licks toward my thighs.

What followed next were the most mind-blowing, extreme orgasms of my life. Orgasms, plural.

"That was incredible, babe," I said once the final shudders had rocked through me. The "babe" had slipped out again, and this time I couldn't care less.

Jenny wiped her mouth before clambering up to me and lying next to me.

"Anytime," she said, grinning.

Jenny ran her fingers over the tattoo that wrapped around my upper arm, tracing its outline. The skin on the underside of my upper arm was ticklish, and her touch made me squirm.

Jenny pulled her fingers away. "Sorry, does that tickle? I've been meaning to ask about this. It's an eagle, right? Is there a story behind it?"

Heat rushed to my cheeks. I'd been hoping Jenny wouldn't ask this question, but I didn't blame her. I'd do exactly the same in her position.

"Yeah, it's a bald eagle." I paused, wondering how much to share with her. I was still tied to the bed and naked after having just made myself extremely vulnerable, so why stop now? "In a total cliché move, I got it after my ex and I..." I swallowed, the pause lasting longer than intended.

"Broke up?" Jenny offered, eyes wide with sympathy. "Sorry, if you don't want to talk about it, that's totally fine."

I took a deep breath. For some reason, I wanted to tell Jenny the story. "No, it's okay. It's complicated. I met Grace in the first week of my residency program in New York, and we became serious—very serious. Living together, talking about marriage, kids, about setting up a medical practice together, all that stuff. And then, one day, she didn't come home for dinner. I got a call, a few hours later, from a woman." I shut my eyes, remembering how panicked I'd felt getting that call. "Grace had been hit by a taxi in Williamsburg."

Jenny's eyes widened even more. "Oh my god. Shit. Was she...okay?"

"Yes, yes, she made a full recovery. And as far as I know, she's happy and healthy. But when it happened, the doctors weren't sure she would survive. I was beside myself with worry. Initially, I didn't think much about the woman, Bec, who'd called me and who was by her bedside when I arrived. She said she was Grace's friend. But as Grace's prognosis improved and I had time to think, certain things just didn't make sense. We'd been together for three years and knew each other's friends well, but I'd never heard of Bec. She was apparently so close to Grace that she checked in on her way more frequently than our other friends. And I also started wondering what Grace had been doing in Williamsburg. She was supposed to be at the hospital in Park Slope, where she was doing her residency. And then, one day, when Bec was visiting, she mentioned she lived in Williamsburg."

Jenny, who'd been frowning, groaned.

"Yeah. For six weeks after the accident, I was her primary caregiver. I kept my suspicions to myself. It was excruciating, but I didn't want to ask her about it until she'd recovered enough to live by herself. Because I knew if she confirmed my fears, I'd find it even harder to keep caring for her. But I wasn't going to leave her when she needed help." I'd felt sick to my stomach for those six weeks, worrying about Grace's health and about us.

I continued, my voice flat. "When she could walk again, I asked her about it. She confirmed she'd been having an affair with Bec for almost six months and left the next day."

"Shit. I'm so sorry, Blake. That really sucks." Jenny stroked my hair.

"Yeah."

It had more than really sucked. I loved Grace. But it wasn't just that. I'd planned my life around her, so much so it felt like I'd lost a lot more than just a relationship. I'd lost a future family, a business, shared hopes and dreams. Moving on had involved a massive grieving process that lasted a long time—well over a year. And the most annoying thing was that this had happened to me before, albeit less dramatically, with Anna and Hanh. At around the two- or three-year mark, when I had my life planned out with each of them, they'd left, leaving me reeling. Anna to work with Doctors Without Borders in South Sudan. Hanh because she didn't think I was "the one." I hadn't learned from my experiences with Anna and Hanh, but after Grace, I sure as hell never wanted to be in that position again. I didn't want to rely on someone else for my happiness. I wanted to be independent, self-sufficient.

The irony of it struck me. And yet, here I was, tied to a bed. And until we'd started this rather heavy conversation, I'd actually been enjoying myself—although I should probably ask Jenny to take off the handcuffs, which were digging into my wrists a little. I realized Jenny was staring at me, and I hadn't actually gotten to the tattoo part yet.

"Sorry. So I left that afternoon, and a few weeks later, I

got the tattoo. After that experience, I decided I'd rather stay single. So I got a bald eagle, soaring through the sky, because bald eagles fly alone." I didn't bother mentioning this was the third time in a row something like that had happened.

"Oh." An expression of something—was it disappointment, or hurt?— flickered across Jenny's face.

Anxiety welled up inside me. *Shit.* I needed to say something, to explain how Jenny fit into everything I'd just told her, but I wasn't sure I knew either. Despite us being casual, it didn't feel like I was flying alone anymore, and I hated to admit...I was loving it.

"It definitely wasn't my finest life choice getting a tattoo immediately after a bad breakup, breakup bangs would have been a less permanent decision, but I've come to—"

The doorbell rang.

We froze.

Who the hell could that be? I wasn't expecting anyone, and it was late for visitors to show up without warning, which, honestly, I didn't think was okay at any time of the day.

"Maybe they'll just go away?" Jenny asked hopefully.

Bang, bang. Now they were knocking on the door.

I groaned. "Shit, it could be one of my patients having an emergency. I'd better get up and check. Can you uncuff me?"

Jenny grabbed the key off the side table, crawled up to the head of the bed, and started to fiddle with the handcuffs.

And fiddle. And fiddle.

Panic rose in my chest, pulling it tight.

"Fuck, I'm sorry. I can't unlock them," Jenny said after what felt like minutes.

The bangs on the door continued. The person was getting impatient.

"Crap. Do you mind seeing who it is?"

Jenny nodded, jumping off the bed, pulling on her clothes, and running out of the room. I remembered thinking at the bachelorette party that the handcuffs weren't very good quality, but that observation had completely fled my mind. An image of the entire Sapphire Springs volunteer fire department standing around me sprawled naked on the bed, shaking their heads in judgment before they freed me from the handcuffs, popped uninvited into my head. I drew in a deep, calming breath. *Jenny will sort this out.*

The sound of the door opening provided a welcome distraction. I listened intently, hoping to god it wasn't someone who needed urgent medical attention. Another image of me trying to assess the patient's condition while naked and tied to a bed appeared.

Why the hell didn't I ask Jenny to pull the duvet over me so I wasn't so exposed?

"Oh hello, Jenny. I thought someone was home. Is Blake here?" a woman asked.

I sighed. I recognized that voice. It was my neighbor and former English teacher, Mrs. Harding. She'd been one of my favorite teachers in high school, although she was very old school, and she liked to talk. A lot. She was in good shape, so at least it was unlikely she was in need of medical attention. More likely she was feeling lonely and had popped over for a chat.

"Um, no, sorry, she's not available at the moment." Jenny sounded awkward, in a rather suspicious manner. I hoped Mrs. Harding didn't pick up on that and barge in here, worried Jenny had done away with me.

"Not available?" Mrs. Harding sounded confused.

"Yes, she's, um, indisposed."

I shifted on the bed carefully, trying to give my arms, which were starting to ache from being fixed in an unusual position for so long, some relief.

"Oh." There was a pause. I was almost positive Mrs. Harding thought I was in the bathroom. "I see. Well, look, I just wanted to have a chat with her about pruning one of my trees that's hanging over her side of the fence. I was hoping she'd be able to give me access to her yard to do it."

An itch in my nose started up, bringing with it a strong urge to sneeze. *Crap.* The walls were thin in my cottage, and the bedroom was right next to the front door. If I sneezed, Mrs. Harding would definitely hear me. I held my breath, trying to fight the urge.

"I'm sure Blake would be fine with that. I'll let her kn—"

"It's just difficult to cut them from my side because the tree has so many branches, you see. You're not really meant to prune in fall, but I couldn't do it in spring because I had a sore shoulder, which I actually had to see Blake about. She was so wonderful, gave me some stretches and anti-inflammatories, and it healed right up. But the tree is now overgrown, and I don't want to spend the next five months looking at that mess, so I've decided to take action."

The need to sneeze was becoming unbearable. If only my hands were free, I could rub my nose, which might give me some relief.

"That makes sense. I'm sure Blake will be more than happy to give you access." Jenny's voice sounded polite, if a little strained.

I'd be more than happy to let Mrs. Harding do whatever she goddamn wanted in my yard if she'd just leave so I could sneeze and Jenny could get back to trying to free me. I tried twitching my nose, a la Samantha in *Bewitched*, hoping to dislodge whatever irritant had made its way up my nostrils. To my immense relief, it worked. The urge to sneeze subsided. *Thank god.* I relaxed back into the bed.

"Do you think Blake will be available soon? I was also hoping to talk to her about a couple of the fence pickets that are rotting and whether we should pay someone to replace them." Mrs. Harding barely paused for a breath before continuing. "I know doctors are always saying to eat more fiber and drink more water to get things moving, but I think a few teaspoons of castor oil is the best remedy. That's what my grandma always said, and it works wonders." It took me a moment to realize what Mrs. Harding was talking about. Yep, she definitely thought I was indisposed in the bathroom. An overwhelming need to laugh rose up my chest. *Do. Not. Laugh.* I clenched my jaw together.

"Uh, thank you. I'll pass on the information to her."

"If she doesn't have any castor oil, I can run back to my place and get it. It doesn't usually work immediately, unfortunately, so it may not give her instant relief."

"That's very kind of you, but I think she already has some."

Please, please let that be the end of the conversation.

"So, you and Blake are close now? That's nice. I don't remember you being friends..."

Mrs. Harding kept talking, but I stopped listening because Fred suddenly jumped on the bed and started rubbing his cheek affectionately on my underarm.

My exposed, very ticklish underarm.

"Fred, no!" I whispered, but as usual, he ignored me. Fred kept going, nuzzling into my underarm, triggering a strong urge to giggle. *Keep it together, Blake.* I took some more deep breaths, trying to focus on the sensation of the air entering and exiting my lungs and not on the excruciating tickles Fred was giving me. I squirmed, but it didn't deter Fred. He continued to bunt against me, every so often stopping to glare at me. Fred clearly wanted to be petted and was wondering why I wasn't cooperating.

"I'm sorry, little dude, but I can't pet you," I whispered to him before refocusing my energy on the deep-breathing exercises in an attempt to counteract the tickling.

Finally, I heard the door shut, and a few seconds later, Jenny appeared at the doorway.

"Shit, I'm sorry that took so long. She just kept talking."

"It's not your fault! But can you please get Fred off me? He's tickling me!"

Jenny shooed Fred away and then spent the next twenty minutes wrestling with the handcuffs.

Just when I thought we would need to call the fire department, the latch clicked, and my hands were free.

"Yes!" Jenny exclaimed.

I sat up, and after I'd shaken my arms out, I wrapped Jenny in an embrace and pulled her into me. "Thank you so much." I squeezed her tight before pulling away. "But I think next time we should invest in some better-quality bondage gear."

Jenny grinned. "Next time, eh? Well, I'm glad to hear this experience didn't put you off."

She leaned in for a kiss but stopped just before she reached my lips.

"Shit! We forgot about the chicken!"

I took my phone off the dresser and touched the screen to check the time. My stomach dropped. The chicken had been in the oven for well over two hours.

We raced down the hall to the kitchen and opened the oven door. A rush of smoke escaped, sending the fire alarm beeping. All the vegetables were blackened to crisps, and the top of the chicken was also black.

Jenny pulled out the food and set it on the stovetop while I ran around opening the windows and turned on the exhaust fan to help clear the kitchen of the smoke.

"Do you think the chicken is edible?" I eyed it dubiously.

With some difficulty, Jenny sawed a piece off. That was not a good sign. When it was cooled, she popped it in her mouth, chewing vigorously. "Nope. It's more like chicken jerky, just without the flavor."

I shook my head, chuckling.

"Pizza?" Jenny asked, smiling.

I nodded. "You'll be pleased to hear I bought cereal for breakfast tomorrow. Even I can't screw that up." And with that, I pulled her in for a side hug with one slightly sore arm, using the other to bring up the pizza menu on my phone.

CHAPTER TWENTY-SEVEN

JENNY

"What?!" Amanda stared at me, her eyes and mouth wide open.

Half of Novel Gossip stared at Amanda because she'd just shrieked at an ear-piercing pitch and volume. It didn't help our table was in the middle of the busy cafe, in prime view and hearing of all the patrons.

"You're telling me that, in the three weeks I've been gone, you hooked up with Blake and now you two are dating?"

I sighed. I'd delayed telling Amanda the news because I'd predicted this reaction. And hearing about her honeymoon in Hawaii was much more interesting than being cross-examined about my confusing feelings for Blake. But now we'd finished brunch and were onto our second coffee, I couldn't put it off any longer.

"Well, you were the one going on about how great she was. In fact, I'd gotten the distinct impression you were trying to set us up. And it's just a casual thing, since I'll be moving back. It's not a big deal."

The only problem was, it didn't feel casual or like not a big deal. Unlike the other casual relationships I'd had—which typically involved catching up at the most once or twice a week and spending most of the time in bed—since our visit to the sculpture park, we'd seen each other almost every day.

Almost every day for two weeks.

And yes, we were spending a lot of time in bed. A lot of very enjoyable time in bed. But we were also doing a lot of other activities that felt very...couple-y, if that was a word. Watching holiday rom-coms on the couch, hanging out at Novel Gossip with George. For god's sake, I'd even agreed to sign up for the Turkey Trot as an excuse to spend more time with her. I did not mention that fact to Amanda. She knew how I felt about jogging.

When Blake joked about giving Walter exposure therapy to overcome his aversion to us making out, I'd wondered whether exposure to Blake might cure me of my attraction to her. But unfortunately, it was having the opposite effect. I'd had a *lot* of exposure to Blake recently, and it had done nothing to dampen my feelings toward her.

"I mean...I was, but I didn't think it would actually *work*. I thought you'd sworn off casual relationships?" Amanda narrowed her eyes.

"I had..." I squirmed. "But things just...happened. There's mutual attraction, we get along surprisingly well together, and you abandoned me, so I had nothing else to do..." I fake pouted.

Amanda shook her head, but her eyes twinkled. "Oh no, you're not going to blame this on me."

I put my hands on my hips, feigning outrage. "Excuse me. This is one hundred percent your fault. If you hadn't asked me to help Blake with the bachelorette party, then had the wedding on a romantic farm and sat us together, and then left me to my own devices for a few weeks, I am confident Blake and I would never have hooked up."

Amanda's face broke into a grin. "Well, all I can say is I hope you and Blake fall madly in love so I can claim all the credit at your wedding."

I snorted. "Okay, that's definitely not going to happen. As much as I'm enjoying being back in Sapphire Springs, there's no work here for me. Serena's been trying to get me new sponsorship deals since I came here without any success."

My lack of income was beginning to weigh more heavily on my mind. While Mom and Dad were generously letting me live rent free with them, and subletting my apartment in LA was covering my rent there, my bank account was starting to look very sad. My follower numbers had dropped since the Melanie93 video and were now perilously close to 2.7 million. If I dropped below that, then the Whamz promotion would be off, and I'd be completely screwed. Even if it went ahead, it was only $10,000, which wouldn't keep me afloat for long.

I glanced over at George, who was behind the cash register, handing a smiling customer a book and their receipt. I'd thought about asking George for a job to tide me over, but I worried she'd feel obliged to help me out, and it probably wasn't worth her while to train me when I was leaving in January.

Amanda stared at me expectantly, so I continued. "And it's not like Blake could move to LA either. She's clearly committed to her medical practice."

And she likes to fly alone.

"It's interesting how all your reasons why things won't work out are practical matters, and you haven't rejected the possibility that you and Blake might fall madly in love."

I glared at her but let it go. Knowing Amanda, denying it would only encourage her. Better to change the subject entirely.

"Oh! I forgot to mention. I'm helping the village board run a fundraiser to create a Sapphire Springs Medical Fund on the Saturday of Thanksgiving weekend. I've already asked Maya if her drama students can give a performance—for entertainment and also to encourage their parents to attend. Do you have any other ideas for ways we could get the students involved?"

"A medical fund, hmmm?" Amanda raised an eyebrow as my cheeks started to heat. I'd avoided any mention of Blake, but Amanda had clearly made the connection.

"What?"

"Nothing... That's very noble of you, and I'm sure it's completely unrelated to our mutual friend, Blake. I could suss out whether the school band could give a performance. They did a medley of pop songs a few weeks ago that was really fun. Something like that would be perfect."

I clapped my hands. "That sounds amazing! If you could ask, that would be great."

AS I WAS WALKING HOME, I pulled out my phone. Two new messages from Serena. I read the latest one first.

> PS: Who's this Blake guy you've been putting on your photo credits lately? Did you find your hot flannel-wearing lumberjack for a fling after all? Maybe you should post a picture of the two of you, or at least send me one of him so I can live vicariously through you.

I laughed. Serena was almost spot on. Blake was basically my hot, terribly distracting, flannel-wearing lumberjane.

I scrolled down to Serena's next message, and my heart beat a little faster.

> Hi Jenny! Just wanted to let you know I've got a few new potential sponsorship opportunities for you I'm exploring. Hopefully have news soon. x

I fervently hoped one of Serena's leads came through.

With slightly more spring in my step, I continued walking down Main Street, past trees already losing their leaves, the smell of smoke from log fires in the air. I'd just reached the turn-off to my parents' house when my phone pinged. I pulled my phone out of my coat pocket and smiled. It was my lumberjane.

> Hi. Are you free this afternoon? Feel like helping prune Mrs. Harding's damn tree? I don't want her injuring herself but wouldn't mind moral support in case she quizzes me about bowel movements and tries to force cod liver oil down my throat.

I chuckled at Blake's carefully punctuated message and at the memory of last night. I still couldn't get over the fact that, of all the people to knock on Blake's door while she was tied to a bed naked, it had been Mrs. Harding. But strangely, despite the situation, for once I hadn't found her intimidating. Seeing her out of her teacher's outfit, in tan slacks and a cozy knit sweater, make-up free with her hair in a loose bun, she suddenly looked like any other woman in her sixties rather than an intimidating figure of authority. Perhaps exposure therapy only helped get over fears, rather than attraction.

Because while I no longer found Mrs. Harding terrifying, the more time I spent with Blake, the more I enjoyed listening to her bad dad jokes and hilarious takes on the often-terrible movies we were watching, the warmth and compassion hiding under her sometimes gruff exterior, the way she did that thing with her tongue... Her text messages were still shockingly terse, but now I knew that was just how Blake texted, they made me laugh.

> Castor, not cod liver, oil. I'll be there for both moral and physical support 😊

As I continued my walk home, it hit me just how strange a turn my life had taken. Six months ago—hell, even three months ago—if someone had told me I'd be looking forward to an afternoon of helping Blake Mitchell and Mrs. Harding prune a tree, I would have assumed they were high and quickly excused myself from their company. But now, if the lightness in my chest were any indication, I was genuinely enthused at the prospect. I shook my head, laughing softly to myself. Life was full of surprises.

But don't get too used to this. Blake doesn't want a long-term relationship, and I don't want to be broke.

CHAPTER TWENTY-EIGHT

JENNY

"You should go on without me," I gasped dramatically through pained breaths as we passed the general store.

"I'm not leaving you, you turkey." Blake slowed her jog to my pace, which could—aptly—at best be described as a trot. "It gets a lot better once we get up Main Street. This is the hardest part."

"I never realized Main Street was so steep before," I puffed, my lungs burning as I inhaled the freezing November air. Yes, it may have *looked* like it was only on a slight incline, but when you were running up it, it was a whole other matter.

Blake chuckled, showing no signs of exertion.

We were jogging-slash-trotting up Main Street with about half of Sapphire Springs and residents from the surrounding towns, for the annual Sapphire Springs Turkey Trot. Amanda, Peter, and Maya had passed us a couple of minutes ago, as had—to my embarrassment—my mom, who'd been training with her friend Becky for weeks. The other half of Sapphire Springs had turned out to cheer us on.

Familiar faces lined the street, yelling words of encouragement. An image of my warm bed momentarily flickered in my mind, making me wistful for my fluffy duvet. But a cheer from Dan, his wife, and his daughter standing outside Builders Arms, refocused my attention on making it up Main Street. I was pleased to see the posters Dan had let me put up outside Builders Arms advertising the fundraiser hadn't fallen off or been pasted over—yet. Fingers crossed we'd get a good turnout on Saturday night.

Distracted with admiring my handiwork, I nearly tripped over my own feet, a jolt of fear sending my stomach skyrocketing, before I managed to right myself. Blake shot a look at me. "Are you sure your ankle is okay?"

"It's completely fine. Just got a little distracted." My thighs, lungs, and heart, on the other hand...

In retrospect, perhaps I should have just cheered Blake on from the sidelines instead of running with her. But since the village board had generously agreed to donate the profits from the Turkey Trot to the medical fund, I'd wanted to fully participate in the experience. We'd gone out for a few slow jogs together over the past two weeks to prepare, but that clearly hadn't been enough.

We were almost at Novel Gossip, and George was out front in a warm puffer jacket and beanie, holding a sign and cheering at us. I temporarily forgot the pain when I got close enough to read it. 'Go Blake! Go Jenny!'

"Aw! Look at her sign!" I managed to pant out.

"Come over for a coffee and pancakes after the race if you're free!" George yelled.

The thought of George's pancakes helped pick up my pace. Novel Gossip wasn't open today, but on days when it was closed, it became an extension of George's apartment above the cafe. I couldn't stay long because I had to get home to help Mom and Dad prepare Thanksgiving, but I'd definitely have time for at least two pancakes. Although, since I was going to have two Thanksgiving dinners today, perhaps I should restrict myself to one.

Olivia, who also lived above her shop, was standing out on her doorstep in her robe, cup of coffee in hand, waving at us and shouting, "Go team!" I longingly eyed her coffee but forced myself to keep going. Not long now, and I'd be devouring pancakes and delicious lattes.

Main Street finally leveled out, and suddenly, it didn't feel like my lungs were about to collapse. In no time at all, we were jogging up the road to the high school, and the finish line was in sight, surrounded by a large crowd of spectators and participants who'd already finished.

"Almost there now!" Blake yelled encouragingly, a wide grin on her face.

The energy of the cheering onlookers gave me a second wind, and for a moment, I was tempted to sprint past Blake so I could tease her about beating her. But instead, I reached for Blake's hand, and we went flying over the finish line together, our hands high in the air.

Sometimes it felt like, with Blake, I could do anything.

BLAKE

I lay back on the pillow, letting out a satisfied sound somewhere between a sigh and a hum.

Today was pretty much perfect. Turkey Trot, well-earned pancakes and coffee with George, Thanksgiving dinner with Jenny's family, followed by Thanksgiving dinner with my family, followed by a lot of dramatic groaning that we would never eat again. Followed by us somehow miraculously feeling better an hour later and falling into bed together.

"It's so convenient our families eat Thanksgiving dinner at different times, but ne—" I slammed my mouth shut. *Shit.* I'd been about to say, *"Next year, we need to be more strategic about our eating and pace ourselves more."*

But there wouldn't be a next year.

Lying here with Jenny, not having a next year, or a year after that, felt...unfathomable.

If Jenny had noticed my mistake, she didn't let on.

I shut my eyes. When I'd invited Jenny to my parents' house for Thanksgiving, I'd known it wasn't exactly in keeping with our "casual" status. Perhaps I was digging a bigger hole for myself by integrating Jenny into my life, into my family. But I didn't have any regrets. Spending today with her just felt so right. And since Jenny had invited me to her family's celebration as well, at least it seemed to be mutual.

"What's the time? I'm feeling like I might just nod off." Jenny rolled over and picked her phone up off the side table. "Oh god, it's only nine p.m. It feels like midnight. Must be all that turkey making me drowsy." She touched the screen and sat up, facing me, a wide grin on her face.

"Wow! I got a text from the mayor. The Turkey Trot raised just over $7,000 for the medical fund. That's better than we were expecting!"

I gave her a squeeze. "That's awesome, babe!" While $7,000 wouldn't go a long way in covering medical expenses, it would be a significant help in paying the wages of Mrs. Gutiérrez, a retired local nurse who'd agreed to help uninsured residents figure out funding options one day a week. Even if all we achieved was hiring her, that would make a huge difference for some of my patients and also take a load off my back.

Jenny nuzzled back into me, resuming her position, and I stroked her hair, looking down at her tenderly.

"Hey. I just wanted to say again, thank you so much for doing all this. Convincing the mayor and board to help, the fundraiser, all the marketing. It's been incredible. It wouldn't have happened without you." A lump in my throat appeared as I spoke. *God, I'm getting emotional.*

Jenny smiled. "You don't need to thank me. I'm so glad I could spend this time doing something worthwhile. And I've really enjoyed it, so it hasn't been a burden at all. Let's just hope it's a success."

"I'm sure it will be." I went back to stroking her hair. The lump in my throat disappeared as I let myself relax into the bed, focusing on the warmth of Jenny's body pressed against mine. I sighed again. "I wish we could just stay like this forever."

The word *forever* lingered in the air. I hadn't meant it like that. Now I'd said it, though, I knew it was true. If upgrading our relationship from casual to serious was an option, right now I'd jump at it. All the heartbreak I'd gone through with Grace faded at the thought of how good Jenny and I could be together. How good we already were together. But it wasn't an option.

After a few moments of silence, Jenny spoke. "You know, I've been thinking...if the Whamz sponsorship deal doesn't go ahead in January—it still sounds like it's up in the air—I might stay another few weeks."

My heart leaped at the prospect. Maybe a few more weeks could turn into a few more months...

Do not get your hopes up, Blake.

CHAPTER TWENTY-NINE

JENNY

I woke before Blake and spent a couple of minutes staring at her, admiring her long, dark eyelashes, the curve of her lips, her strong nose, the smattering of silver threads in her hair. I was definitely being creepy, but when Blake was awake, I didn't have the opportunity to openly ogle at her for this length of time, so I took full advantage of it.

I tried to ignore the pressure from my bladder. I didn't want to move. But my bladder called with increasing urgency. I forced my eyes away from the sleeping beauty next to me, disentangled myself from the warm duvet, and got out of bed, grabbing Blake's robe on the way.

Once I'd peed, caffeine was my next priority. I made a pot of French press coffee, carrying it back to Blake's room along with two mugs. Discarding the robe, I poured myself a mug of coffee and carefully climbed back in bed, sitting against the headboard. I pulled out my phone and began my usual morning routine of checking my emails and social media accounts.

The warm, fuzzy feelings vanished as soon as I opened my emails.

My phone bill was overdue.

Walter's pet insurance premium was due this week.

And the premium for my health insurance was due next week.

Shit.

I logged into my bank account to check exactly what the situation was.

My stomach dropped.

There was enough to cover my phone bill, Walter's insurance, and approximately two more brunches at Novel Gossip, but after that, I would need to start putting everything on my credit card.

I shut my eyes, took a long sip of coffee, and then let out a breath.

Get it together, Jenny.

Instead of stressing out or begging George for work, I just needed to focus on my current job. After the fundraiser was over tomorrow night, I'd make a real effort to increase my posts and chase more likes and followers. As unenthused as I currently was about content creating, it was my job, and I had to apply myself before I fell into a sea of debt.

The duvet covering my legs moved, and I looked down to see Blake staring up at me, bleary-eyed and smiling.

"Morning, gorgeous," she said, her voice husky. "Is everything okay?"

I smiled back at her. After the amazing day we'd shared yesterday, I didn't want to ruin things by telling Blake I was almost broke. "Everything is more than fine now you're awake. Do you want coffee?" I nodded over to the press and mug on the side table.

Blake propped herself up on her elbow. "What I really want right now is a kiss."

I laughed, putting my phone down. Content creating and worrying about money troubles could be put on hold for a little longer. I slid down so I was propped up on my elbow as well, gazing into Blake's eyes, only inches away from her face. "Is that all you want...?"

Blake's smile widened. "You'll just have to wait and see," she said as she pulled me toward her.

———

I'D SENT Blake off to work and was walking home so I could finish up the fundraiser preparation when my phone rang. Serena.

Why would she be calling? If it's to chastise me for not posting enough, at least I'll be able to tell her I'm planning to do more.

"Jenny!" Serena sounded upbeat—excited, even—and some of the tension in my shoulders dissipated.

"Hi, how are you doing?"

"Good, good. Look, I've got some great news for you. Mahler is looking for a new brand ambassador for their Pilates line. Someone relatable, not one of those super-fit women with abs and a thigh gap. They want you!"

"Oh, wow! That's incredible." I stopped, dizzy at the news, and ignored Serena's backhanded compliment. Mahler was one of the most popular new activewear brands on the market. They would almost certainly fix my financial problems, and then some. Hopefully they wouldn't mind that I may have gotten a bit more "relatable" since I've been back home. Despite Blake's cooking and our new jogging routine, my abs, if they existed, were definitely in no danger of being revealed anytime soon.

"There's one catch. They want you back here tomorrow for a photoshoot. The other brand ambassador they had lined up had a surfing accident yesterday, so they need you to step in."

My stomach dropped. The fundraiser. *Shit.*

I groaned. "They're doing it over Thanksgiving weekend?"

Thanksgiving weekend was reserved for eating leftovers and shopping Black Friday sales, which seemed to be lasting longer and longer every year. Not photoshoots. What was wrong with these people?

"Is there any way we could postpone the photoshoot, or they could get someone else to do this one? I've got plans tomorrow night." I bit my lip nervously.

"They were adamant they needed you back here for it. They've got everything organized to shoot tomorrow—permits, film crew, make-up, etc. I know it's not the best timing, but apparently, it was very hard to get the permit, and they had to take what they could get. The photoshoot is the start of a campaign for their latest line, and they want their new brand ambassador to be in it. They've got Joanie Tanner lined up to do it if you can't, but you're their first preference. Unfortunately, if you can't make it there by ten tomorrow morning, they'll need to use her instead."

I was pretty sure I was at least their second preference, given I was replacing an injured surfer, but I had bigger things to worry about. I took a deep breath and tried to think things through calmly. Everything was basically final-ized for the fundraiser. I was supposed to emcee the event and run the raffle, but it didn't *have* to be me. Blake could do it. If I threw myself into the fundraiser today, I should be able to get it to the point that it would run smoothly without me. I'd done all the hard work already.

"Look, assuming I can get on a flight, I might be able to make it. Let me check and get back to you. And did...what's their offer?" My mouth suddenly felt dry. *Please, let it be enough to cover me for at least another month or two. Surely something like this would pay five figures?*

"Don't worry about the flights. I already checked. There are some seats on a JetBlue flight leaving from JFK late tonight, so you'll have plenty of time to pack. I'll text you the details. It's expensive, but Mahler said they'd cover your flight. And in terms of the offer...we should go over it all to make sure you're happy with them. Let me just pull it out." There was a pause, and then Serena cleared her throat. "So, they want you to sign on for a year, have at least one post per week with you wearing their clothes, and three more photoshoots. While they thought your recent country posts were cute, they really want a Californian vibe—lots of photos on Santa Monica Beach, hiking Runyon Canyon, that type of thing. I told them I thought you'd be fine to move back immediately if the offer was right...and you are going to be blown away by their offer, Jenny!" Serena almost squealed the last few words. "One hundred thousand dollars! And if all goes well, they're open to renewing it for another twelve months."

One hundred thousand dollars? My brain stuttered. That sort of money would make an enormous difference.

But instead of the rush of excitement I'd usually experience at news like this, my chest felt tight. It was all happening so suddenly. I thought I had another six weeks—maybe even more, if Whamz canceled—with Blake, with my family, in Sapphire Springs. Another six weeks to prepare myself for leaving. Another six weeks for things to naturally fizzle out with Blake, allowing me to walk away relatively painlessly. My eyes pricked with tears, my throat constricting at the thought. Walking away from Blake right now would *not* be painless.

I took a deep breath, trying to get my emotions under control. I knew it was going to end sooner or later. And for the sake of my finances and career, it was, unfortunately, going to be sooner than expected. It wouldn't make sense to reject this opportunity, one that could give me financial security and enhance my profile, to stay in a town that was a dead-end, career wise, for me. Not for a woman I'd been dating for a month, who'd made it clear she wasn't interested in a serious relationship. As much as I liked Blake, my dating track record was proof it would end soon enough, and then where would I be? Broke and heartbroken.

"Jenny? Are you still there? Should I take this silence as evidence you're dumbfounded by the offer and can't wait to sign on the dotted line?"

I wiped my eyes and tried to keep my voice upbeat. "Yes, it's terrific. Thanks, Serena. I'll do it." Hopefully my aunt wouldn't mind me crashing at her place until my apartment was free again.

Serena let out a breath. "Fantastic! You can sign all the paperwork tomorrow morning when you get in. And Joanie's going to be on standby in case you miss your flight, so make sure you get here!"

CHAPTER THIRTY

BLAKE

Dad cleared his throat. He was standing in the doorway to my office, looking sheepish, holding three large boxes.

"Sorry, honey, I accidentally ordered ten *boxes* of paper instead of ten *reams* of paper for the printer. Do you, uh, happen to have any room in your office for a couple of these?"

I chuckled. "Don't worry. We'll use it eventually. At least it's not milk or something perishable. We should be able to fit a few boxes in the bottom of the closet."

I glanced at the clock. Three minutes until my next patient. I'd been hoping to duck to the restroom, but that would have to wait. I ushered Dad in and opened the closet.

As Dad was walking out, three boxes lighter, he turned. "Oh, by the way, Jenny called. She was wondering if you'd be free to speak to her about something in person. I told her you're fully booked all afternoon but I'd let you know she called."

"Thanks, Dad." I frowned, bending over my computer and pulling up my calendar. It was completely blocked out with appointments. At this rate, I'd never get to the restroom, let alone have time to talk to Jenny. Hopefully whatever Jenny needed to talk about could wait. It was probably some fundraiser-related issue. But it was strange she wanted to speak in person. We'd already planned to meet for dinner tonight. Unease unfurled in my stomach. I glanced at my watch. My next patient was in one minute. I had time to text her.

> Dad said you called. I've got patients all afternoon. Can we talk tonight?

My phone rang. "Mr. Ortega is here, Blake," Dad said.

I put down my phone and walked to the door to greet my patient, trying to push Jenny out of my mind. Mr. Ortega deserved my complete focus.

FINALLY FINISHED FOR THE DAY, I pulled my phone out as I walked out of the clinic, eager to call Jenny to see if she was free. That sense of unease hadn't dissipated all afternoon, so I was keen to put it to rest.

"Blake."

I looked up from my phone to see Jenny sitting on the bench outside my practice. My stomach turned. She was waiting for me.

"Hey, what's up?" I asked as Jenny stood. Her smile didn't reach her eyes, and there was something about the way she held her body that put me on high alert. Something was not right.

"Sorry to ambush you, but we need to talk." My stomach dropped. That didn't sound good.

"Is everything okay?" I tried to keep my voice light.

Jenny looked around. The trees had finally lost their leaves, and the cold weather seemed to have kept people at home. Main Street was almost deserted.

"Why don't we start walking toward your place?"

"Okay," I said, my mouth dry.

We started walking down the street, and for the first time in a long time, an uncomfortable silence descended. Jenny clearly had something important to say, and I didn't want to make small talk until she told me what it was. Jenny's body language—hands stuffed in her pockets, the tension in her jaw, and her eyes fixed on the pavement—had me worried. And it was very unusual for chatty, bubbly Jenny to be silent for this long. After a few minutes, I couldn't take it any longer.

"Jenny, what's going on?"

She looked across at me, and I noticed her eyes were bloodshot. "I got a call earlier today. It was a job offer. To be the brand ambassador for Mahler. And it's too good to pass up."

I let out a breath, my face breaking into a smile. "But that's amazing! Why are you...why don't you sound happy about it?"

Jenny's eyes welled with tears. "They want me back in LA for a photoshoot tomorrow. I have to leave tonight to make it in time."

Shit, the fundraiser. My stomach dropped. No wonder Jenny was upset. It definitely wasn't ideal. I hated public speaking, and organizing events was not a strength of mine. But there was no way I was going to ask Jenny to stay and give up a once-in-a-lifetime opportunity. She'd already helped me so much.

"Hey, look, I understand. Of course this is more important than the fundraiser. We'll work it out. I'm sure George and Olivia and my parents will help out, and I can emcee it."

Jenny's lips quivered. I put my arm around her and pulled her to me, feeling her shaky breaths rattle her lungs.

"Hey, I know it sucks after all your hard work, but we'll make it a success. And we'll take lots of photos to show you when you get back." I paused. She hadn't mentioned when she'd be back. "How long will you be there for?"

Jenny looked away and cleared her throat. "So...it's a condition of the deal that I stay in LA for the next twelve months, at least."

My stomach plummeted to the pavement as I absorbed the news. Jenny was leaving. Tonight. For good. The six weeks I thought we had left vanished. The six weeks I thought I had left to prepare myself for Jenny's departure...gone.

"Oh," I managed to get out. Now Jenny's reaction made sense. Now I was experiencing a very similar one. Tears pricked in my eyes.

"I'm so sorry, Blake. But this is just too good to pass up. We always knew this had an expiration date. I was always going to leave. This is just bringing it forward. Their offer, it's life changing. It just wouldn't make sense to say no."

I blinked away the tears, nausea flooding over me. Of course it didn't make sense for Jenny to give up the offer of a lifetime for another few weeks together. Rationally, I knew that. But that didn't make it feel any better. *Shit.*

"I get it. It sucks, but I understand." I dug my fingernails into my hand.

"We can still keep in touch?" Jenny's voice wavered. "And I usually try to visit twice a year, so we can see each other then?"

The ache in my chest grew. Even though a long-distance relationship wasn't a viable option, I wished Jenny had suggested it. But long distance just didn't make sense when we had no plan to actually be together. It was just dragging out the inevitable heartache.

You could move, Blake. It's not like it would be hard for you to find a job in LA. I pressed my lips together. I couldn't make that mistake again, building my life around a partner, leaving me to pick up the pieces when they inevitably left, and it all fell apart. Especially not when Jenny wasn't willing to do the same for me.

And as for keeping in touch... I took a deep breath. "I'm not sure if it's a great idea if we keep in touch, at least not initially. The therapist I saw after my last breakup said having a clean break was usually best. I just think...I think it might be too confusing, at least in the beginning. I'm sorry."

"Keeping in touch" suggested we'd be friends. But we had never really been friends, and I didn't know if I could be that for Jenny. I liked her too much. If we kept in touch, I'd want to speak to her every day. I'd get terribly jealous if she started dating someone else. And that wouldn't be healthy either.

Again, part of me hoped Jenny would disagree, that she'd fight to keep us together in some form, do something to show the last six weeks had been as special to her as they had been to me. But she nodded slowly. "I hate the idea of not speaking to you, but I'll respect what you need. But if you change your mind, let me know. Will you...will you at least text me to let me know how the fundraiser goes?"

"Yes, of course."

Jenny stopped walking, and I realized we'd reached the turn-off to her parents' house. She looked at her watch and then turned to me. "I'm so sorry, Blake, but I need to get my bags and head to the train station. Thank you...for everything. I'm really going to miss you. I...I'm sorry we didn't have more time together." She swiped under her eyes as the tears started to escape, and I went in for a hug before she saw me start crying too. I squeezed her as tightly as I could without hurting her.

"I'm going to miss you too," I muttered into her hair.

There was so much more I wanted to say, so much more I didn't have the words to say, but I knew it wouldn't achieve anything letting Jenny know just how much she meant to me, just how much I'd miss her. So instead, I tried to just savor the hug, commit the feeling of her warm body pressed against mine, the softness and smell of her hair to memory. I didn't want to let go. Eventually, we disentangled ourselves, me blinking furiously to hide my tears.

"Good luck with the fundraiser tomorrow." Jenny managed a weak smile. "I'll email you the schedule and all the info, and please call or text me if you have any questions."

"Good luck with your photoshoot. You'll be amazing." I forced my mouth into something hopefully resembling a smile.

And with that, Jenny crossed the road toward her parents' house. I watched her go, standing on the pavement with my chest and throat aching, trying to keep the tears under control.

CHAPTER THIRTY-ONE

JENNY

I spent the train ride to Grand Central and the Uber from Grand Central to JFK attempting to suppress the image of Blake's face crumpling when I told her the news. I scrolled through previous Mahler campaigns, trying to drum up excitement for tomorrow. But it did nothing to alleviate the sick, heavy feeling in my stomach. Walter lay slumped in his carrier, his brown curls drooping over his eyes, looking as morose as I felt.

The Uber dropped me at Terminal 5. I grabbed a trolley, setting off to check in my bags and go through security. My face was puffy from crying. I had a few minutes before boarding, so I wandered around the duty-free store, searching for miracle beauty products that would avoid Mahler canceling the deal on the spot when they saw me. I was paying for a serum and a moisturizer that made big promises in the rejuvenation department when the boarding call for my flight boomed over the loudspeaker.

I didn't have time to dwell on my problems as I rushed to the gate, scanned the ticket, shoved my backpack in the overhead compartment, and got Walter comfortable in his carrier under the seat in front of me. But as soon as I was buckled in and the plane began to taxi in preparation for take-off, doubt set in.

I was going to miss Blake. A lot.

It blew my mind that I could have fallen for someone so hard in such a short time.

And it wasn't just Blake I'd miss. Mom and Dad, Amanda, George... While I'd once found Sapphire Springs suffocating and dull, over the past weeks, I'd developed an appreciation for what it offered. A sense of community and belonging. Quality small businesses who really valued their customers. The lack of traffic. The close proximity to nature. Reduced cost of living. Plenty of space for Walter. More time to stop and think.

But while there were so many good reasons to stay in Sapphire Springs, there was one major impediment. Work. Sapphire Springs businesses weren't exactly lucrative sources of sponsorship deals, and so far, despite my recent rural-themed posts, no brands specializing in flannel or hiking gear had offered me a gig. If I couldn't do that, what could I do?

All the other jobs I could think of would make me miserable.

As much as I loved George and my parents, I'd quickly get bored waitressing at Novel Gossip or working in the family construction business. But maybe it didn't matter if I was surrounded by the people I loved? Could I suck up a tedious job I wasn't passionate about to be with Blake and close to my family and friends? I sighed loudly, attracting a pointed look from the middle-aged woman sitting next to me, who was clearly trying to sleep. I knew deep in my soul that I wouldn't be fulfilled, that I'd be unhappy, and that unhappiness would affect everything. And if history repeated itself and my relationship with Blake just fizzled out, I'd be even more miserable.

But I wasn't satisfied with my current job either. I was dreading going back to my regular schedule of posting and promoting products and services. The Mahler deal would provide me with some financial stability...but if I didn't want to keep doing this, was it worth the money? And what would happen as I got older? Would there be work for a social influencer when I was fifty?

The montage of Blake started up again. As my memory lingered on the image of Blake and me hanging up prints in her living room, another realization struck me. I was so worried about my casual relationship with Blake fizzling out, never getting serious. But it *was* already serious. Everything we'd been doing for the last month screamed *serious*, except for the label we'd put on it. I'd had enough experience with casual relationships to know this wasn't one. I shook my head. *Why the hell hadn't I realized that earlier?*

And yes, Blake might have said she was an eagle flying alone, but she hadn't been flying alone the last few weeks, and she'd certainly seemed to be enjoying my company. Perhaps she did feel the same way.

I chewed my lip. I needed to come up with a career I actually liked, one that would be long term, sustainable, and pay my bills. And ideally, one I could do from Sapphire Springs.

Until now, everything had fallen into place for me. I hadn't set out to become an assistant to a Hollywood actor or a social influencer. It had just...happened. Moving to LA when I was eighteen had been the last big decision I'd proactively made. But if I wanted to be truly happy, I had to work out what I really wanted and pursue it.

I unlocked my phone and started to research job ideas. After five failed career quizzes, which served me more and more unlikely career suggestions, including slaughterhouse worker and garbage truck driver, I shut my eyes and tried to visualize what my ideal life would look like.

Me and Blake, Walter and Fred cozying up on the couch in Blake's cottage. Blake leaning over, her mouth beginning to explore... *Get a grip, Jenny. This is meant to be helping come up with a career change, not a sexual fantasy.* Seeing my parents for Sunday lunch. Gossiping with Amanda over brunch. Catching up with George at Novel Gossip and...and... *Think, Jenny, what would make you happy?* I sat in my seat, unable to sleep, racking my brain for inspiration.

The comment Blake had made a couple of weeks ago came back to me. "But you have lots of skills, and you're smart. I'm sure you could do something different if you wanted to. I mean, you were incredible stepping in to do Amanda's wedding and—"

All of a sudden, I was wide awake, excitement replacing the heavy feeling in my stomach. Of course. It was so goddamn obvious.

I didn't know why I hadn't thought of it before.

CHAPTER THIRTY-TWO

BLAKE

I stood in the large, empty auditorium at Sapphire Springs High, overwhelmed at the task ahead of me. The only thing keeping me from going home and curling up on the couch under a blanket with Fred was just how much the fundraiser would help my patients. God, the couch sounded good right now.

I took a deep breath and straightened my posture. *No, this fundraiser has to happen. It's only a few hours. You can get through this.* George, Amanda, and Olivia would be here any minute to help set up. That would make things easier.

I'd broken the news about Jenny to George this morning when I'd trudged into Novel Gossip in search of caffeine and moral support. George had plied me with lattes and gently offered me every edible option on the menu at least twice, concern written all over her face. But today I didn't feel like eating—not even her lemon-blueberry cake. Once I'd downed my second coffee, I'd texted Olivia. Jenny must have told Amanda already, because she'd messaged me last night to see how I was.

At about three a.m., I'd seriously considered moving to LA. In some strange, half-sleep, half-awake state, I'd imagined becoming a doctor to the rich and famous. All my financial worries and the stress associated with having patients who couldn't afford medical treatment would vanish, and I'd spend endlessly sunny, carefree days with Jenny, walking along the beach and hiking. But even in my sleep-deprived, emotionally confused condition, I knew leaving everything I'd built here was not an option. I'd spent so much time establishing my practice, caring for this community, I couldn't just leave it all behind. If Jenny ultimately left me—which, given my track record, seemed likely —I knew I'd regret leaving Sapphire Springs for her.

The door banged. I looked up from the paper in my hands to see Olivia, George, and Amanda walking over. Before I knew it, I was enveloped in bear hugs. I lingered in their arms, drawing comfort from their warmth.

"How are you holding up?" Amanda studied my face, her brow furrowed.

"Not great, but definitely a bit better now you're all here."

"I'm so sorry, Blake. It really sucks." The compassion in Amanda's voice reactivated my tear ducts, initiating another round of blinking.

"So, what can we do to help?" George clapped her hands together.

I put them to work unstacking the chairs and setting up the refreshment and silent auction tables. I threw myself into it as well, hoping the physical activity would distract me from my anxiety over the fundraiser and thoughts of Jenny.

A few hours later, I surveyed the neat rows of chairs, the refreshment stand piled high with George's baked goods, wine, and a coffee and tea station, and the silent auction items spread out on long tables. We'd put up the Thanksgiving decorations Jenny had sourced or, in some cases, made. Hanging up the gigantic cardboard turkey I'd helped her paint on Tuesday night nearly set me off again. She'd had such an intense look of concentration on her face, trying to trace an outline of turkey, and eventually got so frustrated I'd taken over. The memory of her grinning at me after we'd finished cutting it out and painting it sent a pain deep into my heart. "I couldn't have done it without you," she'd said. I couldn't have done this fundraiser without her. But now, I was going to have to get used to doing everything without her. I squeezed my eyes together, as if willing the memories of Jenny to dissolve, and then opened them again, taking in a deep breath.

Everything was ready. Now all we needed was a good turnout, for people to give generously, and for me to keep my shit together long enough to make this a success. Tomorrow, I could curl up on the couch under the blanket with Fred, but for now, I had to finish what Jenny started.

CHAPTER THIRTY-THREE

JENNY

My flight touched down at JFK just before three p.m., almost thirty minutes late due to mechanical delays. I'd hardly slept at all, my mind whirring with excitement. I'd tried to make a call before I got on the flight back to New York to confirm if my idea would work, but I couldn't get through, so it was unclear whether I'd just thrown the deal of a lifetime away for nothing. But by the time I'd arrived in LA, my return ticket already booked, I was so convinced of the merit of my plan that once I collected my bags, I walked straight over to the departures gate, a spring in my step.

All things considered, Serena took the news surprisingly well. Although, I'm sure it helped that Joanie, Mahler's backup option, was also one of Serena's clients. Serena would be getting her commission regardless.

As I walked through JFK to the luggage carousel, holding Walter's crate, my phone rang. Twenty minutes later, I hung up the phone with a wide grin on my face and a weight lifted off my shoulders.

I itched to call Blake to tell her the news, to hear her

voice, to let her know I was on my way back. I hadn't called her at LAX—I didn't want to get her hopes up, only to dash them if my proposal was rejected. And now...and now I was less than three hours away from seeing her in the flesh. This was the sort of news you told someone in person, not via a text message or phone call. I drew in a deep breath. It would test my patience, but I could wait another three hours.

Speaking of patience, we'd reached the luggage carousel, still empty, so I kneeled down to check how poor Walter was doing. "You've been such a little champ, suffering through a train ride and two flights without complaint. We'll be back home soon, buddy," I said, feeding him a treat through the grill. He looked skeptical but eagerly devoured the treat and licked my fingers afterward, suggesting he wasn't about to disown me, despite being dragged across the country and back again in less than twenty-four hours.

I jiggled my legs impatiently as the bags took ages to load on the carousel. I'd booked a ticket for the 4:13 p.m. train, but with the plane delay, I wasn't confident we were going to make it. It was currently 3:25 p.m. If I was lucky, it would only take thirty-five minutes to taxi to Grand Central. That didn't leave much time for getting through Grand Central to the tracks.

Thunk. Thunk. The first bags appeared on the carousel, and my heart rate slowed a little. I spotted my large, purple suitcase, heaved it off, and then strode—Walter in one hand and the suitcase in the other—toward the exit.

Thankfully, there was no problem getting a taxi. Before long, we were rattling down the Van Wyck Expressway and then the Long Island Expressway before entering the claustrophobic yellow-and-blue striped Queens Midtown Tunnel, finally emerging in Midtown Manhattan.

The taxi dropped us off on 43rd Street and Vanderbilt. Gathering Walter, my backpack, and my suitcase, I struggled down the stairs to Grand Central and sprinted to the tracks, pulling my suitcase behind me. My heart bounced as I caught a glimpse of the clock. 4:10 p.m. Three minutes. *Shit.* It would be hit or miss whether we made it.

To my relief, the train was sitting there when we arrived at the platform. Not wanting to risk it, I jumped in the nearest car, and then walked down the center of the train.

I collapsed on the first spare seat I found, out of breath, my heart beating a million miles per hour. *Thank god.* I put Walter's crate on the floor and shut my eyes, letting my breathing slow.

We'd made it. The train would get us into Sapphire Springs around 5:40 p.m. When I caught my breath, I'd call Mom and Dad and see if one of them could pick me up from the station. With luck, I'd be at the auditorium just before six p.m., leaving plenty of time for a reunion with Blake before the fundraiser started at seven p.m.

Thirty minutes later, I was looking out the window, admiring the view of the Hudson River as the sun set, when I noticed some weird floaters on my eyes. *Please let me not be having a stroke now. That's the last thing I need.* I blinked and realized those white things in my vision weren't floaters, but snow. The first snowfall of the season. I watched the flakes dance, suddenly euphoric. I'd forgotten how beautiful snow was.

The sky began to darken, and the snowflakes increased in density, flurrying about, as if they, too, were in a hurry to get somewhere.

My view on snow changed drastically when, half an hour later, the train ground to a halt, and a voice boomed over the speakers.

"Due to the unexpected snowstorm, we are experiencing delays on the Metro North line. We have been asked to stop until some further investigations are carried out. We thank you for your patience."

Crap.

The snowflakes suddenly lost their appeal. Nope, they weren't beautiful or romantic. Those damn ice crystals were just a pain in the butt.

I drummed my fingers impatiently on my thighs as I looked out at the rapidly darkening sky, willing the snow to stop. I took some deep, calming breaths. We'd be fine. The fundraiser didn't start until seven p.m. While, ideally, I'd get there at least an hour before, to give me time to talk to Blake and help in whatever way I could, we had time to spare. Surely the train would start again soon. It wasn't like the snow was *that* heavy—we'd had much worse. I looked out of the window to assure myself, and all I could see was snow. It was so thick visibility was reduced to zero. *Shit.* I took another deep breath. *We'll be fine.*

Ten minutes later, the calming breaths and reassuring comments to myself had gone out the window, replaced with panic. I kept telling myself it didn't really matter if I missed the fundraiser, but I really, *really* wanted to make it. To be there to support Blake. To help ensure it was a success.

I was seriously considering breaking out of the train, trudging through the storm to the nearest town, and calling an Uber, when the train jolted to life and slowly picked up pace. *Thank god.*

I sat back in my seat and texted Mom—who'd agreed to meet me at the station—an update. Assuming there weren't any further delays, I should be with Blake by 6:30 p.m.

That didn't give me as much time as I was hoping for our reunion, but it was still fine. I shut my eyes.

I jolted awake a little later. Someone was touching my shoulder.

"Sorry, ma'am, but your ticket was for Sapphire Springs, and we've just passed it."

Disorientated, it took me a few seconds to process what had happened. When it did, my stomach lurched into my chest. I'd fallen asleep and missed my stop.

"Oh no!"

The ticket collector looked at me sympathetically and glanced at her watch. "We'll be arriving in Milford Falls in a few minutes. The next train back to Sapphire Springs will be in about an hour."

Shit. I'd miss most of the fundraiser if I waited for the next train.

Mom. Maybe Mom could pick me up. I called her, and to my relief, she agreed.

While I was waiting for the train to arrive in Milford Falls, I quickly did the math. It was nearly 6:30 p.m. It should take less than fifteen minutes to get back to Sapphire Springs, so I should still get there before the fundraiser started...just. I might not have time to talk to Blake, but at least I'd be there to support her.

As soon as the train pulled up at the station, I rushed out and ran to the parking lot where I'd agreed to meet Mom. While I was waiting, I let Walter out of his crate so he could stretch his legs. Ten minutes later, Mom's pickup truck pulled up. I threw my luggage and the crate into the backseat, and then jumped into the front seat with Walter.

Mom looked at me. "Hi, honey. So, are you going to tell me what's going on? Not that I'm not thrilled you're back so soon, but..."

I ignored Mom's question, giving her a hug and asking her another question, which effectively gave her the answer she wanted. "Great to see you too, Mom. Can you drop me off at the fundraiser?"

"Ah, I see." Mom grinned. She started the engine before I'd even had a chance to shut the door. I'd almost pulled it shut when the truck jerked backward before proceeding speedily out of the parking lot toward Sapphire Springs.

I clutched the side of the door. "Mom, come on. You're not driving me to see Blake because I'm having a medical emergency. I know the fundraiser is starting soon, but you can slow down. At this rate, I'll vomit on her as soon as I get out of the car. And that's *not* the look I'm going for. As you may have guessed, I'm trying to win her back, not revolt her."

Mom rolled her eyes and sighed. "Okay, okay," she said, reducing her speed.

Ten minutes later, we arrived back in Sapphire Springs, heading toward the school. I'd only been away from Sapphire Springs for twenty-four hours, but driving up Main Street, lit by the old-fashioned cast-iron lamp posts, passing the familiar, gorgeous old red brick buildings, the American flags, Builders Arms, Novel Gossip, Olivia's flower shop, it felt like it had been much longer. Warmth radiated through my body.

I was home.

With that pleasant thought, I pulled down the sun visor to check how I looked in the mirror. *Good lord.*

My hair was falling out of the sad ponytail I'd been wearing for twenty-four hours, my eyes were bleary with dark bags underneath them, and my face looked wan.

I searched in my backpack for my brush and found the serum and moisturizer I'd bought at the airport. I lathered them both on my face, hoping they would rejuvenate as promised, and started brushing my hair. Mom turned off Main Street and drove down the dark side street toward the school.

I was just putting my brush back in my bag when a sudden impact flung my body to the left, smashing into the side of the door. I grabbed Walter, holding him as our bodies bounced in strange directions. My stomach clenched as I tried to process what was happening.

And then everything stopped moving with a sickening jolt. What the...?

The car was on a strange tilt.

We must have veered off the road. Fear constricted my throat as I looked over at Mom. Thankfully, she was still in one piece, muttering about icy roads.

"Are you okay?" we asked each other in unison, both nodding in response. *Thank god.* I quickly examined Walter, who, to my relief, also appeared unscathed.

With some difficulty, we struggled out of the truck and surveyed the damage. The truck itself didn't look damaged, but it did look...stuck. Very stuck. In a ditch.

"Shit." It was 6:52 p.m. I tried calculating how long it would take to jog the rest of the way, putting my Turkey Trot training to good use, but I couldn't in good conscience abandon Mom.

I shivered, drawing Walter, who was in my arms, closer to me. It was still snowing lightly, and the temperature had dropped now the sun was down.

Out of the corner of my eye, I spotted car headlights approaching. A small, red sporty-looking coupe slowed, pulling off the road next to us. *Please, please be someone we know.*

"Jenny? Sue?" Tom Harrison, the very same mechanic

who had been on that panel with Blake and me what felt like months ago, hopped out.

"Hi, Tom. We, uh, had a little incident," Mom said sheepishly.

"I can see." Tom paused, walking around the truck, examining it closely. "Are you on the way to the fundraiser?"

"Yes!" I said, a little too loudly. Tom gave me an odd look, and I realized I was bouncing up and down on the spot, presumably a way for my body to release the nervous energy that had been building up all day.

"Me too. You'll be hard pressed to get someone out here tonight to tow you. Why don't I take you to the fundraiser, and we can sort this out tomorrow?

I started striding toward his car, Walter in my arms, keen to get back on track as soon as possible. "That sounds great! Thank you!" I'd collect my luggage tomorrow. Tonight, I had bigger things to worry about.

I opened the passenger door to squeeze into the back of Tom's coupe, but Mom grabbed my shoulder. "I'll sit back there so you can get out faster."

Safely seated, Tom switched on the ignition, and we were off. A few minutes later, the welcome glow of the school lights appeared up ahead. I glanced at my phone again. Three minutes to seven. My heart, which had been thumping loudly in my ears for the last hour, sank. My plan to talk to Blake before the fundraiser was officially dead. But we still had a chance of reaching the auditorium before the event started.

Tom parked in a spot that definitely wasn't an official spot, effectively blocking two people in. "I'll duck out and fix it in the intermission," Tom said with a shrug as he shifted into park.

"Thanks so much, Tom!" I jumped out of the car and raced toward the entrance with Walter. I felt guilty not waiting for Mom, but I knew she'd understand. Dad was saving her a seat anyway.

Olivia was sitting at a table just inside the hall, selling tickets.

"Can I have one ticket please?" Butterflies fluttered in my stomach as I directed this question at Olivia's bent head.

Olivia looked up from the cash she was sorting, her eyes widening with surprise. "Jenny! What are you doing here? I thought you were in LA."

"Yeah, I...I was, but..." My voice trailed off. It didn't feel right to tell Blake's sister my plans before I'd had a chance to speak to Blake.

I couldn't help flicking my eyes up to the front of the auditorium to look for Blake. Over the sea of heads—it looked like we'd had an amazing turnout—I spotted Blake moving toward the stage. While I knew Blake hated public speaking, it felt too late to run up and offer to take over. I knew she'd be fine. More than fine. Great.

Olivia followed my gaze and grinned. "I see."

"I don't want to distract her while she's talking. Is there somewhere I can sit so she won't spot me, but I can still hear what's going on?" I looked around.

Olivia pointed toward some screens behind George's refreshment stand. "You could hide behind those screens. I think George is using them to store some extra supplies. Do you want me to look after Walter?"

"That would be amazing, thank you!" Blake had reached the stage and was nearly at the podium, so I power-walked over to George, whose jaw dropped as she spotted me.

"Jenny! What the—?" George hissed.

"I'll explain later. Is it okay if I hide behind here? I don't want Blake to see me, in case it throws her off."

George nodded, grinning, and gestured for me to come around the back of the stand. She pushed one of the screens so I could squeeze through into the space. I took a seat on a box of wine bottles. To my delight, there was a small gap in the screens I could see the stage through.

"I'm glad you're back," George said before taking her seat.

I breathed a sigh of relief. I'd been worried Olivia and George might be annoyed with me for fleeing to LA, but they seemed genuinely pleased to see me.

Hopefully, Blake would feel the same way. I'd been in such a rush all day, I hadn't spent much time considering how Blake would respond. What if she didn't forgive me for leaving? What if she really was an eagle flying alone and didn't want to try anything long-term with me?

The thought sent my stomach tumbling, but it was cut short by a high-pitched squeal.

CHAPTER THIRTY-FOUR

BLAKE

While I was blown away by the turn-out, it did nothing to lessen my nerves as I made my way to the front of the auditorium.

Memories of me sitting on the very same stage for the careers panel, my heart bouncing as Jenny sauntered into the auditorium, looking incredible in her jumpsuit, flooded back to me. It was hard to believe that was less than two months ago and that now I'd give anything for her to saunter back in. So much had changed. Including my feelings about relationships. Jenny had reminded me just what I was missing out on by closing myself off to them. And while I was in pain now, I had no regrets about the time we'd spent together.

It was just past seven, so I took a deep breath and walked up to the microphone on the stage. *You've got this, Blake. You've spoken to almost everyone in the audience before at the clinic.*

Clearing my throat, I moved closer to the microphone, causing a high-pitched squeal to reverberate around the hall. I winced and shut my eyes for a second as heat rushed to my cheeks. *You can do this.*

"Sorry about that. Um, thanks, everyone, for coming out tonight and braving the weather to be here. As most of you know, my name is Blake Mitchell, and I run the Sapphire Springs Medical Practice." I looked around the auditorium, which was now almost full, locking eyes with George who gave me an encouraging smile.

"Having access to medical care is crucial for a secure, healthy, happy life in our country, but unfortunately, for some of us, it's just not affordable." I paused for effect, already feeling more comfortable.

I kept going, describing how people's immigration and financial status could make them ineligible for government benefits and how finding other sources of funding could be difficult, before explaining how the Sapphire Springs Medical Fund would help uninsured Sapphire Springs residents who couldn't afford medical care.

"I encourage you all to give generously tonight to support this initiative. I would like to give a special thanks to the mayor and village board, for setting up this fund, and also to Jenny Lynton, who unfortunately couldn't be here tonight but is responsible for organizing this entire evening." My voice wavered. I took a deep breath.

A loud crash made me jump, interrupting my attempt to gather myself.

What the hell was that?

I scanned the crowd, looking for the source of the noise, as my heart thumped in my chest.

Most of the audience seemed to be doing the same thing. A low murmur filled the room.

One of the screens behind George's refreshment stand had fallen over.

And there was someone on the ground, slowly getting to their feet.

My heart somersaulted.

That someone was Jenny.

I blinked in disbelief.

But the audience was staring at her as well. This wasn't just some figment of my imagination.

Confusion and euphoria flooded my veins, lighting me from the inside.

It was definitely her. Somehow, Jenny was here.

JENNY

Oh my god.

My face burned with embarrassment. Near the end of Blake's speech, to get a better view of her, I stood up and moved closer to the gap I'd been peering through. I'd tripped over the leg of one of the screens in the process, sending both me and the screen flying.

I struggled to my feet, hoping I wasn't too disheveled, and looked up at the stage where Blake stood, still and blinking, staring at me. In fact, the entire audience was staring at me.

So much for not distracting Blake during her speech.

I took a deep breath and cleared my throat, running a shaky hand through my hair to smooth it down.

"Hi, everyone. Sorry about that," I said, awkwardly waving, my eyes locked on Blake.

I started walking toward the stage. Now Blake, and the rest of Sapphire Springs, knew I was here, it seemed pointless to keep my distance. Blake finished her speech, handed the microphone over to the mayor, and walked down the stairs toward me. I had to restrain myself from running the last few feet and throwing myself on her and, instead, settled for a brisk walk. But as I got closer to Blake, my stride faltered.

Shit.

I couldn't read the expression on her face, but she wasn't smiling.

BLAKE

My mind was still struggling to process Jenny's reappearance. I was lost for words.

What on earth was she doing back in Sapphire Springs?

Unfortunately, with the mayor in the middle of her speech, there was no way of finding out. This fundraiser was my responsibility. I couldn't exactly run out the door with Jenny and demand answers, and conversations as important as this one couldn't be done in low whispers or furtive text messages.

My heart racing, I grabbed Jenny's hand, warm and soft, and gently tugged her toward two spare seats. When seated, I didn't let go of her hand, and neither did she.

That was a good sign. Could she...was it possible she was back for good? My chest expanded at the thought. I shot Jenny a sideways glance. She sensed my eyes on her and turned to me, shooting me a gorgeous smile, and squeezed my hand.

That was even more promising.

We sat in excruciating silence, holding hands while we watched the students' performances, counting down until Jenny could tell me what the hell had happened in the past twenty-four hours. I couldn't focus on the performances, too distracted by Jenny's presence next to me.

As soon as the intermission started, I looked around for somewhere we could talk in private. If we didn't escape quickly, we'd be waylaid by well-meaning audience members.

"Will you be warm enough if we go outside?"

Jenny nodded, grabbing her coat and beanie, and we marched toward the closest exit.

The cold air hit us as we escaped through the door.

"Wow." During the afternoon, while I was stressing about the fundraiser and feeling shattered by Jenny's sudden departure, the world had transformed into a winter wonderland. A thick blanket of white covered the trees next to the auditorium and the school oval, which were lit by flood lights. And here Jenny was, in the flesh, looking as gorgeous as ever, smiling at me.

I wanted to envelop her in my arms and kiss her so badly, but I didn't dare. First, I had to find out why she was back.

The air burned my lungs as I took in a deep breath. "So, um, what are you doing here?" I managed to ask, wincing at my less-than-smooth question.

"Well, hello to you too." Jenny smiled, but it quickly wavered. She bit her lip nervously. "So, I've decided to stay. In Sapphire Springs."

Excitement, relief, and worry welled up inside me.

Was she staying for me? What was she going to do? As much as I wanted to be with her, I didn't want her to give up everything for me or to build her life around me. From personal experience, I knew just how badly that could end. Above all, I wanted Jenny to be happy. But would she really be happy in Sapphire Springs? Or maybe she didn't want to be with me at all, and something else was going on? *Stop hypothesizing and just ask her.*

"You...you have? What made you change your mind?"

Jenny tugged her beanie down, her hair escaping in waves from underneath it, perfectly framing her face. Her cheeks and nose were pink, and her eyes were sparkling.

"Yesterday, I didn't feel like I had any choice but to accept Mahler's offer, for the reasons I told you. But as soon as I got on the train, I started having doubts, and by the time I'd arrived in LA, I'd come to two realizations. One, I *do* have a choice. Two, I'm tired of being an influencer, and despite what I previously thought, I do have some other skills. It was actually something you said that made the lightbulb turn on. What have I been doing the entire time I've been in Sapphire Springs? Planning events. And I love it. It uses my creativity, my organizational skills, my people skills...and I get to help people celebrate special days and support worthy causes."

"So, I rang Miriam with a proposition for us to become business partners. She was already run off her feet before she became pregnant, and she's thrilled to have someone she can share the load with. Once she's back on board, we're going to look to expand into other types of events. My social media experience will come in handy for building our brand, but it will only be a small part of what I do."

"That sounds amazing." I let out a deep breath. The excitement in Jenny's voice was clear. Jenny wasn't moving back for me. She wasn't making my mistake of planning her whole life around a love interest. She'd found something she was genuinely passionate about and was pursuing it with fervor.

I was thrilled Jenny hadn't decided to stay for me. But had I played any role at all? I'd been hoping she'd say something to indicate that my presence in Sapphire Springs was another reason she wanted to stay, but she hadn't even mentioned me. How would I fit into her new life in Sapphire Springs?

I felt like I was back at high school again, asking this question, but I needed clarity. I didn't want to spend the rest of the fundraiser not knowing how things stood between us.

"So, um, what are you thinking about us? I mean, would you be interested in dating for real? Like an, um, actual relationship?" I winced as the words came out of my mouth. Major awkward-teenager vibes.

Jenny's eyes widened. "Are you sure you...? Do you want that? What happened to being a bald eagle?"

I stared at Jenny blankly. "What?"

I was clearly missing something.

"You know, you're a bald eagle flying alone." She ran her hand over my arm where my tattoo was, sending my body humming.

I chuckled. "Oh. Yes. Well, about that. The thing I didn't know about bald eagles, but that my brother was very quick to point out to me after I got the tattoo, was that while bald eagles fly alone, they're monogamous. They stay in their relationships year after year, until one of them dies. So, while I might fly alone, I'd love nothing better than to come home to you, night after night." I kept my voice light and grinned to hide the terrifying realization that, despite our short time together, I absolutely meant it.

Jenny giggled. "If that's an invitation to move in, I think we should wait a few more months just to fight the U-Haul stereotype, but I'd love nothing better than to roost with you." I rolled my eyes at her terrible pun, trying to contain the elation flowing through my veins.

I wrapped my arms around her waist and smiled at her.

"I am so happy you came back." My voice was gentle and low.

"I'm so happy to be back."

She leaned in, and we kissed as if we'd been apart for months, rather than hours. I shut my eyes, inhaling her familiar scent, holding onto her as if I'd never let go.

And I wouldn't have if snow hadn't started to fall, first slowly, dusting our heads and settling on our shoulders, and then faster, whirling around us in a beautiful, icy dance.

CHAPTER THIRTY-FIVE

JENNY

I knocked on the door, my stomach full of butterflies. If this went badly, it could mess everything up. We wouldn't be able to move in together next year. In fact, we'd probably need to live apart until one of them died—a scenario I didn't want to contemplate for multiple reasons. The stakes were high, much higher than when we'd officially met each other's parents over Thanksgiving, which, unbelievably, was just a little over a week ago.

"Now, behave, okay?" I said, looking down at Walter. "Just because @charlietheinstagramcat was a dick doesn't mean all cats are. It would be very narrow-minded of you to make that assumption. Fred is really quite lovely."

I heard footsteps approaching and took in a deep breath, only releasing it when Blake opened the door.

"Hi, babe." Blake grinned, leaning out to plant a quick kiss on my lips. "Hey, Walter, are you ready to meet Fred?"

Walter began tugging on the leash to go inside.

"We'll take that as a yes!"

Blake opened the door, and Walter and I walked in.

"Fred's down in the living room."

We walked down the hall, my stomach churning, and into the colorful living room, where Fred sat curled up on his usual corner of the couch. *Please like each other. Please like each other.*

As planned, Blake kept a close eye on Fred's body language, while I focused all my attention on Walter.

Fred immediately spotted Walter but remained seated on the couch, looking curious but unconcerned. Fred, it appeared, was totally chill about the intruder.

Walter, on the other hand, still hadn't spotted Fred. He was sniffing the carpet, potentially picking up Fred's scent or, perhaps—more likely—a scrap of pizza we'd dropped last night.

"Walter, look. There's Fred!" Blake said, crouching down next to him and pointing at Fred.

Walter started wandering in the other direction. I shook my head, giggling, some of the tension dissipating. "God, he's hopeless! Walter, look, there's a cat! I might need to go get his eyes tested."

"He could see well enough at lunch today to snap up that piece of prosciutto I dropped within seconds, so I'm not sure that's the issue." Blake chuckled. "Maybe I should put Fred onto the carpet, too, so they're at the same level?"

I nodded, and Blake picked up Fred and plopped him on the carpet. Fred promptly sat down, still eyeing Walter with interest but, as far as I could tell, no malice.

Finally, Walter noticed Fred's feline presence. He froze.

My heart skipped a beat. This was the moment of truth. I gripped his leash, ready to pull him back or, if need be, throw myself between Fred and Walter to avoid either ending up at the vet.

Walter tentatively took a step toward Fred.

Fred stood up and took a step toward Walter.

"Oh god, this is stressful!" I muttered to Blake.

They both took another step forward. And another. And another.

And then they stopped about a foot apart. My pulse thumped in my ears. *Please don't pounce.*

They appeared to be engaging in some sort of stare-down.

And then, all of a sudden, Walter's tail moved.

"He's wagging his tail! That has to be a good sign, right?" I exclaimed.

Blake nodded, grinning.

Walter, tail still wagging, quickly took three more steps toward Fred. They were almost face to face now.

And then Walter leaned forward, sniffed Fred's little pink nose, and gave it a lick.

"Yesss!" I murmured as I let out a breath, trying not to be too loud in case I threw either of them off.

All of a sudden, both of them jumped back. *Shit, maybe I'd gotten my hopes up too soon.*

They started walking in a circle, eyeing each other from a safe distance.

Then Walter picked up pace, ran over to Fred's butt, and sniffed it.

"A butt sniff! That's promising," Blake said softly, smiling.

We spent the rest of the afternoon keeping an eye on them while we finalized the administrative work for the fundraiser. We'd raised enough to pay Mrs. Gutiérrez to help with financial aid applications for at least the next year, plus a sizable amount that would go toward paying the medical expenses of Sapphire Springs residents who couldn't otherwise afford them. I'd been meaning to do this work during the week, but I hadn't had a chance because I'd been so busy meeting with Miriam to get up to speed on the weddings she had lined up and to discuss our plans. Miriam and I had been getting along really well, and I was still bubbling with excitement about my career change. While it didn't come with a one-hundred-thousand-dollar check, it would cover my bills and then some, and if we expanded the business like I planned, it could become quite lucrative. But even if it didn't, at least I'd be doing something I loved.

After dinner, as soon as I'd dried the last dish and Blake had wiped down the kitchen counter, she pulled me into her arms, giving me a slow, soft kiss that sent me throbbing.

"Mmmm," I groaned.

"Since it seems like the kids are getting along well enough"—Blake nodded her head toward the couch, where Walter and Fred were sitting on opposite corners—"how do you feel about us moving to the bedroom?" Blake kissed along my jawline and started gently biting my earlobe.

"Yessss," I exhaled, suddenly incredibly impatient to rip all Blake's clothes off.

One hour and multiple orgasms later, Blake pulled her head back.

"Jenny?"

"Uh-huh," I mumbled, keen to get back to kissing.

"Do you realize we've been in bed for, like, an hour, and you've had two very loud orgasms?" I winced, hoping Mrs. Harding hadn't heard me next door. "Walter hasn't once scratched me, whined, or otherwise engaged in any sex-policing behavior."

"Oh, wow! Maybe we should go check everything's still okay." An image of blood streaming out of Walter's leg after the @charlietheinstagramcat incident flashed into my mind.

We disentangled ourselves and, still naked, made our way down the hallway, peering in each room for any sign of our pets. Blake reached the living room first and, after looking in, waved me over.

When I reached Blake, she pointed to the couch, and my heart almost combusted on the spot.

Fred and Walter were on the couch, curled up together in a perfect circle.

"Oh my god! That is so freaking adorable!" I exclaimed, putting my arm around Blake's waist and pulling her to me.

We stood there, in the hallway, watching them for a few minutes.

"Maybe Walter just felt left out. Perhaps now he has a buddy to keep him company, he won't sex police us anymore?"

"Well, there's only one way to test that hypothesis out!" I said, grinning, as I tugged Blake back to the bedroom.

CHAPTER THIRTY-SIX

JENNY

"Jenny!" a high-pitched voice squealed.

Engrossed with typing an email about floral arrangements, I jumped in my seat, losing balance and nearly capsizing onto the Novel Gossip patrons sitting behind me.

Steadying myself, I looked up to see Blake grinning at me, dark hair falling over her eyes. Dark hair she couldn't brush away because she had an excited twin hanging off each hand. Ava and Liam let go and raced over to me. Blake ran her hand through her hair in relief.

"Well, hello!" I said, enveloping the twins in a hug. "How are my two favorite four-year-olds?"

Ava and Liam clambered up onto a chair each, and Blake settled down next to me, leaned forward, and kissed me for longer than was probably appropriate in front of the twins.

"Good! We went to the playground, and Auntie Blake pushed us so high on the swings we nearly went to space," Liam announced, completely unfazed by our PDA.

"Wow! Auntie Blake must be very strong." I looked at Blake, and our eyes connected, my chest full to bursting.

"Auntie Blake is exhausted." Blake leaned forward and poured herself a glass of water, taking a long gulp. But despite her words, she looked radiant. I didn't know what it was—whether it was the medical fund taking a load off her shoulders, my return, or something else altogether—but in the last week, she was more energetic, more upbeat than she had since I'd moved back the first time, in October. "Now, what do you kiddos want?"

"Milkshakes!" the twins screamed in unison.

"Inside voices, you two," Blake said, trying to sound stern and failing completely. "Now, where is George?" Blake turned around and waved at George, who was already walking toward us.

"Did I hear someone say milkshakes?" George placed two coloring pads and some crayons in front of the twins. They grabbed the crayons and started scribbling.

"I think everyone in Sapphire Springs heard someone say milkshakes," Blake said, grinning at George. "Sorry about that."

Untroubled, George took down our orders. I'd just finished putting in my coffee order when the front door opened. George looked up quickly, an indecipherable expression crossing her face as a couple entered.

"Hello! Please take a seat. I'll be with you soon." She looked at her watch and furrowed her brow.

"Is everything okay?" Blake asked.

George looked up, a wry smile on her face. "Yep, sorry. It's just the *TimeOut New York* crew is coming today to take photos for the article, so I'm a little distracted. They should be here any minute."

"Oh sh—I mean, oh!" Blake glanced at the twins, who

were engrossed in coloring and hadn't noticed her swearing slip-up. "Maybe we should get out of your hair, then. These two are quite, er...energetic today. Olivia is going to meet us here to take over soon, but we can easily just play in the park some more until she closes up the shop." Blake's family had gifted her brother a kid-free weekend so he could celebrate his tenth wedding anniversary with his wife, so they were taking turns to mind the twins.

George looked down at Ava and Liam, who looked angelic as they scribbled peacefully.

"No, no. Don't leave. We're a family-friendly establishment, and I want them to see that," George said firmly before turning and walking back to the counter.

Blake and I exchanged a concerned look. It was only a matter of time until the twins lost interest in coloring.

The front door opened again, and Blake and I looked up, my grin broadening.

Amanda spotted us as she walked through the door with Maya and beelined toward us.

"Hello! How are my favorite lovebirds?" Amanda asked, her grin mirroring my own. "Apart from you and Jasper, of course, Maya—who tie for that honor," she hastily added. "You know, I've been thinking about starting up a dating agency after my recent successes. My wedding brought y'all together."

I laughed. Blake and I were taking full credit for Maya and Jasper getting together, but now probably wasn't the time to admit to our *Emma*-like scheming. Maybe one day we'd tell them about it—perhaps at Maya and Jasper's wedding, which I'd hopefully get to plan. Just the thought of helping another friend celebrate their special day made my body buzz with excitement. My mind started whirring with possible locations, color schemes, and themes.

"Well, if you're looking for clients for your dating agency, keep me in mind," George said, smiling as she placed two gigantic milkshakes in front of the twins and coffees in front of me and Blake.

I shot Blake a quick glance, but her face gave nothing away. She'd given me the impression George was happily single, but perhaps that wasn't the case. Intrigued, I made a mental note to ask Blake about it later. The twins pushed the crayons away and grabbed their milkshakes, downing them with ungodly loud slurps.

Amanda grinned. "I certainly will! Well, we'll leave you to enjoy your drinks in peace. I'll see you for brunch tomorrow, Jenny?"

I nodded vigorously. After years of seeing Amanda in person only a couple of times a year, it was amazing being able to catch up with her on a regular basis. Amanda and Maya headed to a table nearby, and as I watched them go, I spotted Mrs. Harding in the corner of the cafe, her head in a book. Despite my plan not to U-Haul it with Blake, I had spent a lot of time at her house in the past few weeks and had run into Mrs. Harding a few times. The intimidating figure she'd once held in my mind had been replaced by the reality of her now. I could see she cared about her students, even if the way she'd dealt with me had been misguided.

The front door opened again, and two attractive women in their late twenties walked in. One of the women, who had short black hair and wore a red bomber jacket, was carrying a large camera.

"Here goes," I said, tilting my head toward the newcomers, who were making their way toward the counter. I shot a glance at the twins, who were still loudly making their way through their milkshakes, and breathed out. We were okay for now.

The *TimeOut* crew spoke to George for a few minutes and then began snapping some photos of Novel Gossip's interior. Watching George pose behind the counter for a shot, a wave of relief washed over me that it wasn't me. I did not miss being in front of a camera at all.

"Jenny! Can George make us another milkshake?" Liam asked loudly, sliding out of his chair in a swoosh.

"No, I think one is enou—"

Liam was suddenly weaving through the Novel Gossip tables toward the counter.

"Liam! Come back here!" Blake said, jumping up from her seat and following.

"Where is Liam going?" Ava asked with interest.

Before I had a chance to respond, she slipped off her chair as well and chased after Liam.

Shit.

I could see Blake behind the counter, pleading with someone, presumably Liam. Ava stopped, peered through Blake's legs, and then set off through the aisles of the bookshop section of Novel Gossip. I started to jog after her, increasing my speed when I realized George and the *TimeOut* crew were now taking photos at the back of the bookshop.

Passing Blake, I saw she was trying to wrestle a half gallon of milk from Liam, who'd clearly decided since George was busy, he'd take milkshake making into his own hands.

I entered the aisle. At the end, I could see George standing in front of a wall of books, trying to pose for the photos while watching Ava and I run toward her. The *TimeOut* photographer had her back to us, oblivious to what was going on.

"Ava, no running in the shop please," I begged, trying

not to make a scene. Still running, she turned to look at me and ran directly into a Penguin book display case at the end of the aisle. The adorable penguin-shaped display, full of Penguin classics, did a sickening rock side to side. George ran forward to try to right it. A book flew off the display case and hit the photographer, causing her to jump forward in surprise. George and the photographer collided at the same time the Penguin display case smashed to the ground.

Ava let out an ear-piercing shriek. "I killed the penguin!" she wailed.

Just then, Blake, holding Liam in her arms, arrived on scene.

I looked up at them and did a double-take. Blake and Liam were drenched in milk.

Oh my god. What absolute chaos.

Olivia walked past Blake, shaking her head in amused exasperation. She righted the Penguin bookcase and began picking up all the books. "I'm sorry about this, George."

"Damn, I think we're still dripping." Blake dabbed at Liam's face with a tea towel, looking back down the aisle, which was covered in milky drips. "When I heard the crash, I was worried someone had been injured. I'm so sorry we've interrupted your photoshoot." *And trashed the joint*, I thought. Presumably there was a half-gallon of milk spilled behind the counter. Holding Ava's hand, I helped Olivia and George pack away the remaining books.

George, to my relief, didn't look too pissed off. "Don't worry about it. It'll be easy to wipe down." She chuckled. "And you did warn me that something like this might happen."

"Are you both okay?" I asked, looking at George and the photographer with concern, worried they might have injured themselves in the collision.

"I'm all good," said the photographer, smiling at George, and suddenly my meddling *Emma* instincts were activated. *I wonder if she's single.* I inwardly shook myself. *Calm down, Jenny.*

We made our way back to the cafe section of Novel Gossip, where we found Mrs. Harding on her hands and knees behind the counter, mopping up the spilled milk. Blake and I rushed over to help, and Olivia ushered the twins out of the cafe, on a mission to take them back to the playground to tire them out without causing any more property damage.

Five minutes later, the floors were clean, and peace had descended back on Novel Gossip. Back at our table, just the two of us now, we leaned back in our seats.

"You know, I don't think I'll ever get tired of this," I said, smiling at Blake.

"Of ruining George's photoshoot and causing general chaos?" Blake grinned, raising an eyebrow.

I laughed. "No, not that. I mean our life here. The close-knit community, our families, each other."

"Well, I'm glad to hear it, because I don't think I'll ever get tired of it either."

Blake held my gaze, leaning forward to squeeze my hand, and the desire to U-Haul it immediately had never been so strong.

EPILOGUE

18 MONTHS LATER

BLAKE

Hot and sweaty, my heart pounding in my head, I was having some misgivings about my plan. Perhaps hiking up Breakback Ridge in the middle of summer wasn't the best way to go about this.

I shot a worried glance at Jenny. Despite being pink-cheeked and out of breath, she'd broken into a wide smile. I followed her gaze, and my shoulders relaxed. We'd arrived.

We'd reached the same rocky outcrop we visited on our first hike together. But unlike that eventful hike, Jenny was dressed in proper hiking boots, and I was on high alert for even the slightest hint of a cloud in the bright-blue sky.

My eyes darted to the spot we'd picnicked at last time. It was empty. I breathed a sigh of relief. Hopefully, we'd be undisturbed for the next few hours.

We walked up to the edge of the outcrop and took in the view. Instead of the sweeping views of red and orange foliage that greeted us last time, today the trees were all a dark, deep green.

"It's absolutely gorgeous." Jenny sighed, wrapping an arm around my waist.

"Not as gorgeous as you," I said, kissing her on the cheek.

Jenny giggled and rolled her eyes. I smiled. Making Jenny giggle never got old. And since her career change, her giggles were even more frequent. She adored helping people celebrate important milestones, whether it be engagement parties, weddings, or birthdays. After a self-imposed social media hiatus, she now only posted on her personal accounts when she felt like it, mainly when Fred and Walter were doing something particularly cute.

"Should we get our picnic set up? I could really do with a sit-down and some food." I don't know if it was nerves or the heat, but my legs were a little shaky.

Once the picnic blanket was sprawled out, and all the food, except the cookies, was unpacked, I took a long swig out of my water bottle and then leaned back against the boulder.

"I don't remember you being this out of breath last time we came up here," Jenny teased.

"I was trying to impress you last time. I must've done a good job of hiding my exhaustion."

"Oh, so you're not trying to impress me anymore?" Jenny grinned and then did a fake pout.

I gave her a gentle shove. "Ha ha. Very funny."

But in some ways, it was true. I was so comfortable with Jenny that I could be my whole self with her. Not comfortable in a boring, all-the-spark-is-gone kind of way—we still went on date nights, had incredible sex, and didn't take each other for granted. More comfortable in a safe, accepted, I'm-confident-we-love-each-other-very-much-and-you're-not-going-to-leave-me way.

Although, despite that confidence, butterflies fluttered in my stomach.

"Thanks for picking up all this food. It's delicious," Jenny said with a mouthful of chicken sandwich in her mouth.

"Good lord! And you were accusing me of no longer trying to impress you," I joked as a piece of chicken fell out of Jenny's mouth. "Make sure you leave some room for dessert. I've got a surprise for you."

I took yesterday afternoon off work to prepare for the picnic. Thankfully, work had been much more manageable since we'd set up the medical fund. No longer overwhelmed with paperwork, I could take a day off here and there without stressing out.

After finishing the sandwiches, we lay back on the boulder, watching boats make their way up and down the Hudson.

Fifteen boats later, I took a deep breath. It was time. "Would you like a cookie? It's one of George's chocolate-walnut ones."

Jenny shook her head. "No thanks. I'm too full at the moment. Maybe later."

Shit.

"Not even a little bite?" I couldn't help myself.

"Seriously, I can't eat anything more at the moment, or I might explode. I might need to wait until we're home."

I spent the next half hour trying to enjoy the view and Jenny's company and hide my inner turmoil. What if she didn't want to eat the damn cookie?

"Mmmm, I think I'm feeling more like that cookie now. How about you?" I looked at her hopefully.

Jenny furrowed her brow, as if trying to calculate exactly how much room remained in her stomach. *Please say yes. Please say yes.*

She nodded, and I let out a breath. "I think I could at least have a bite."

I tried to play it cool, even though my heart was thumping in my chest. I turned to my backpack and rustled through it, lifting out the Tupperware container I'd carefully placed at the bottom of the bag. With my back to Jenny, shielding the Tupperware container and its contents from view, I carefully pulled out the cookie, took a deep breath, and turned back to Jenny, who was still staring out over the valley.

I cleared my throat.

Jenny turned to look at me, her eyes widening as she took in the giant cookie in my hand.

The giant cookie with a ring stuck in a big chunk of chocolate in its middle.

I had a whole speech planned about how incredible Jenny was, how much I wanted to spend the rest of my life with her, and how wonderful the last eighteen months of my life had been.

But as Jenny's eyes connected with mine, all my words flew off the rocky outcrop and into the valley, sailing away on the breeze. Jenny's face broke into a big, beautiful smile, and my heart felt like it might explode.

"Oh, Blake." Jenny took the cookie out of my hands, examining the ring closely. "It's gorgeous."

"Um, so, is that a yes?" I asked.

Jenny leaned in, pressing her warm, soft lips gently against mine, before pulling back a few inches. "Of course it's a yes." As relief and excitement washed over me, I tugged her back for another, more passionate kiss.

"Do you want to try it on?" I asked once we'd disentangled ourselves.

"Sure."

I yanked the ring out of the chocolate, brushed off the cookie crumbs, and handed it to Jenny. She pushed it over her finger, beaming.

"It's beautiful. Thank you."

I breathed out. "Thank god you said yes, because I got this done yesterday." I pulled up my shirt and showed Jenny the upper right corner of my back, where a small tattoo of two cute little bald eagles, sitting side by side on a branch, now occupied prime position.

Jenny's delighted laugh rang loud in my ears.

"Oh, I love it." She traced her fingers around the skin next to the tattoo. "Maybe I'll have to get a matching one." Jenny's eyes twinkled, and I couldn't tell if she was joking or not.

Thirty minutes of making out later, my watch chimed. "That's our cue to start heading back to the nest." I winked at my bad eagle joke, eliciting another fond eye roll from Jenny. "We need to make it back in time for dinner so Fred and Walter don't get mad at us."

Not that Fred and Walter had probably even noticed we'd left. They were so obsessed with each other these days. We'd likely come home to find them exactly where we'd left them, curled up together on their favorite spot on the couch. We started packing up.

Before we left our picnic location, we stood, backpacks on, taking in the view one last time. I reached for Jenny's hand.

"If we were eagles, we could fly off this ledge and swoop down the mountain, back to Fred and Walter in no time," Jenny said, smiling.

I imagined us soaring together over the green, leafy trees down to the river, where we would fly low to the water until we reached Sapphire Springs' pier, astonishing kayakers and passengers on boat cruises with our impressive wing-span and aerial acrobatics. And then gliding up Main Street, enjoying the birds-eye view of our family, friends, neighbors and tourists going about their daily life, before finally flitting back to our cottage. Any bird enthusiast who happened to see us would be amazed to see two bald eagles flying in tandem.

I grinned. "That would be incredible. But unfortunately, we're going to have to rely on our own two feet to get us home and it's getting late. Are you ready for our first hike as an engaged couple?"

Jenny laughed. "When you put it like that, it sounds a lot more appealing. I'm ready. For the hike, and also for so many more firsts together." She squeezed my hand.

And with that, we turned and walked, one foot after another, down the mountain.

THE END

DEAR READER

Thank you so much for reading Not Just Gal Pals.

If you enjoyed it, I would really appreciate if you could leave a review on Amazon, Goodreads or share your thoughts on #booktok or #bookstagram.

If you'd like to get a free bonus scene of Jenny and Blake's wedding, and also hear when the next book in the Sapphire Springs series is published (George's story!), please sign up to my newsletter: https://elizabethluly.com/newsletter-sign-up

Thanks again,

Elizabeth

ACKNOWLEDGMENTS

Many thanks to my family for their ongoing support and encouragement.

Thank you Ann Leslie Tuttle for your thoughtful comments, Lauren C. for your guidance when I got stuck and Jenn Lockwood for your excellent proofreading.

To my amazing beta readers, Rhiannon, Jess, Rita, Carolyn, Jeanette, Dimitra, Hannah, Holly and Ginny, your helpful feedback and supportive comments meant the world to me.

A huge thank you to Sam at Ink & Laurel for bringing Jenny and Blake to life through your fantastic cover design.

Amy, thanks for letting me use your Instagram handle novelgossip as the name of George's cafe.

Thank you to all the amazing writing podcasts that inspire me and teach me so much. A special shout out to *The Shit No One Tells You About Writing*, *The Manuscript Academy*, *Lesbians Who Write* and *How Do You Write?* podcasts.

And to everyone else who provided feedback and support along the way, thank you.

ABOUT THE AUTHOR

Elizabeth Luly lives with her wife, toddler, and Schnoodle in Melbourne, Australia, in a home overflowing with books. She loves (in no particular order) rom coms, coffee, dogs and traveling.

Sign up for her newsletter and stay up to date on her book news: www.elizabethluly.com.

And find her here:

Website: www.elizabethluly.com
Facebook: www.facebook.com/elizabethlulyauthor
Instagram: www.instagram.com/elizabethlulyauthor
Goodreads: https://www.goodreads.com/author/show/229862 18.Elizabeth_Luly

ALSO BY ELIZABETH LULY

From LA to London, With Love

A celebrity romance set in London, featuring Sophie Shah, a bisexual single-mom-by-choice, Chris Trent, a humiliated movie star, and a cast of queer characters.